Alice's Story: A Search for Light

Mary Taylor Martof

Prologue

New York, 2005

This little light of mine, I'm gonna let it shine,
This little light of mine, I'm gonna let it shine,
This little light of mine, I'm gonna let it shine,
Let it shine, let it shine, let it shine.

Ev'ry where I go, I'm gonna let it shine,
Ev'ry where I go, I'm gonna let it shine,
Ev'ry where I go, I'm gonna let it shine,
Let it shine, let it shine, let it shine.

Tears welled in Alice's eyes and began a path down both cheeks as she sang out with the rest of the congregation, tapping time to the music on the pew in front of her. *If I had found that light early on, I wouldn't have needed the drugs and alcohol to fill the emptiness inside and cope with life. But how was I to know the light was there? No one else had ever seen it.*

New Orleans, Louisiana, 1948

Fear shone in the eyes of eleven-year-old Alice Hollister as she looked about the small living room for her baseball bat. It would protect her until she got to her bedroom where she could lock and bar the door. She could not find the bat, but her eyes were smarting from the heavy scent of alcohol in the room.

Her mother, Belle, had picked up a stranger from Grande Isle in a local bar and brought him home. Belle had just staggered into the master bedroom of the little shotgun house to change into 'something more comfortable', leaving the man to ogle Alice. He had a strange look on his face when he said, "I done had me a girl about your age—sweet little thing." His voice trailed off as he slicked back his long, black hair.

He bore a striking resemblance to pictures Alice had seen of Jean Lafitte. *Probably a descendent of the gentleman pirate,* she thought, *most folks from Grande Isle are.* He even called himself Jean. Was it a namesake? His eyes, so dark one might call them black, held a danger that had probably attracted her mother, but horrified Alice. A bushy mustache and a scar cutting diagonally across his cheek added to his mystique. A more pleasant expression might have made him appear handsome,

3

but the constant scowl gave his face an ominous foreboding. She felt those eyes penetrating her blouse and caressing the pink nipples beneath.

Belle stepped out of her bedroom, dressed in lounging pajamas that were slit to the thighs on the sides, exposing her shapely legs. She was a beauty with long black hair, high cheekbones, sensuous red lips and flashing black eyes to match those of Jean. Her low-cut top bared plenty of cleavage and bronze skin—skin so bronze that some claimed she was sure to have black blood in her family tree.

Flipping her luxurious black hair back, Belle glanced at Alice, a disdainful look on her face. The child wondered if her mother thought that she was actually flirting with Jean. *I'd rather walk on razor blades,* thought Alice.

The child finally reached her bedroom door, opened it and quietly slipped inside. Bolting the door, she grabbed a heavy chair she kept for occasions like this, which happened quite frequently. She jammed the chair under the doorknob as extra assurance that no one could open the door.

Suddenly realizing that she had to use the bathroom, she thought *Oh, no. Wild alligators could not force me to open that door again.* What to do? Placing her index finger against her chin, she looked about the bedroom. Finally, she climbed reluctantly up on the windowsill, stuck her small bottom out the window, and peed. *Hope no one saw me.*

Deciding to sleep in the clothes she was wearing, she reached for Teddy, her favorite stuffed animal. The fur on his belly was missing in spots from her constant rubbing when she felt anxious, but the spots made him even more lovable to her. The child hugged him to her chest and whispered in the dark, "What should I do, Teddy? What if that stranger took a notion to rob and kill us? I heard on the radio where Sam Spade, my favorite detective, breaks down doors all the time. Could that pirate man break mine down? The chair might not hold. That man looked awfully strong to me. And what about Belle? Would she protect me? Sometimes I think she'd be happier without a big, ugly kid like me around. After all, she pitches a fit if I call her anything but *Belle*—probably wants folks to think I'm her little sister."

She frowned thoughtfully," I need to have a little talk with Dad, for sure this time. I've waited this long because I didn't know what would happen if I did. But you can bet that whatever happens will be my fault. And Dad won't be here to take up for me."

She hung her head as she thought: *But Belle's not all bad. Sometimes she's even nice—like the way she treated Fannie, the Bag Lady. Why I've seen old Fannie many times on the streets of New Orleans-- always in rags, the number of layers depending on the outside temperature, always wheeling that shopping cart. Guess it contains all her possessions.*

Belle, Pirate Man, and I ran into her on our way home tonight. Belle walked right up to Fannie like she knew her. Handed her a bill. Old Fannie smiled and said, "Praise the Lord for you, Miss, you always helps old Fannie." When Pirate Man sneered and said that the old hag would just spend it on booze, Belle stood up as straight as she could and replied that she did not care as long as it made Old Fannie happy.

The child rubbed the teddy bear's stomach, whispering, "Maybe if I wait a little longer, things will work out. Just wish she would show more of that kindness to me, instead of criticizing everything I do. If I wash dishes, she says I didn't get them clean. My room is never straight or clean enough to please her. Why once I made pancakes for her breakfast, and she threw them in the garbage—saying, I didn't wash my hands first. Makes me feel like I can't do anything right, Teddy."

Her eyes turned upward as she said, "If I didn't have my dad and my teachers to praise me once in a while, don't know what I would do. Just go around feeling miserable all the time, I guess. And never know why. I think Belle resents having a kid to take care of."

Alice paused, wrinkling her brow and clenching her right hand into a fist. She did not understand why but clenching that right fist seemed to fill her with the strength she needed to rise above her circumstances.

Turning back to Teddy, Alice said, "No, no excuses, this time. Things have gone too far. Dad needs to know what goes on around here when he's away."

The house was quiet—too quiet. Alice put Teddy down and crept to the door. Placing her ear against it, she listened but heard nothing.

She was about to open the door a crack when she remembered another night like this. That other night, she had actually opened that door and made her way stealthily out and into the living room. Two nearly full wine glasses had been sitting on the coffee table in front of the white leather couch. She had picked up the one with lipstick and sipped. It tickled her nose and made her cough, but she liked the taste. And besides, it made her feel good. She covered her mouth with a towel and went over to peek through the partly open door to Belle's bedroom. No one had noticed, so she took another sip and before long another. She felt like she was

floating on clouds and sailing on a gigantic
rainbow. Looking down, she saw the Bengal-tiger
rug at her feet move. Or was it the room? Suddenly,
her tummy felt funny, and nausea was clutching at
her throat. She clapped her hand over her mouth
and ran for the bathroom, arriving just in time to
spew her partially-digested supper into the
commode. The taste and smell of puke made her
even more nauseous.

The day after, she had been too sick to go to
school. And school was the highlight of her life.
Alice had decided then and there that she would not
try that again.

Tonight, she just checked the chair barring the
door again and walked back across the floor in her
bare feet. Climbing into bed and under the covers,
she reached for Teddy. Holding this precious gift
from her dad closer, she whispered in the darkened
silence, "Unless I talk with Dad, you're the only one
I can tell family secrets to, Teddy. Other people
might not understand and think I was a bad person."
With one eye on the door, she rocked the bear back
and forth, until she fell into a restless sleep.

She was awakened by the sound of glass
shattering. The noise had come from the living
room. Lying very still, she was afraid to move.
Stealing a glance at the window, she saw that it was

still dark outside with a sliver of moonlight creeping across her bed.

A male voice was shouting, "Where's the money, Tramp? I know you got it stashed away. I know that excuse for a man o' yours makes plenty on that oil rig."

There was no answer. Alice wondered whether Belle had passed out, been knocked out, or worse. Then came the sound of drawers being opened and slammed shut. The child pulled the covers over her head, slinking down beneath their warm comfort. But the shivers started anyway—they started at the bottom of her spine and worked their way up to her shoulders. She reached for Teddy but couldn't find him. Much too rattled to think clearly, she remained in her paralyzed position and waited.

Am I imagining things, or is that someone outside my door. I'm pretty sure I heard a noise. Can't tell what it was. She strained her ears and soon discovered that she had not imagined it: There was no doubt. Someone was at her bedroom door. The doorknob rattled. And then it shook more forcefully. She couldn't imagine being more terrified but soon discovered that the nightmare got worse when the door began to vibrate. She couldn't breathe. Just as she was sure that she was turning blue, the noise ceased as suddenly as it had begun.

Did the chair hold, or did I dream all that? Silence filled the darkness. A gunshot rang out.

Chapter 2: Belle Hollister

What seemed like hours later, the police arrived, and Alice knew that it was safe to leave her room. Opening the door, she sniffed the strong aroma of Luzianne coffee. Belle was making coffee in the small kitchen. She had thrown a terrycloth robe over her revealing outfit and twisted her hair into an upsweep. A uniformed policeman stood in the hallway surveying the damage.

The house looked like a hurricane had blown through. Empty drawers were strewn all over, their contents spewed out like debris left by the passing storm. Furniture and vases sat upside down next to bare kitchen cabinets over a floor covered with beans, sugar, rice, and flour.

The policeman made his way around all the debris and sat down at the kitchen table, taking a notepad from an inner pocket. Belle sat across from him, her feet planted demurely on the floor. "I shot at him, but he got away," she was saying. His eyes narrowed as he studied her. Then focusing on the overturned bottle of champagne, he commented, "Looks like someone was celebrating," He was watching her face as he said this.

Belle did not meet his eyes but remained focused on her hands as she replied in her most innocent voice, "Oh, yes, I had some friends in earlier this evening. So if I sound a little fuzzy, it's because I had a little too much champagne."

The policeman made a note on his pad. Then levelling his gaze on her, he said in an authoritative voice, "Wanna tell me exactly what happened?" He was still watching her face.

"Well, as I said, me and some friends was celebrating a recent birthday. I might have had a little too much to drink 'cause I got awfully sleepy about eleven. They left, and I went to bed."

"Let me get this straight. They left before you went to bed, right? "Belle nodded.

"I must a left the door unlocked 'cause that's how he got in." She walked over to the stove and picked up the pot of coffee. "Would you like a cup of coffee, Officer?"

He nodded, so she took a mug from the cupboard and poured the rich, brown liquid in it. "Sugar is on the table. Would you like some cream?"

"Black is fine. Thank you." He took a sip and said, "Good coffee."

Belle nodded, as she placed a strand of hair back into her upsweep.

The policeman turned around and saw Alice standing in the doorway.

"Where was the child?"

"Asleep in her room, weren't you, Alice?" Belle crossed her arms and gave Alice a steely look that told the child she'd better keep her mouth shut.

The policeman also saw the look, "I'll just let her speak for herself, if you don't mind, ma'am."

Alice placed her hands behind her so that he would not see them shake and just nodded, too afraid to say anything. No telling what Belle would do to her when he left. It would be better to wait and tell her dad.

I've got to hand it to her, Belle can lie with the best of them, thought Alice. At the same time, the child couldn't help but feel grateful for protection during the night. Had Belle intended to protect her? She didn't know. Still shocked by what Belle had done, Alice had not been aware that a gun was in the house. This woman, so critical of everything Alice did but unable to see her own faults, might do anything.

Chapter 3: Tom Hollister

The following morning Alice was awakened by the ringing of church bells and knew that it was Sunday. *Are there voices coming from the kitchen?* She stuck her head out from under the covers and strained her ears, soon recognizing the low, booming voice of her dad. Stuffed animals and covers went flying as she jumped onto the cool, hardwood floor, tripping over the school books she had dropped there on Friday. Not bothering to don robe or slippers, she made a beeline for the kitchen. And there he was—spooning the rich, chicory-laden coffee into the pot. When he turned and saw Alice, his whole face lit up. He grabbed her and lifted her small body high in the air before clasping her close to his chest. She wrapped both arms around his neck, rocking back and forth.

Tom Hollister was six feet, 3 inches tall and weighed 185 pounds. His lean body was all muscle. Handsome in a rugged sort of way, he stayed tan most of the year from his work on the oil rigs— work he had done since the age of 19, first in his native Texas and later in Louisiana where he had met Belle. He was a man who had the respect of his coworkers and most who knew him—all except those who had borne the brunt of his explosive temper, a temper he had never lost with his precious

Alice. Alice thought he was perfect and wondered why her Grandma Hollister was always saying, "You just ain't no good unless you got some temper in you."

He sat her down on a stool saying with a grin, "I thought I heard the patter of small feet, and look who showed up. A little beauty with red hair and pretty freckles."

Alice wiggled her toes, "Do you *really* think my freckles are pretty, Daddy? The kids at school tease me all the time, saying the cow blew bran in my face."

He straightened his broad shoulders, feigning surprise, "What you talkin' bout, cher? Everyone of 'em is a beauty mark."

Alice glanced sideways at her mother before saying, "Belle thinks I'm a redheaded, freckle-faced ugly duckling."

"That's all in your head, Alice," Belle mumbled. She frowned as she adjusted the heat under the deep fryer to 360 degrees. "This deep fryer should be ready by the time the beignets are."

Alice tightened her lips. Looking at Belle, she said, "Well how come every time I visit your family, they laugh and want to know what tree stump you found me under?"

Tom patted his daughter on the head, saying, "Why, honey, only the prettiest of fairies and angels like you are found under tree stumps. Didn't you know that?"

Alice smiled. "You always make me feel like I'm the best, Daddy. Sure hope you're right." She glanced at Belle, who busied herself checking the temperature of the deep fryer for a second time.

Alice remained perched on the stool where her father had placed her, toying with the silverware on the counter. Tom put the coffee on the open flame to boil and turned to his daughter, "Your mother was telling me about the robbery last night. Were you scared?"

Belle interrupted by saying, "I told you I took care of it, Tom." She gave Alice a riveting look. Alice knew what that look meant. And she'd better not make any waves.

Tom said firmly, "The child needs to express her feelings, Belle."

Alice looked from Belle to her father, the color draining from her face. Her lips trembled but nothing came out. Tom looked at his daughter and changed the subject. There'd be time later, when they were alone. Tension in the room was palpable, so Tom turned on the radio. Zydeco music filled the air, soothing Alice's soul. For some unknown reason, it always seemed to affect her that way. Calmly, she pulled her pink flannel nightgown over her knees and looked at her dad for a clue as to how

16

they should proceed. He obliged with a question, "How's school, Alice?"

"Oh, Daddy, it's great. One day Sister had a microscope, and we got to look at a very common Diptera under it."

"A what?"

Alice laughed, "A fly, Daddy."

"Alice, you're very smart. If you work hard in school, I'm willing to bet you can become anything you want to be."

"Made all A's on my report card again. Sister thinks I should be able to get into medical school one day."

"Will that make you happy, Alice?"

"Oh yes. I want more than anything to be a doctor so I can help others."

"Well, just keep working hard, and your old dad will do his best to see that you get there."

Alice hopped down from her stool and went out to the small porch to retrieve the Sunday newspaper. Returning, she spread it out on the kitchen table and began searching for the comic strips. "I'm glad you got here to read the funnies with me, Daddy; they're not half as much fun without you. Let's read Peanuts first. He's my favorite."

Tom pointed to the comic strip. "Look at Snoopy with sunglasses, ain't that a blast?"

Alice smiled. "Who's your favorite character, Dad?"

"No question about that, sunshine, Dick Tracey is my man."

Belle was removing the chilled dough from the refrigerator and placing it on a floured board on the counter. Searching through several drawers, she finally located her rolling pin. Then, all of her attention was focused on rolling the dough out exactly 1/8th of an inch. Cutting the dough into 21/2 inch squares provided further distraction. She then carefully picked up each square and dropped it into the hot oil. Turning back to the refrigerator, she reached in and pulled out a box of confectioner's sugar. She poured the sugar carefully into a plastic bag. Keeping an eye on the frying beignets, she pulled each of them out as soon as it reached a golden brown. The hot beignet was inserted into the bag, and the bag was shaken until it was covered with the light, sweet sugar.

Alice watched her out of the corner of her eye, wondering whether her concentration on the beignets kept her from being with the family. *She's lost in her own world. I wonder if she can even see the truth around her.*

Belle placed the beignets on a platter, saying, "Better eat these while they're hot." Brushing back her long, black hair, she left a trace of flour as a highlight.

Alice had cafe au lait while the adults swilled the luscious Louisiana coffee they were addicted to. Everything made better by the hot beignets. Belle looked at Alice critically, "Wipe your mouth, Alice; you have a white mustache." Filled with shame because she couldn't even eat beignets correctly, Alice obeyed her mother.

"Oh, leave her alone, Belle. She looks cute"

Alice stopped twisting her hair and gave her dad a big grin.

From outward appearances, they were like dozens of other Louisiana families enjoying a peaceful Sunday morning together. Only the tremor in Belle's cup, fear in the eyes of her child, and tension in Tom's muscles belied the idyllic family scene.

Alice had not finished her hot drink before Belle was ushering her out of the room, "I'll clean up. Alice, go to your room and get some clothes on. You'll be whooping and coughing next week," She said this as she adjusted her apron and turned the water on full force to rinse the cup in her hand.

She's afraid I'll tell Dad the truth. She's always doing things to keep us apart. Alice went to her room and quickly donned a pair of jeans and a white blouse. When she went outside to look for her bike, Tom was waiting for her on the porch steps.

"Leave the bike, Al. Let's walk along the levee," he said, as he took her by the hand.

Alice's other hand went into her mouth, and she started chewing on her nails. The moment she had been dreading but, at the same time, hoping for had arrived. She had to tell her dad the truth.

When they reached the levee, he stared into the distance, not meeting her eyes. "*I*'ve heard Belle's side of the story, Alice. Now I'd like to hear yours."

Alice told him everything, the truth rushing out like water from a broken dam. Then turning and seeing his face, she frantically wished that she had chewed on her words instead of her nails. His mouth was drawn in a straight line as taut as the skin over his white knuckles. The lines on his forehead had deepened as he smacked one of his fists into the other. The furrow between his eyebrows combined with the crinkles around his eyes to give him an ominous look. He was about to explode. She had no road map to tell her how to act or what to say because she had never before seen this stranger standing beside her.

After what seemed like an eternity, her legs could move. Staring straight ahead, she turned around and started toward home, not knowing what else to do. But Tom stopped her saying, "No, Alice,

I want you to go to your friend Cecile's house and stay there until you hear from me. Do not go home. Do you understand?"

Alice was dazed, "But can't I get my bike?"

"I'll bring your bike to you. Just stay here until I get back with it."

Alice sat down on the levee, dazed and confused. Her whole life had been turned upside down. She had no compass to guide her, not even knowing whether she could trust this stranger walking away from her. She watched him with fear and a perplexed look on her face. She watched until he disappeared around the curve—his broad shoulders drooping, his gait slow and painful, like that of an old man. But he was all she had.

It was a while before he returned with the bike in tow saying, "I called Mrs. Guidry. They'll be more than happy to have you stay with Cecile for a day or two." Pointing to the small suitcase in the basket on the handle bars, he said, "I brought you some clothes and a key to the house in case you should need something in there. But I don't want you to go back to that house unless you absolutely have to. You hear me, Alice?" She nodded.

Then he walked away, the broad shoulders by now taut and defiant against a world that had betrayed his dreams. She watched him until she could no longer see him through her tears.

Chapter 4: The Quarter

Alice, Cecile and Mrs. Guidry sat on the levee, waiting for the ferry that would take them across the Mississippi to the French Quarter, that most famous part of New Orleans, known the world over as 'The Quarter.' Alice guessed that Mrs. Guidry had planned the trip to distract her from her problems at home.

Sniffing the jasmine blossoms in the warm, October breeze, Alice felt better already. The silence surrounding them was broken only by the squawking of an occasional sea gull and music from a calliope. This music machine was calling tourists for a ride on the steamboat that would churn the muddy river to mix the blueness under the shadows with the shimmering yellow left by the late afternoon sun. It was almost impossible to visit the French Quarter and stay sad. The spirit of the place engulfed everyone who went there with a carefree attitude that sang out, "Laissez les bon temps rouler (Let the good times roll.)"

Serious and studious, Alice didn't want to waste her time on frivolous things, preferring instead activities that would help her become a doctor, a person so important that others wouldn't look down on her. She pulled on her favorite strand of straight, bobbed hair and said shyly, "I want to go to the old slave market first."

Cecile frowned and said, "Oh, Ally, that ain't no fun."

Alice flipped her hand playfully at her friend. "Sure it is. What could be more fun than seeing how things were long ago and learning history?"

Mrs. Guidry raised her eyebrows at Alice. "Wouldn't you rather go to one of the more cheerful places, cher? How about listening to jazz at the Cafe Du Monde?"

"Maybe later we can have lemonade at the Cafe Du Monde. But we are studying about the slave market in school now. I'd rather go there first to see what it's like today."

Mrs. Guidry gave a big sigh and said, "Well, if that will make you happy, cher, we'll go to the slave market first." She paused before continuing, "But only if we go to Cafe du Monde afterward for cold drinks and jazz."

Then with a more serious expression, she continued, "Actually, it was right here in Algiers that the ships unloaded their human cargo of slaves so long ago."

Alice looked at her. "But the market is across the river."

23

"True. But they were kept here in high-walled pens with their entire families until healthy enough for sale. Can you imagine the sight of their bleeding sores where the shackles gripped their ankles as they walked in the Louisiana heat?"

Alice peered through the fine mist covering the water, "I don't have to do much imagining; the vision still lingers."

Mrs. Guidry turned up her nose adding, "Yes, and the humid winds still carry a trace of the stench from human waste mixed with the smell of bacon."

"Bacon? Come on, Mere. How did the bacon get in there?" exclaimed Cecile.

"The bacon was used to fatten them for sale."

Alice grimaced. "Sometimes I can hear the moaning and wailing of the fourteen-year-old girl Sister told us about. I hear the sounds in the echo of the palm trees as they blow in the wind."

"What else did Sister say about the fourteen-year-old girl?" asked Mrs. Guidry.

"She was moaning and wailing as she was being torn from the arms of her family to be sold on the market for about $550.00."

Cecile looked intrigued in spite of herself. "How did they ever survive all that?"

Mrs. Guidry folded her hands in her lap and said thoughtfully, "Well, they had each other and their religion, voodoo, which they brought with them

24

from Africa. Some say pockets of voodoo are still in this city today."

"There's the ferry," exclaimed Cecile. "You can have your facts, Ally. I'm ready for some fun in the Quarter. You hear that saxophone in the distance. You see them tourists swaying to and fro in time to the calliope." With that, she kicked up her heels and danced her way onto the ferry. But the ride to the Quarter was not conducive to dancing: the boat rocked from the rough waters of the Mississippi.

Chapter 5: Kat Trahan

"Folks keep asking me how old I is. Ain't nobody's business. I don't even know myself. I knows that I was born sometimes after the War ' tween da states, the seventh daughter of a seventh daughter, and I got the gift. "The old woman twitched her nose, adding another wrinkle to the others on her ancient face. Her long, white, stringy hair fell forward on her face, leaving a small space for the dim eyes to look out on a faded world that had long since passed her by. She was rocking in her dilapidated chair and daydreaming about the past.

The years melted away. Once again she was young and beautiful with tawny skin, long black hair and matching black eyes. She could no longer see the dust and cobwebs in her one-room shack. She was stepping barefooted onto the rich, cool soil of Bayou St. John. The sound of the drums and tambourines surrounded her, working the other dancers into a frenzy. But she was a priestess of voodoo; her movements were slow and calculated.

As the rhythm picked up its tempo, a tall, muscular African male, wearing only a loin cloth, handed her a box. She reached into the box, and the head of a snake emerged. The snake wound its body around her arm, across her shoulders and down her back until its full twelve feet of mud-colored and spotted roundness had emerged. "Come, le petit Zombie, let's us dance for yo' namesake, Zombie, snake of the great Marie Laveau," she uttered aloud.

The drums, tambourines, and dancers quickened the beat as snake and voodoo priestess became one in a slithering, enchanted movement that made it impossible to separate woman from snake. "Come, spirits of the dead. Come you who been to that Great River, you who has crossed over and you who is still waitin' to cross. You walks among us, the living, today and sees all our troubles in a light that only the dead can see. Give us yo' wisdom. Come to us. Come to us." She remembered those words as if it were yesterday she had spoken them.

The daily newspaper had written about the rituals, calling them "uncontrolled orgies" and "devil worship." She had read the words and muttered, "What does they know?"

"Meow." She was brought back to reality by Minuit, her black cat. She reached out and stroked the cat's back. "Where you been, Minuit? Did you bring me some more spiders?" The cat purred and rubbed against her outstretched hand. "I was gittin ready to get up from here and make somethin' for us to sell and git us some money. Them spiders will make a good addition to my so-called 'hex,' which some fool with less sense then money will pay for."

She pulled several spiders from the cat's fur and dropped them into a bright red canister next to a makeshift table, made from two pieces of lumber and two sawhorses. Reaching in a drawer behind her, the old woman pulled out a small kitchen cleaver, useful for chopping meat. On the makeshift table something was wiggling. Chop! The cleaver came down on the critter, and part of it flew off to a corner of the room. It was the head of a snake. She ignored it and continued chopping until the length of the wiggling form was in pieces. She pulled a sausage grinder from her cupboard and carefully placed the pieces in it, adding the spiders from the canister. Squinting and looking about, she limped over to pick up the severed head with its jaws still snapping. The head went into the grinder with the other parts.

She then turned the handle until a small portion of the gruesome mixture oozed through the outlet openings and into the red canister. It was all camouflaged with flour, oatmeal, several spices, and powder from an old rusted tin. The mixture was carefully stirred with water and placed in the oven as she muttered unintelligible words over it. The heat of the oven made the room smell like the bowels of hell itself had opened up.

Oddly enough, when the canister emerged 20 minutes later, it looked the same. It was a hideously bright red with a large yellow eye in the center of its front side. The eye had a dilated black pupil with orange snakes winding around each other.

Chapter 6: The Storm

Mrs. Guidry dropped onto her easy chair, exhausted from their trip to the Quarter. "You girls wore me out today. I gotta rest a bit." She kicked off her shoes and rubbed her bare feet before elevating them on an ottoman. "Tomorrow's a school day. Is the homework done, Cecile?" She paused." I know Alice did hers—don't even have to ask."

Cecile pulled herself erect and looked her mother in the eye, "I did mine, too, Mere. Alice is no better than I am."

Her mother smiled. "No better, cher. Just different."

Mrs. G. wiggled her toes to get the circulation going, "Now, go lay out your clothes for tomorrow and take your baths. I don't want to have to tell you twice." She looked at her daughter. "You hear me, Cecile." Alice obediently got up and started for the bedroom. Cecile frowned and put her guitar back into its case.

Her mother sighed. After a brief respite, she arose and went into the kitchen." Removing some cold, vegetable soup from the icebox, she put it in a saucepan and placed it on the stove. As she opened the bread box to remove a loaf of French bread, she turned to see Alice enter the kitchen.

With a sheepish look on her face, Alice said, "My dad forgot to pack my uniform blouse. What should I do?"

"Can you wear one of Cecile's?"

"It's too big, and Sister will give me a demerit for my uniform."

The lady gave a big sigh, turning up the palms of her hands. "Well, we don't want you getting demerits, do we?" She paused before saying, "First, we'll have an early supper, and then we'll just have to go over to your house to get you a blouse; you must have it for school tomorrow." She placed the bread in a basket and covered it with a towel before returning to the icebox for fresh butter.

Alice rubbed her hands together, hoping to find a way to ease the lady's burden. "Cile and I can ride our bikes over there."

Mrs. G. returned to the stove to check the soup, saying firmly, "No, I am going with you."

Alice lowered her eyes, "Sorry I'm so much trouble, Mrs. Guidry."

"No trouble, cher. Just lay out everything else, and take your bath."

"Cile has the bathroom right now. Okay with you if I take mine when we get back?"

Mrs. G. squared her shoulders, "Suit yourself, cher."

"May I help you with supper?"

The lady smiled, "Napkins are in that middle cabinet. Soup bowls are just above them. I'll get the silverware."

Cecile entered the room toweling her wet hair and sat down at the table. "I'll just have bread and cheese," she said as she tore off a large piece of the fresh, French bread.

Her mother filled her bowl with the hot soup and looked at her daughter, "Eat."

Alice poured glasses of milk for Cecile and herself from a frosted pitcher on the table, placed a napkin in her lap, and dug into her meal. The broth and barely cooked vegetables tasted so good.

As Mrs. Guidry buttered a piece of the crusty bread, she turned to Cecile, "That wind is picking up out there. Hear it? Go turn on the radio, cher. Let's hear the weather report."

A jingle for the latest detergent was soon interrupted by an announcer from the Weather Bureau in New Orleans. "Looks like that area of disturbance in the Gulf of Mexico is turning into a hurricane. That would make it Hurricane Charlie with winds of 78 miles per hour; Charlie is predicted to move east of New Orleans and reach Biloxi, Mississippi about dawn."

Mrs. Guidry sighed with relief, "Sounds like Charlie will miss us, so if we hurry, we can get over to your house, grab some blouses and get back before the remnants of that storm hit. But there's no time to waste. Can't tell what those hurricanes will do. I've known them to make a u turn and head in the opposite direction. Let's finish our supper when we get back." They scraped their chairs back and left the unfinished meal on the table. Cecile grabbed a hunk of bread and cheese before heading out the door.

The winds had continued to pick up by the time they reached the little, shotgun house. Mrs. Guidry swept the hair from her face and turned to Alice. Looks to me like the house is empty. Any radios in there? We better get another weather report."

"There's one in the master bedroom. I'll get it first thing." Bracing against the wind, Alice carefully placed her key in the door and opened it. She stuck her head in and called out. But no one answered. Everything looked the same as it had when she left to go for a bike ride. Dishes were still in the drainer just as Belle had left them. Otherwise, the house looked a mess—just as it always did. Disappearing into the master bedroom, she soon reappeared, saying, "Couldn't find the radio. Belle must have taken it with her."

Mrs. Guidry frowned. "I'll just look around the kitchen and rest of the house, if you don't mind."

"Help yourself, Mrs. G. I'll grab a few blouses, and we'll be out of here in no time." She went to her room and began searching through her closet for a blouse but found none. A pile of dirty clothes on the floor of the closet were searched with no better results. *I know I've got some blouses here somewhere. But where?* She went to the laundry room and found another pile of dirty clothes by the washing machine. This pile yielded better results. She grabbed several blouses and was looking for something to stuff them in when she was distracted by Cecile's voice coming from the living room. "What is that? Ugliest thing I ever saw."

Alice rushed in to see her friend pulling something out of the trash can. It was a flyer of some sort like the ones used for advertising products for sale. On the front of the flyer was the picture of a hideously bright red canister. Not just any canister. It had a large yellow eye painted on it. In the center of the eye was a dilated black pupil with two orange snakes coiled around each other.

Mrs. Guidry pointed a finger at her daughter, "Cecile Guidry, you got no business mucking around in other people's trash."

"But this ain't no ordinary trash, Mere. It's an ad for a hex. I'd be willing to bet on it. I better go outside and take a look around, just in case." Her voice trailed off as she opened the front door.

Alice looked at the flyer and shrugged her shoulders, "No idea how that monstrosity got in our trash." Then she walked into the kitchen, where she found a pile of paper bags. She took one and stuffed several dirty blouses into it.

Carrying the bag into the living room, she lowered her eyes before addressing her friend's mother, "May I use your washing machine when we get to your house, Mrs. Guidry? The only blouses I could find are dirty. She took a deep breath and added, "I'm so sorry to cause you so much trouble."

"I'll do them for you, cher, you need your s....."Her sentence was interrupted by a scream from outside. They both ran to the door. A blast of wind hit them in the face, knocking some old- dirty dishes from the table in the hallway. Broken glass mixed with dried food cluttered the hallway.

Cecile lay at the bottom of the steps, holding her ankle and rocking back and forth.

Her mother helped her up, supporting the side with the injured ankle. "Have you tried standing on it, 'Cile?"

"I tried, but it hurts too…." She broke off, heaving heavy sobs.

"Hold on. We'll think of something." Alice and Mrs. G. looked at each other, concern etched on both of their faces. "There's no way we can get back to our house if you can't stand on that ankle.

Guess we better get you inside out of this wind and try to figure out what to do. Maybe if you rest it a while, and I wrap it good and tight, we could make it home."

"Alice you get on one side. I'll take the other. "Cecile, can you put your bottom on the step and use your arms to pull yourself up to the next one? Alice and I will help you." Taking what seemed like an eternity, they moved up the four steps so that Cecile could sit on the porch. Her helpers stopped to rest and take a deep breath. Then each grabbed an elbow and placed their arms around her back. In this way, they were able to get her into the house and on the couch.

"Let me take a look at that ankle." Mrs. G. gently placed the ankle on a nearby ottoman for elevation. "Can you move your toes?" Cecile wiggled all five.

Alice came into the room carrying an elastic bandage. "I found this in our medicine cabinet."

"Good girl, Alice." Mrs. G. took the bandage and expertly wrapped the swollen ankle, using a figure eight. "Remember the word RICE, girls. It will help you treat any injury:

R stands for rest.

I means ice. It is used until the swelling is gone.

C is for coil. Wrap it snugly—but not too tight.

E means elevation."

"Oh woe is me! Why did this have to happen?" Cecile wailed. "I was just trying to make sure we had not been hexed."

A loud noise came from the front porch. Alice opened a crack in the door to peer out. The wind had blown the metal container for milk delivery into the yard. A low rumbling howl had begun.

Mrs. Guidry started to wring her hands but stopped abruptly, changing her facial expression into a quiet calm. The calm appeared to move slowly down her body and permeate her entire being. "We must be getting the tail end of that storm in the Gulf. It's not safe to go out there right now." Her face took on a look of resignation. "Alice, round up all of the flashlights you can find. I'd say we could lose power any minute." She looked about, "Is there a way to shutter these windows?"

"The shutters are outside in the garage."

"Too late to get those and put them in place now. We'll just have to do the best we can with what we have in here." She looked around. "Alice, can you help me move that wardrobe over to cover the dining room window? That seems to be where the wind is hitting hardest." Luckily the large wardrobe in the hallway had rollers, so the two of them were able to maneuver it up against the window.

Alice left the room and soon returned holding four flashlights and a head band with a light attached. Mrs. Guidry placed the head band on her head and gave each of the girls a flashlight, keeping an extra one for herself.

The wind was now howling like an angry god and blowing rain against the window. The tapping sound of the rain brought some comfort. "Well, at least the window is still intact," sighed Mrs. G. She checked the front door, shining her head light on it for a clearer view. Rain was coming in through the cracks surrounding the door. "But thank the good Lord! It's not coming under the door yet." She turned to her frightened wards. Cecile was crying, her whole body rocking back and forth with sobs. Alice felt sorry for her but at the same time a bit angry that she could not help.

Mrs. Guidry found two mops in the kitchen closet. Handing one to Alice, she began mopping water wherever it appeared. "Stay away from those windows, Alice. They could shatter at any minute."

"Oh woe is me! Please protect us, our Lady of Mercy," exclaimed Cecile as she searched in her pockets for her rosary beads.

"You can pray for us, 'Cile, while we do all we can. God expects us to use the brains He gave us to do all we can for ourselves, and He will be with us," her mother said as she made the sign of the cross.

Alice went into the kitchen to see if more rain was being blown in from that direction. The kitchen was dry for the time being, but that could change at any moment. Cecile's voice could be heard, repeating the rosary over and over.

"Alice, how do we get into the attic?" asked Mrs. G., her eyes glued to the bottom of the front door. "Looks like that storm changed course and headed for us."

Alice put down her mop and went closer, whispering, "You're worried about the storm surge and flooding, aren't you?"

"That and all the water coming through the cracks," Mrs. Guidry softly replied."

Together, they found a pull-down staircase to the attic next to the pantry in the kitchen, just as the overhead lights began to flicker. "Stay calm, girls, we're about to lose power." Alice thought the lady was doing a pretty good job of doing that for herself.

Just then, the lights went out, leaving them in total darkness, where only the howling winds and beating rain could be heard. Alice walked over and hugged Cecile to her chest. "It'll be okay, 'Cile." The action helped Alice calm her own fears.

She returned to help Mrs. G. pull the staircase down. They climbed by flashlight into the humid, hot attic and huddled briefly near the entrance. "We'll have to find a way to get Cecile up here."

"Maybe she'll be able to put a little weight on that ankle after your fine treatment."

"Let's hope so."

They climbed back down and found Cecile swinging the light from her flashlight around the room. "Save the batteries in that flashlight, 'Cile. We may need them."

Just then the kitchen window blew out. The howling wind hurled broken glass around the room.

"Leave it, Alice, you'll cut yourself. Besides, getting Cecile into the attic is our first concern."

She carefully made her way through the darkness to her daughter. "Cecile, can you try standing on that ankle? Alice will be on one side, and I'll be on the other. We'll keep as much pressure off of it as possible."

They helped her to the attic stairs, Cecile moaning every step. "You're doing great, cher. Now, you need to climb these steps. Let your arms do the work. I'll be right behind you keeping the weight off of that ankle. " After struggling for what seemed like hours, Cecile heaved herself onto the attic floor. The attic was vibrating in the howling wind.

"It's hot and scary up here. Besides it smells like mold."

"Cecile, get ahold of yourself. We're all scared, you know." Mrs. G. directed her light down the steps to check on the level of water on the floor. "Looks like the floor is barely covered, so we should be okay here for a while. That window we covered must have been blown out, too." Grabbing another flashlight from Alice, she used it and her head light to search out the attic. "Alice, how do we get onto the roof?"

"Guess we'll have to cut a hole through. I don't know of any other way."

"Oh, Laws! We gotta climb on that roof?" cried Cecile. I knew a girl in school; she drowned after her and her family waited on their roof for days."

"You're not helping, 'Cile, so shut up!"

'Thank you, Alice, Now tell me where I'll find an ax or a hatchet to cut our way through to the roof."

"Dad keeps several tools on the floor of the pantry."

"Okay! It may take me a little more time to find what we need. Cecile, where are your rosary beads?"

"In my pocket."

"Use them." She turned and started down the steps.

Cecile clasped her rosary to her chest, "Hail, Mary, full of grace," She was stopped by the sound of a gigantic crash in the rear of the house. Alice guessed that the old oak tree out back had just been uprooted. They looked for it to come through the roof, but, oddly enough, the structure remained intact.

Cecile's teeth were chattering, so Alice placed her arm about her and held her close. They rocked back and forth, searching the darkness for Mrs. Guidry's flash of light.

Alice started singing, "Abide with Me."

Cecile joined in with "Fast falls the eventide...." They harmonized, and it helped calm them for a while.

"I'm guessing we're not close to the eye of the storm,"

"How do you know, Ally?"

"Well, we'll get a period of extra fury sent by the wall of the eye, followed by silence. The eye of the storm is silent."

"Shh! Right now I'm more concerned about that noise over in the corner, Ally."

"Shh-hh, 'Cile. It'll be okay." Alice thought of the rats her dad had once found in the attic but kept her mouth shut.

"Alice, I know something is moving across the floor. I can feel it. It's a rat, ain't it?"

"You still have your shoes on 'Cile?"

"I got shoes, Ally, but I have other parts uncovered."

Alice said nothing. She could see the dim light from Mrs. Guidry's head light as the lady ascended the stairs.

"Oh! Thank the good Lord—you're back," cried 'Cile.

"I found an axe, but no saw. This will have to do."

"You gonna chop through to the roof with that axe, Mere?"

"If we have to, Cecile. But that's not necessary yet. There's no water coming under the front door. The floor is covered but seems to be holding steady for now. I'll keep watching."

"What do we do after you cut through the roof?" Cecile's voice was shaking.

"Well, child, we climb up there and try to attract attention from somebody in a boat. Do either of you have a white handkerchief or anything that would attract attention?"

"I have a white blouse on, Mrs. G."

"We may have to use it, Alice."

"Ain't there snakes in that water? I seen pictures of floods—them slithering things are everywhere." Cecile shuddered.

"Cecile, go back to your rosary; you're letting fear take control of you. How many times do I have to tell you?"

Water was now coming through cracks in the wall of the attic. Mrs. Guidry removed her dress and started mopping.

"Should we try the axe now?" Alice tried to keep the panic from her voice.

"We can wait a few more minutes." Mrs. G. was reluctant to let more water in through the roof.

Something hit the front of the house with such force that Alice wondered whether the little house would stand. Then came the sound of shattering glass. The attic vibrated with more force. The wind howled. Total darkness. More flying debris hit the house from time to time as the endless night went on and on.

After the wall of the eye passed, the wind began gradually losing its force, and only the rain could be heard, beating on the roof. When this continued for what seemed like forever, Mrs. G. decided that it was safe enough to leave the attic and look for beds. By then, Cecile was able to put more weight on her ankle and got down the steps with the help of her mother and Alice.

The kitchen clock gave the time as 5:14 a.m. Alice limped about, trying to get the cramps out of her legs. The beds stood in about two inches of water. They were covered with oil cloths from the kitchen table and nearby closet. Alice fell onto the oil cloth. She was exhausted mentally and physically. Sleep had been waiting for her. It grabbed her whole body in an instant. Cecile and her mother slept in Belle's bed.

Chapter 7: After the Storm

Alice awoke and sat up in bed. The oil cloth beneath her was stiff and stuck to her skin. Although it was cloudy outside, she knew it was late. *How in the world did I sleep so soundly on this thing? I must have been really exhausted.* Opening her eyes wider, she looked about as familiar objects in her room gradually came into focus. She looked for Teddy before realizing that she had left him at Cecile's house. She still wore the jeans and white shirt she had put on so long ago. *Was it only yesterday?* The outfit was still damp in places. The terror of the night before came rushing in, arousing her into a fully conscious state, and she wondered what damage had been done. Peeking out the window, she saw a landscape she hardly recognized.

She stepped out into the damp, overcast New Orleans morning, attempting to smooth her wrinkled shirt as she searched for anything that looked familiar. The sharp, fresh smell of ozone filled the hot, humid air. Rapidly flowing water was pushing trash and debris in the flooded street in front of the house. Black silt covered everything else, and insects were swarming from the silt, as if they had been hatched there. Broken limbs were everywhere. A tree in her neighbor's yard lay on its

46

side, its roots naked in a mound of mud that had once held it in place. The scene, so familiar to her for a lifetime, now took on a haunted mien. Even the sweet-olive bush and the nearby orange blossoms were covered in silt, their fragrances smothered by the acrid smell of gas fumes and the smell of dead fish. She braced herself to descend the steps of the porch and check on her favorite oak tree in the backyard, the one that had held her tire swing.

Placing one hand on the railing for support, she started down the steps, one at a time. Suddenly, she stopped. *"What is that?"* Sucking in her breath, she gazed at the bottom step, as ice crystals crept up her spine.

The step was streaked with a rusty-brown substance. It was not paint but appeared to be dried blood. Her stomach felt queasy, and her hands started to shake. Next to the smear was a small wooden coffin. The shaking traveled up both arms and into her torso as she grabbed the porch railing for support. *"What does this mean? What have I done?"* She went back up the steps holding onto the railing for support. Silence was everywhere; only the rushing water in the street could be heard.

Cecile lay sleeping next to her mom, her arms and legs spread out on the bed so that little space was left for her mother. Alice shook her until she awakened, rubbing the sleep from her eyes. Cecile groaned and stretched. "This better be good, girl." Then seeing Alice's face, she sat up and grabbed her friend. "'What's wrong, cher? You look like you seen a ghost."

Alice opened her mouth to speak, but nothing came out.

Cecile shook her, "You're scaring me, Alice. Say something."

Finally, through chattering teeth, Alice muttered, "I...I'm afraid, 'Cile. I...I think I've put a curse on this house." She pulled her friend out of bed, down the hall, and through the front door. They stepped out on the porch and Cecile rubbed her eyes again. She stared at the step with the dried blood and the coffin.

"Laws have mercy, Ally. You right. You been hexed." Alice, who stood on the porch above her, fainted.

When she came to, Mrs. Guidry was standing over her with smelling salts. Cecile came out the door carrying a steaming cup and saying, "Here, drink this."

Mrs. G. looked at her daughter. "Wait until she's fully conscious, Cecile."

Alice opened both eyes wider and took a sip of the hot tea, holding the cup in both hands. When she was able to speak, she frowned, saying, "Cile, what do you mean, I've been hexed?'

"Voodoo, girl, voodoo. They done put a hex on somebody in your fam'ly."

Guilt, shame, and fear cluttered at the base of Alice's spine, struggling to erupt. "It must be me. I did something bad, really bad." The picture of her dad's face flashed before her, as she told him the truth about Belle.

At that point, Mrs. G. interrupted their conversation." Naw, cher, children can't be hexed nor can they hex others. The good Lord sees to that." Cecile gave her mother a strange look but kept her mouth shut.

All of a sudden the tea didn't taste so good. Alice could feel the heat coming to her face. Her stomach was a pit of acid. She started heaving and ran for the bathroom, spewing brown liquid as she went.

Mrs. G. washed the child's face and led her back to the bedroom. Locating a relatively dry space in a corner, she placed a comforter over it and motioned for Alice to lie down. Locating a dry stuffed animal on a closet shelf, she placed it next to the child, who soon dozed off again from exhaustion.

Alice was awakened by the sound of voices coming from the kitchen. She got out of bed and tiptoed to the kitchen door. Peeping through the crack between the door and its frame, she saw Mrs.

Guidry seated across from a policeman at the kitchen table.

"Nice of you to come all the way out here by boat, Officer; I know the streets are still flooded. Will you have a cup of tea, or would you prefer coffee? I found both in the pantry and just made a pot of coffee."

"Coffee, ma'am, straight up and black, the blacker the better." He paused, looking about the room. "No trouble getting here; we was out patrolling the neighborhood. We have to. Crime don't stop for hurricanes." She handed him a mug of the rich, black coffee. He took it and sipped a bit of the Louisiana brew. Leaning back in his chair with a grin that reached both eyes, he sighed, "Aaah, now that's good coffee—good ole Louisiana style."

"I also found some beignets in the bread box. I didn't make them, but they appear to be fresh enough. Want 'a try one?" He took one from the plate she offered him and bit through the powdered sugar to the tasty fried dough.

"I called out to you because we are all upset by that bottom step out front and the coffin. You realize that Cecile and I don't live here, but the other child does. She's very upset by the whole business and trying to put all the blame on herself."

He sat up straighter in his chair, "Yes, ma'am, we'll run some tests on the smear and dust for fingerprints—take the coffin into the station. Of course, it'll take some time. Can't do it all today; we're not equipped in the boat. And we can't call it a crime scene since no crime has been committed that we know of. "

Mrs. Guidry folded her hands in her lap and looked up at her guest, "What do you make of it, Officer?"

He emptied his cup and set it down, "I'd rather not say, ma'am. There's some strange things going on in this city. And folks are looking for something to protect them from the evil eye. Doctors and nurses over at Charity tell about people coming in and dying for no good reason they can find." He paused, lowering his voice a bit, "Not long ago, an Italian woman across the river found a black wreath and some blood on her front porch—very similar to this situation. She and another lady in the neighborhood had had a falling out. A few weeks after that, the Italian lady was brought by ambulance into Charity—her eyes rolled back in her head, talking nonsense."

Mrs. G. frowned. "You mean the woman who found the blood and the black wreath?"

He nodded, "The very one, ma'am. Before long that lady fell into a coma and died; they couldn't find a thing wrong with her." He paused again, looking around the room. "Sensible folks, like you

51

and me, don't even like to talk about things like that. But once in a while I have no choice but to deal with it in my work."

"You talking about voodoo?"

His voice returned to its usual volume, "Between you and me, ma'am, I don't believe in the supernatural, but there's them that do. Of course, there's many more out there who take advantage of the fear and superstition to make a quick buck, if you know what I mean." He made a clucking sound with his tongue as he grinned.

"You mean the shops that sell gris-gris's and other voodoo paraphernalia?"

He squared his shoulders, "That's only part of it, ma'am. Criminals can always find a way to make a dishonest dollar. As for voodoo, there's no simple answer. Would you believe them voodoo queens go to mass in Saint Louis Cathedral more often than we do?"

Mrs. Guidry raised her eyebrows, "That's shocking. Why doesn't the Catholic church expose them for the devil worshippers they are?"

He turned his palms down on his thighs, "As I was about to say, ma'am, some folks don't believe it to be devil worship. Them priestesses call on the dead, whom they believe walk among us, to help the living with their problems. And they make sure to keep close ties with the church, claiming that many of the African deities survived as Catholic saints." Nodding his head, he continued, "Marie Laveau done a lot of good for our soldiers in the War Between the States. Lots of folks see her as a heroine." Looking about him again, he added, "But I've talked too much already."

With that, he removed his cap from the clothes tree in the hallway and placed it on his head. Then tipping the hat to Mrs. Guidry, he walked rather quickly toward the door. "I'll be in touch, ma'am." The door opened and closed.

Alice returned to her pallet on the floor, her mind swirling in a desperate attempt to make sense of it all. Assuming the fetal position, she felt cold in spite of the humid heat around her. She lay there scrunched up and too scared to move. When she finally dozed off, she drifted between troubled sleep and fearful wakefulness, trying to erase the images of witches, coffins and dried blood. But the harder she tried NOT to think of them, the clearer the images emerged. Whenever she sensed the presence of Mrs. Guidry, she feigned sleep, wondering where Cecile had gone. The house was too quiet.

She dozed off again but was soon awakened by the sounds of the front door opening and Cecile calling out, "Where are you, Mere?"

"I'm in the kitchen, trying to put together some lunch for us, 'Cile. This pantry's pretty bare. Did

53

you find any possibilities of getting to a grocery store that's open?"

"Dominique, a girl from my class, said Allemande's is open. They're on the hill up the street. We could get there by wading through a little water here and there."

"Too dangerous, cher. We'll have to make do with what we have until the streets are clear."

"Where'd you see Dominique?" asked Alice. She stood in the doorway, twisting a strand of her hair.

"She and her big brother were paddling up the street in a canoe."

Mrs. Guidry knitted her eyebrows in concentration. Then turning to her daughter, she said, "If you see them again, Cecile, ask whether they could get a few groceries for us. That's a possibility I hadn't considered." Cecile nodded.

"Dominique said you need to get a gris-gris, Ally."

"You told *her*, 'Cile," Alice groaned. "It'll be all over school when we go back."

"Don't worry, Ally; she'll have forgotten all about it by the time we go back." She placed her hands behind her and crossed her fingers.

"When *do* we go back?"

"Soon as the water goes down. We have to listen to the radio every day. I can practice my guitar and have a good ole time." She looked at her mother, "If only we had some good eating." Alice's eyes glazed over in boredom.

Mrs. Guidry assigned them daily chores, gave reading assignments from Alice's collection of books, and entertained them with stories from her childhood memories of previous hurricanes. "I remember the lights strung along the seawall after many a storm; they were set up to attract shrimp. Folks would go out on the lower steps of the seawall to cast their nets and haul 'em in by the bushel. Those steps were usually covered with seaweed, making them very slippery. So there were many accidents—kept the coast guard constantly patrolling back and forth to keep watch."

Alice looked out the window one day and saw that the street was dry in front of her house. She ran to turn the radio on and heard that schools would be open the next day.

"We go back to school tomorrow, Mrs. G. I know 'Cile will be happy," she grinned.

"She won't, but I will, Alice. I can't wait."

They were interrupted by a knock on the front door.

Chapter 8: An Unexpected Guest

Alice went to the door. Opening it, she recognized her Aunt Izzie from Lafayette.

"Alice, bless your heart. How you doing, chile?" She took Alice in both arms and hugged her to her ample bosom. Alice could smell the faint fragrance of lilacs. "Chile, I thought I would never get here—what with Rachel being sick and then this storm. Wasn't that something—all that wind and rain? Well, least we didn't have thunder and lightning in this one. I'm a scared of lightning, ain't you?"

Alice nodded but said nothing. She knew that thunder and lightning were rare during hurricanes.

Just then, Aunt Izzie noticed Mrs. Guidry and Cecile. "Oh, hello, I'm Alice's Aunt Izzie, her daddy's sister. Name's Lizabeth Broussard, but everybody calls me Izzie" She walked over and gave them a hug, too. "I thank you so much for taking care of our Alice, but I've come to fetch her, I'm afraid. Tom called me right after that attempted robbery." She placed her hand on the side of her mouth and whispered, "If you can believe anything Belle says." She raised her voice again and continued, "He wanted me to come over and get Allice—take her back with me to Lafayette. Then, as I said, Rachel took sick and right after that—this storm. Got here just as soon as I could." She paused to catch her breath.

Mrs. G. eyed her guest, a frown lifting her brow, "But we were hoping Alice could stay with us as a companion for Cecile, Mrs. Broussard. At least until the end of the school year."

Both girls chimed in at once. "Please, please."

But Aunt Izzie squared her shoulders and stood firm, "I'm afraid I must respect my brother's wishes. He was most insistent—did not want Alice staying in New Orleans a minute more than she had to. I promised him that I would see to that, and I mean to stand by my promise." She paused, making eye contact with her hostess. "And by the way, my name is Izzie. Mrs. Broussard was my mother-in law. Rest her soul."

Alice was chewing her fingernails. "Can't we get in touch with Dad and get his permission?"

"No! He's off the platform of the oil well now. We won't be able to reach him until he gets back. Besides, I don't know when I'll be able to make that trip over here again." She looked at the disappointed expressions on the faces of the girls and quickly added. "I'm sorry, girls. It's the best thing for Alice; the sooner she adjusts to Lafayette the better."

Mrs. Guidry wiped the disappointment from her face, replacing it with a cheerful smile. "How about a bite of lunch, Izzie? Such as we have. We had very little to eat for days, but a neighbor was good enough to go to the store for us day before yesterday, so we have plenty of bread and tuna fish. Won't you share it with us? Actually, we're getting kind'a tired of tuna fish."

"Don't mind if I do. We can polish off that tuna in a hurry. Sounds like you're ready for some gumbo."

"Oh, boy, are we! Did you bring us some?" Cecile was hushed immediately by a stern look from her mother.

"I just need a restroom to freshen up a bit, and I'll be ready to eat. That trip from Lafayette to New Orleans gets longer and longer."

"Alice, show your aunt where the bathroom is." Alice did as instructed. She had to please this woman who would be in charge of her life indefinitely.

"Cile, open four cans of tuna fish while I put together the rest of the ingredients for a salad. We'll have to use lemon again instead of mayonnaise, but we can make do."

Cecile groaned, "I'm so tired of 'making do."

Her mother nodded and said, "We all are, Cecile."

Alice took a loaf of French bread from the breadbox and started setting four places at the table.

Aunt Izzie returned, her face shiny clean, her hair neatly combed. She picked up the forks Alice had placed on the table and put them to the left of each place setting, saying, "That's where forks belong, cher." Alice smiled at her and finished setting the table. *It will be okay. I'll make it okay* she thought, trying to reassure herself.

Aunt Izzie tore off a large piece of bread and bit into it.

"You may want some butter or olive oil with that bread, Izzie; it's been around a couple of days—getting pretty hard."

"Oh, I like it this way, but I will take some of that olive oil—good for what ails you."

"How about a glass of sweet tea?" Mrs. Guidry offered the glass of un-iced, brown liquid. It was accepted without hesitation and gulped.

Turning the palms of her hands up, Mrs. G. looked at Aunt Izzie sighing, "I haven't been able to get Alice to eat. Poor thing, she'll be skinny as a toothpick."

"Come on, chile. You need to eat something it's a long trip back to Lafayette. Did I tell you that already? Sometimes I just talk and talk and half the time forgets what I just said." She laughed again, this time, patting her protruding belly. Alice and Cecile exchanged glances across the table.

Alice choked down some lunch, wanting desperately to please her aunt.

"Hurry along, cher, and get your things together. We need to get on the road soon as possible. Much as I hates to eat and run, I'm sure your friends will understand."

Mrs. Guidry shot a look at her daughter, warning her to keep her mouth shut.

Alice excused herself from the table and headed for her bedroom. "Come with me, 'Cile."

"Be there in a minute, Al," Cecile quickly finished her sandwich, gulped her tea, and grabbed a bag of potato chips to take with her. The door to Alice's room had been left open, so she went in, closing the door behind her.

Alice was bending over an open suitcase and looked up when the door closed.

Cecile walked over to her and placed her hand on top of Alice's head, rustling her hair." You look like you lost your last friend, Ally."

"Guess I'm about to," Alice sighed. "Aunt Izzie is just being an unreasonable witch."

"Cheer up, Ally. Lafayette ain't that far away, and I'll come see you as often as I can. Maybe you can come stay with us at Mardi Gras and in the summer."

"If they let me." She shrugged, "It'll be okay...I guess. Better than living with Belle." But the sadness in her eyes belied her attempt at cheerfulness. "Aunt Izzie and Uncle Bill are nice, but their kids are just plain mean."

Cecile brushed aside her own feelings and tried again to lift the spirits of her friend. "Oh, don't worry Ally. Your cousins will love you soon as they get to know you."

"I sure hope so." Then adding under her breath, "If they just don't make fun of me and exclude me from their stupid games." With that she yanked open a dresser drawer and started rummaging through her things. She had never packed for herself and quickly realized that she had no idea how to start.

"You be sure to do all your homework, 'Cile. I won't be here to help you with it anymore."

"My guitar is my homework, cher. I got a recital in a coupla weeks;" Alice shook her head. "You got to keep up with that school work, too. I better not hear about you flunking out. Hear me, girl?"

Cecile rolled her Cajun eyes.

"Cecile, you come on back in here, and let Alice pack," her mother called from down the hall. Before going, Cecile went over and embraced her friend. They clung to each other until 'Cile turned away to hide the tears. She walked out quickly, closing the door behind her.

The tears in back of Alice's eyes were stinging.

Looking around the room where she had spent her entire life, she tried to remember the good times, the times her dad had been home. But memories of her hiding there with Teddy in the dark flooded in, knocking aside the good memories. Alice took a few items from her dresser drawer but left room for the things she could not bear to part with—a collection of rocks she had gathered on the levee, strings of beads and gold coins from the last Mardi Gras, a snail shell Cecile had given her, and her favorite books. *Got to remember to get Teddy. Can't go to Lafayette without him.*

Aunt Izzie appeared in the doorway, "Can I help you, Alice?"

Alice looked at her helplessly. "We have to go by 'Cile's house for Teddy; I think it's on our way out." Her aunt nodded.

"And I left my best sneakers in the garage last Saturday. I'll need them for sure."

"Well, go get the sneakers, chile. And hurry. I'll just redo this packing a bit while you're gone." Aunt Izzie was mumbling to herself as Alice went out the door. Something about needing clothes for school, play, and church.

"Fore you go to the garage, bring me a shopping bag for some of these things you already packed," Aunt Izzie called out.

Oddly enough the old garage still stood there, apparently undamaged by the storm. The hinges squeaked as the old door cut a wide swath in the dirt of the garage floor, adding more dust to what was already accumulating there. *Guess Dad needs to fix those hinges,* she thought. *But will he ever be back to fix anything around here?*

Just then, a cloud of dust hit her nostrils, making her sneeze and cough. She took a tissue from her pocket and wiped her nose. Looking around, she soon spied her sneakers under the work bench, but a gigantic spider web was between her and the shoes. She was searching for something to destroy the spider web when she saw the trash can; it was sure to have a stick or something she could use. As she rummaged through the trash, she saw something that looked vaguely familiar. Where had she seen that shade of red before? When she picked it up and examined it, her blood turned to ice water. It was a canister with a large eye in the center. The eye had a dilated black pupil and inside the pupil were two orange snakes coiled around each other. She had last seen that hideous canister on an ad that had been discarded in the trash of this very house. She remembered 'Cile's reaction to it—had claimed it was an ad for a hex. *Did that canister have anything to do with what I saw on the porch step? Did I make my dad do something terrible? And where is Belle?*

The canister was empty but emitted a foul odor. Alice pushed it to the bottom of the trash and covered it over.

Chapter 9: Lafayette

Lafayette, Louisiana, 1948-1949

Alice had been in Lafayette one week when one of her favorite desserts, fudge-covered brownies, was served for Sunday lunch. She waited patiently until everyone else had been served and then took the last and smallest one for herself. Her mouth watered as she brought the delicious morsel toward it.

All of a sudden, Rachel, who was sitting beside her, jumped up from the table knocking the brownie to the floor. Her cousin, Mary, smiled as sixteen – year-old Matthew watched her reaction with that look in his eyes that gave her the creeps.

Alice had learned that she could maintain a somewhat peaceful existence with her cousins by keeping a low profile, finding it necessary to suppress her own wants and desires to accommodate theirs. She would get out of bed long before sunrise to ensure that both bathrooms were free for the others when they got up. This schedule had worked well for her, after all: She found that her mind was fresh to do homework early in the morning, that there were no distractions, and that it gave her a good excuse to go to bed early. But holding back on dessert was troublesome because she loved sweets.

Determined to get along at any price, she forced herself to give them their way, telling herself that she would be free to do as she pleased soon enough. Besides, Uncle Bill and Aunt Izzie usually treated her fairly. What more could someone like herself ask for?

The Broussard home, an unpretentious rambler, was located in an older section of Lafayette, where the live oaks formed a cathedral-like arch over the street, and Spanish moss hung from their limbs like old lace. The soil was so rich that flowers Aunt Izzie had never planted would pop out of the ground as if they had a will of their own.

One evening into her third week, the cousins invited her to join them in one of their favorite games, kick-the-can. *I don't know about this, but it's a chance to show them that I'm a good sport and more than willing to meet them half-way.*

They drew straws to see who would be *it*, and Alice got the shortest straw. Sixteen-year-old Mathew kicked the can into a distant neighbor's yard, and they all went to hide from Alice. She ran to the yard where the can had landed and was trying to retrieve it when a large pit bull came charging out of the doghouse barking and baring teeth at the intruder. Alice stood there staring at the dog. *Look away. I've heard that you never make eye contact with a dog attacking you.* But fear held her in its clutches so that she couldn't even move her eyes.

"Quiet down, Butch; it's okay." The voice came from the doorway of the owner's house and had the most amazing effect on the dog, who stopped barking and turned back toward its own shelter.

Alice picked up the can and began her search for the other players. After checking the front yards and finding no one, she began to feel anxious. *What if I've been hoodwinked? I wouldn't put it past them. I'll just check out back to be sure.* She looked through damp clothes still hanging on the lines, behind trees, in coal bins, and even in large garbage cans but found no sign of the other players. Getting angrier and angrier with herself for being so gullible and at her cousins for being so mean, she gave up the search, and headed back to Aunt Izzie's. The Spanish moss, so silvery and beautiful in the sunshine, now appeared like small ghouls waving from the live-oak branches.

Venus had just appeared in the western sky when she met a neighbor who lived on the next street over. "Beautiful, isn't it?" the lady asked, as she looked up at the star. "Looks like a plane requesting permission to land."

Alice felt her insides take a tumble, but she looked up to see a smiling face. "The first one in the evening sky and the biggest."

The neighbor fixed Alice with a stare, "How come you didn't go to the show with your cousins, cher?"

Alice's jaw dropped and tears stung the back of her eyes. "They went to the show?"

"Climbed into that old pick-up and took off. I was wondering why Matt parked it on our street."

The neighbor placed her arm around Alice's shoulder, giving her a little squeeze, "Come on, child, I'll bet your Aunt Izzie can find some cookies and hot cocoa in that big kitchen o' hers. Let's go see."

When they stepped on the porch, the family mutt, Puddles, ran to meet them. Alice bent down and hugged him to her chest.

Aunt Izzie opened the screen door and greeted her neighbor, Tabatha, with a warm smile. "Well if it ain't Tabby Cat. Come on in, neighbor, love to see you. How's about a cup of tea?"

"Let's have hot cocoa instead, so Alice can join us." Aunt Izzie caught the look in Tabatha's eyes and quickly agreed. They went to the kitchen, and soon hot cocoa was simmering on the large kitchen range.

"Stir the cocoa, Alice, while I go to the pantry." The aunt soon returned with a bag of marshmallows and offered the open bag to Alice and her guest. Plopping one into her own mouth, she winked at Alice. "Nothing like hot cocoa and marshmallows to make your day straight. Don't you think so, Tabby Cat?" The neighbor nodded in agreement.

Alice was placing two fat marshmallows in each of three large mugs and pouring hot cocoa over them. When Aunt Izzie opened the oven door, steam from the chocolate rose in the warm air to mingle with the aroma of freshly baked chocolate-chip oatmeal cookies. "O' course, these cookies also help. You like chocolate chip cookies, Ally?"

"One of my favorites," said Alice as she took a warm cookie from the pan.

They gathered closer around the cookies, not bothering to switch them to a platter. "Let's us tell some ghost stories," suggested Aunt Izzie. "Bet you know some doozies, Tabatha." The two women exchanged glances.

Tabatha cleared her throat and began. "Why I do remember one time when I was about five or six years old, something very strange happened. Mama always said we saw a death light."

"Goodness sakes alive, tell us about it," chimed in Aunt Izzie, as she dipped her cookie into the hot cocoa. Alice perked up her ears.

Tabatha's wide-set, green eyes grew larger as she began the story. "We lived on a farm so far back in the sticks the crows couldn't find us." She paused, looking at Alice. "Well, one night as we was about to go to bed we saw a strange light moving over the tree tops on the other side of the cornfield."

"What did it look like?" asked Aunt Izzie.

"Well, it looked like the light from a giant flashlight or lantern."

"Could somebody been walking over there with a lantern?"

"Above the tree tops, Izzie?"

"Oh yeah. Forgot about that. Well, how was it moving?"

"Just let me tell the story, neighbor. Then you can talk all you want." She squinted both eyes and twisted her mouth. "That light moved slowly along the tops of them trees as we watched it. Then all of a sudden, it scattered apart like a firecracker, shooting sparks in every direction. Finally, it went back together in a ball the size of a car headlight. That thing danced over the trees for several minutes before taking off and heading straight for my grandpa's farm a few miles even farther back in the sticks."

"Sounds to me like aliens," said Aunt Izzie. "Did you report it to the authorities?"

"Never did. Guess we were scared they'd think we was crazy."

"You think it might have been swamp gases?" asked Alice with a shy look on her face, not wanting to appear smarter than her elders.

"That ain't all. Don't you know a field hand came running up to our house the very next day to tell us that grandpa had been found dead in his barn. They said it was a heart attack. I always wondered if he saw that strange light like we did."

"Well, danged if I can beat that one," exclaimed Aunt Izzie. "That was the strangest true story I ever heard. It did really happen, didn't it, Tabby?"

"I wouldn't say it was, if'n it won't, Izzie."

It was so warm and friendly around the old oak table that Alice soon forgot about the feelings of rejection and resentment toward her cousins. But the next day as she recalled the details of how her cousins had tricked her, the feelings returned. Remembering that she often felt better after talking about such feelings to the school counselor, Sister Bernadette, she went to her office. But Sister had gone to a meeting at another school, so Alice had to carry the weight of those feelings around with her all day. She snapped at people, and they snapped back. She stormed through the hallways daring anyone to knock the brick off her shoulder and found quite a few volunteers. Her music teacher pulled her aside, "Alice, it is not okay to act out our feelings."

The next day, Alice found Sister Bernadette in her office. The nun looked up, and seeing Alice, she motioned for her to enter. Alice did so, and closed the door behind her. Sitting across from her teacher and mentor, she folded her hands in her lap and recited the incident with her cousins.

"That was a terrible thing they did to you, Alice, but it is a reflection on their own poor character and has nothing to do with you. At the same time, you may want to examine your attitude toward your 'country cousins.' Remember the lesson of Saint Francis—that it is in loving and accepting others just as they are that we will receive love."

"Love?" Alice rose, practically shouting the word. "I hate their guts."

The nun said nothing, realizing that forgiving is never easy and takes time, often a lot of time. She accepted Alice right where she was at that moment, and Alice felt the acceptance and love. After several minutes, the nun touched Alice's hand saying, "Ah, child. It is a shame that one so young should have to wrestle with one of the great challenges in life. How *do* we love people who are mean to us? There are no easy answers. But for the sake of our souls, for our own peace of mind, our own chance to live happy and fulfilling lives, we must find a way. Most of the time, people are just being themselves. Don't expect them to fit into your world like puppets. Look for friends who like you just the way you are. And enjoy them every chance you get."

"I don't have anyone here who likes me."

"You will. Just be sure to keep your eyes open so you can see them." After Alice left the office, Sister called out to her young assistant, "Paula, get me the telephone number for Izzie Broussard. Think I'll just put a bee in her bonnet."

When Alice got home from school later that day, Aunt Izzie was waiting for her, "Come into the kitchen, cher; let's look for some more of those cookies you like." She poured a glass of milk so cold that it frosted the glass. Then placing several cookies on a small plate, she sat down across from her niece. Taking Alice's small hand in hers, she looked her in the eyes, "Ally, I have some bad news."

Alice wondered what could get worse.

"There's no good way to say this, so I'll just come out with it." She paused, squeezing Alice's hand. "Your mother, Belle, is dead." Alice did not ask what happened, fearing that she already knew. Nevertheless, Belle's death was a shock. And she searched her heart for tears, but they would not come. She tried to remember the times Belle had been good to her, but all of them were times Belle had been trying to please her family or showing off for the neighbors. The child tried to put on a mask of sadness to please her aunt.

Puddles came running into the kitchen wagging his tail when he saw Alice. "Hey, Boy, did ya' miss me? She offered him one of her cookies, but Aunt Izzie intervened, "Don't give him chocolate, Alice, it'll make him sick."

Alice just sat there staring straight ahead, allowing the numbness to take over.

Chapter 10: The Jazz Funeral

Belle's funeral began with a march from the funeral home. The hot, humid air carried the fragrance of magnolias mixed with the faint smell of garbage—so typical of New Orleans in spring. Family, friends, and the brass band were followed by onlookers and just-plain-jazz lovers. They all stepped in time to the somber playing of *Just a Closer Walk with Thee.*

After the body was in the ground and folks had said their final goodbyes, the band cut loose. A swinging version of *When the Saints Go Marching In* was followed by the latest hot jazz tunes. The second line danced and twirled parasols or waved handkerchiefs.

Alice thought it was a fitting way for Belle to go. *You would have been happy with your funeral, Belle. I'm glad.* She did not understand why thinking that made her feel better.

Alice looked for her dad but could not find him. At the funeral home, her eyes wondered through the crowd of Belle's relatives and then more slowly and carefully through the few members of the Hollister family present. Familiar family features in the latter group touched a deep ache and longing within her. At the gravesite, she peered around trees and gravestones and checked out every car as it passed.

With each failure to spot him, the emptiness returned, creeping up her spine and settling around her heart, mingling with the fear that was her constant companion. He wasn't there. Why wasn't he there?

Other family members, friends, and neighbors stopped by the little shotgun house following the funeral. They brought steaming dishes of crawfish etouffee, chicken-sausage gumbo, shrimp, carrot soufflé, okra smothered in Creole tomatoes, jambalaya, and other New Orleans favorites. And although the food was gourmet delicious, it did not touch the emptiness and fear inside Alice.

As at all social gatherings in the city when crawfish were in season, there were platters piled high with the tasty, delectable little 'mudbugs.' Hot bread pudding with whiskey sauce was everyone's favorite dessert. Bottles of French wine were dispersed throughout the room, for any social gathering without wine was a dark and dull occasion for the French, who saw a funeral as an occasion to celebrate life.

Alice stopped to stare at one of the crawfish platters, asking out loud, "How do you eat them? Dad never let us have them in the house."

Cecile, who was there with her mother, stepped forward, "Let me show you, cher." She grinned as she picked up a special bib from a table nearby and placed it around Alice's neck.

"You're in for a treat, my friend." Alice looked at her with raised eyebrows.

Holding the crustacean in one hand, Cecile twisted off the tail with the other. "Next you suck the hot, spicy juices out o' the head." Alice watched as her friend actually put the ugly, beady-eyed little head into her mouth and sucked. "YUM YUM, soo good!" She rolled her eyes toward heaven and smacked her lips. Alice was still skeptical.

"Now, place the top o' the tail between your thumb and forefinger at the sides o' the tail and squeeze." She demonstrated. The shell broke open, and the meat popped into her mouth. "Dee lish ous!"

Alice raised her index finger to her chin, still pondering whether she wanted to try this Cajun delicacy when everyone's attention was drawn to loud voices coming from the kitchen. Belle's mother, Mellette, had raised her voice so that everyone could hear, "Whahr dat Tom? Too shamed to show he face?"

Aunt Izzie pulled herself erect and faced the angry woman, "Don't be a fool, Mellette."

The remark fed Mellette's rage. Red in the face and scowling, she raised her voice a few decibels higher, "Fool am I? Everybody know he put hex on her. My poor chile die in agony. Dem doctors and nurses at Charity say her stomach pains worst they ever see. Growin' snakes in her belly, she was. I seen 'em." She stood with her hands on her hips, declaring that the discussion was closed.

Aunt Izzie looked around for Alice. Spying her still standing as if paralyzed beside the crawfish platter, the older woman took her by the hand. "Come on, child, we're going home. Don't you pay no mind to crazy talk."

Uncle Bill appeared in the doorway and quickly loaded his wife and Alice into his new Ford. Aunt Izzie had insisted that the other children stay in school. They drove away without another word. With a little luck, they could make it to Lafayette before dark, using the Old Spanish Trail.

While Alice was enjoying the peace and quiet of a respite from her cousins, it gave her more time to worry. *Why didn't Daddy come today? Did he really put a hex on Belle? Sister Bernadette said voodoo was nothing but superstition. I wish I could talk to her about it, but I'm too ashamed. If she finds out how bad we are, I might lose my only friend.*

Chapter11: Honors for Alice

"Hold still, Alice," Aunt Izzie gave one last vigorous brush to the shiny red hair and was tying it with a white ribbon at the back of Alice's neck. The ribbon was a perfect match for the new white dress from Maison Bleu, a graduation gift for promotion to eighth grade.

Her cousin, Mary, rolled her eyes and huffed, "Why are they making such a big deal out of her being promoted to eighth grade? They never gave me a ceremony or anything else, for that matter, when I was promoted."

"Alice always gets special attention cause she's teacher's pet." Her sister, Rachel, chirped. "Haven't you heard, Sister bought her that new dress to wear?"

"Now hush up, Girls. Alice didn't have anyone else to buy her a dress." Aunt Izzie finished the bow and turned Alice so she could see herself in the hall mirror.

A skinny, freckled face, well-scrubbed kid stared back at her. People were always telling her to smile, so she tried it. She didn't look half bad in her little white dress with the big sailor collar and a big smile showing her white, even teeth. *Yeah, I'll try smiling more often—makes me feel better.*

It was a sweltering June day. Girls in white dresses and boys in navy gabardine jackets filled the auditorium. They were surrounded by loving parents and other family members. The smell of books, closed for the summer, filled the large room where the distinctive fragrance of vegetable soup from the cafeteria still hung in the air. Straight rows of uncomfortable seats added to the ambiance.

Birdsong from the nearby woods could be heard through the open windows. An occasional cough could be heard above the whispered chatter in the audience. One of the seventh graders started playing the piano, and all stood for *The Star Spangled Banner,* placing their right hands over their hearts.

When a sixth grader was reading a poem she had written, the squirming started. Several boys jostled and punched each other, snickering and giggling. A blistering look from Sister Bernadette brought the behavior to an abrupt halt.

Alice was watching the door, keeping her fingers crossed that her dad might suddenly appear. *Where is he? Will I ever see him again?* The emptiness and loneliness swept over her again, clouding what otherwise might have been a pleasant day.

Her thoughts returned to the present moment when she heard the principal saying, "And graduating from seventh grade with highest honors.........Alice Hollister with a perfect record of straight A's." Her friends applauded. Alice looked down, blushing. The child mounted the stage with her head down, looking no one in the eye. The principal hugged her and handed her a diploma.

They closed by singing the school alma mater. As they sang, Alice realized she would miss school but, most of all, she would miss her friend and teacher, Sister Bernadette.

Trying to sneak out the back door unnoticed, she was surrounded by several teachers, students, and other adults, offering their congratulations, smiles, and lots of hugs. Armand, one of the boys in her class, slipped up from behind and lightly kissed her on the cheek. Glaring at him, she swiped it off with the back of her hand.

As they started for home, thunder boomed from the distance, and dark clouds gathered overhead. The smell of rain permeated the air as a cool breeze blew against her; she grabbed the white ribbon from her hair, placing it in her pocket before making a mad dash for shelter. Luckily she reached the house just ahead of the drenching downpour. Wanting to stay on the porch to watch the storm, she reluctantly obeyed Aunt Izzie's call to come inside. "If you can see the lightning, Alice, it is close enough to strike," she warned. Inside, Alice sat where she could hear the sound of rain hitting the tin roof. Staying close to nature brought her comfort.

When the rain ended three hours later, Alice checked the rain gauge; the line was above the eleven - inch mark. The neighborhood children were wading in the overflowing ditches, but Alice stayed on the porch, holding Puddles and watching them. She told herself that wading in the microbe-filled water where broken glass was apt to be encountered was not safe, but at the same time, she was longing to join the laughing frolicking kids her own age.

"Hey, Alice, wanna go crabbing with us? They'll be biting something fierce after this rain."

Alice turned to see Armand with a boy from eighth grade and two girls she had never met. She thought about what Sister had said—finding friends who would like her. Placing both hands on her hips, she looked in Armand's direction, "You promise you won't do what you did this morning?"

"Cross my heart." He made the sign of a cross over his heart and added, "Wear your boots. It's kind'a wet out here." She laughed. Then joining the little group, she headed for the river with them. Puddles followed behind.

"Here, Alice, you wanna carry the net; it's the most important piece of equipment." Alice accepted the net; it made her feel like one of them.

Reaching their destination, they set to their tasks without wasting time. Raw chicken parts were tied to a long string, and the chicken parts were slung into the water. Before too long, a tug on his string told Armand that a crab was probably gnawing on his chicken, so he slowly and carefully pulled it toward shore. The other boy grabbed it with the net.

The clawing crustacean was then dropped into the large basket nearby. Puddles barked and wagged his tail. As more crabs were added to the melee of fighting, clawing crustaceans, many of the creatures lost their limbs. Alice was watching them with a look of pity on her face when she felt a tug on her line. The boy with the net was watching and quickly went over to stand beside her.

"Pull him in easy, Alice. Looks like a big one." Alice wasn't sure she wanted to catch the poor creature and send him to his doom, but she wanted even more to be a part of the group. When the crab was safely in the net, she got a thumbs up from Armand and a smile from one of the girls.

The girl's name was Aimee and looked to be about Alice's age. The smile was returned, and Alice felt good inside, realizing that she was actually enjoying herself.

When the basket contained as many crabs as the little group could safely carry, they started for home. Alice turned to her new friend and asked, "What will we do with them?"

"Cook 'em and eat 'em, o' course. My mom knows just how to cook 'em. Haven't you ever eat crab afore?" Aimee asked as she swept her black hair from her face, her dark eyes showing surprise that here was someone who could be so different from the world she knew and loved.

"Never have."

Aimee smiled again, displaying a row of beautiful, white teeth, "Well, you're in for a treat. Come on home with me, and we'll show you how to eat 'em—really good eating with lots a melted butter and lemon." Shaking her head, she smacked her lips in anticipation.

Alice picked up one handle of the basket to help Armand carry their catch to the house. Giving a little scream, she quickly dropped the handle when a claw grabbed for her hand. "Knock him back down with the handle of the net," cried the other boy. Using the handle of the net, he quickly returned the creature into the midst of its fighting companions. He then picked up the handle to help Armand.

Show off, thought Alice. But then she remembered that she was trying to make new friends, so she brushed the thought aside.

Aimee's mother was thrilled to see the basket of crabs and quickly began boiling a large pot of water. A white oil cloth was spread on a table nearby with more spices and seasonings than Alice had ever seen set out at one time.

She watched in horror as the live, clawing crabs were dropped into the boiling water. "Does it hurt them?" she asked.

"Cher, they are going to crab heaven. They are serving the purpose for which the good Lord made 'em." Aimee chirped as she set a large bowl of melted butter on the table.

When the cooked crabs were spread out on the oil cloth, Aimee said, "Here, Alice, let me show you which parts to eat and which to leave alone." Alice picked at the crab because she did not want to displease her new friends, although she really wanted to leave and not participate in this barbaric feast. Eating enough to be polite, she soon took leave of her new friends, bidding them a fond farewell and thanking them.

"You come back anytime to see my Aimee," smiled the girl's mother.

Alice skipped and hummed a happy little tune all the way home. *Wish every day could be like today, but I know it won't.* Thunder rumbled in the distance.

Chapter 12: The Explosion

Arriving back at the house, she was surprised to see the adults gathered around the radio in the living room. Something was going on. Aunt Izzie was crying.

Alice felt a new fear creeping up her spine, "What's wrong?"

Uncle Bill took her out on the back porch.

"We don't know yet, Alice. But there's been an explosion in the Gulf."

Alice went limp and everything around her went black.

When she opened her eyes, her cousin, Mary, was standing over her with smelling salts.

Uncle Bill was saying, "Now just stay calm, girl, Matt is trying to get through to Texas Oil right now. We don't even know if'n it was one o' their rigs. And even if it was, I'd be willing to bet—your pappy was the first to get on one of those lifeboats. Most experienced men like Tom find a way to survive."

"Wh-where's Aunt Izzie?"

"She's in her room lying down."

Alice wanted to be near her father's other close relative, but Uncle Bill held up his hand to stop her. "No sense in you two upsetting each other. Why don't you help Mary in the kitchen? Folks might start dropping by, 'fore long."

Puddles came bouncing through the open screen door and stopped at Alice's feet. Alice grabbed him to her. The dog licked at her face as the tears welled up in her eyes. The ever present fear around her heart was beginning to move out to other parts of her body. It was engulfing her, choking her. She prayed that her dad would be okay.

Everyone turned expectantly toward Mat when he came out. "It was their rig all right, but that's all they can tell us for now. They'll start calling every 10, 15 minutes once they know something."

"Oh, no," sobbed Alice. Puddles licked her face. Before long, she reluctantly put the dog down and washed her hands before going to the kitchen. Mary was lining up ingredients to prepare her favorite cookies--flour, eggs, sugar, vanilla, and lemons.

"Alice, you can crack the pecans."

Mary's being nice to me, thought Alice. *The last time I cracked nuts for her she fussed at me because they were broken into small pieces. I'll just try extra hard to keep each of them in two large pieces this time.* So she carefully cracked each nut and began extracting the halves.

Mary frowned, slapping the counter,

"What are you doing, you little dope? Don't you know anything? These cookies need pecan pieces."

She grabbed the hammer out of Alice's hand and gave it to her sister who was watching with glee.

Alice turned red with shame; *I really am good for nothing,* she thought *as* she went to look for Puddles, who had escaped to the backyard. She had just opened the screen door when the telephone rang. No matter how much Alice wanted to grab the telephone, she didn't dare. Uncle Bill picked it up on the third ring, "I see....Yes....we'll be waiting to hear from you. Thank you for calling." He hung up, looking at Alice, "That was a representative from Texas Oil. No word on your dad yet."

The doorbell rang. Josephine, a neighbor, stood there holding a covered dish. With concern written on her face, she handed the dish to Uncle Bill. "My cousin, Robert, works for Texas Oil. Was it their rig?"

Uncle Bill looked at her in sympathy, "I'm afraid so ma'am. Would you care to stay here and wait for word with us?"

She nodded, "I'd like that. Thank you."

Uncle Bill held the door for her, and she entered.

Other neighbors stopped by or drifted in all evening, bringing casseroles, cakes, cookies, crawfish bread (frozen since last Christmas), and other rich Louisiana dishes. Those who stayed clustered around the radio, hugged each other a lot, and jumped every time the telephone rang.

Uncle Bill took a call around 10 p.m. and returned to the living room, "About a dozen men are returning to the dock in New Orleans in an emergency support vessel. Let's drive over there. Our men could be there waiting for us. Alice, you can go with us. The rest of you kids go to bed. Mat, you stay by the telephone. If they call, write down everything they say. Mary, you might make another pot o' coffee. Looks like folks will be here awhile." The telephone rang.

Chapter 13: The Wait

Matt, who had answered the telephone, replaced the receiver and turned to the group. "One of the lifeboats turned over, but they think they got all the men."

"Write it down, Son. Others may want to know."

Uncle Bill and the others drove through the night to New Orleans, all ears glued to the sound of the radio. Alice prayed on her rosary all the way, hoping that if she just prayed hard enough that her dad would be waiting for her on the pier.

A half-moon was rising over the Mississippi when they reached the river. And although it was still hot and humid, Alice could not stop shaking. Uncle Bill maneuvered through the traffic and was lucky enough to find parking near the pier; he pulled into the newly vacated space. People were arriving by car, truck, and on foot. Some of the trucks were loaded, with people standing in the beds. No matter how they came, their faces were marked with fear and desperation. They scanned the pier and the black Mississippi beyond, searching for anything that would feed the hope lingering like a candle placed before an altar.

Uncle Bill joined a small group who were nodding their heads from time to time as a policeman talked and gestured toward the river with his hands. After a few minutes, the uncle returned to the open window of the car announcing, "No sign of 'em yet. Guess I'll mosey about and talk to some more folks—see what I can find out."

"Let me go with you," pleaded Alice.

"Ally, this ain't no place for a little girl at night. Try to get some sleep."

"I can't sleep. I just want to know that he's okay."

Josephine reached over for Alice's hand, "I know what we can do. Let's sing some songs. What's your favorite, cher?"

Alice withdrew her hand, "I don't feel like singing."

Josephine began anyway in her rich soprano voice, "Be still my soul, the Lord is on thy side…." The others joined in one by one. Alice refused to sing. Her heart was weighted down with worry. She sat stiffly in the corner looking out the window, glowering, and wishing they would just shut up. Her right hand was clenched into a fist, assuring herself that she would overcome the difficulties life was throwing at her. But no one noticed or cared.

Uncle Bill's face soon reappeared in the car window, "An emergency support vessel has been spotted up by the buoy." Alice opened the door and jumped out before anyone could stop her. She peered out into the black water hoping to spot the familiar form she loved so well. But she could see only darkness and hear the seagulls taunting refrain. The waters of the Mississippi were in control—not to be mastered. The waiting was torture.

After several minutes—hours to her mind, she thought she detected movement out on the water. A crowd was gathering at a spot several feet away. She guessed that the vehicle carrying the men would be docking there. Squeezing between a fat lady holding a baby and a bearded man, she placed herself in the center of the group where she had a good view but couldn't be seen by Uncle Bill or the others. The emergency vessel pulled up to the dock; it contained what looked like eight men. The area had been roped off to hold back the crowd and give the men some space to maneuver. The first man got off the boat and walked unsteadily across the weathered planks. A young woman beside the fat lady with the baby screamed and ran toward him. He grabbed her, the fat lady, and the baby in both arms. They stood there embracing and talking excitedly before walking off together.

Alice strained to get a closer look at each man as he disembarked. As her fear and apprehension grew so did her courage; finally she clenched her right fist in one last effort to bolster her strength and courage. She approached the next man walking in her direction, "Mister, do you know Tom Hollister?"

"Sure do, little lady. He's not in this boat, but another boat picked up some of us a few miles out. Bet you ole Tom is with them."

"Where's that boat now?"

"Don't exactly know. But it should be along any minute now."

"There you are, Alice. We been lookin' all over for you. Let's go back to the house and see what Texas Oil has to say. Bet they've located Tom by now." Uncle Bill reached for her hand, but Alice was too quick for him. She darted into the remaining crowd of despondent people still peering into the darkness covering the river like a shroud.

Alice wandered about on the pier until she spotted a place between two boats where she could not be seen by the crowd. It felt good to get away by herself—she could cry and watch for the other emergency vessel. No one would disturb her. She removed her shoes and reached for the water with her toes, but her legs were too short.

With a grunt of disgust and frustration, she replaced her sneakers and was about to tie the strings when something clamped over her mouth. She tried to scream, but nothing came out as the hand from behind pushed her lower jaw against her upper teeth. Her lips were caught in the middle. She felt something warm trickling down her chin and tasted blood in her mouth. Then she was being lifted into the air by a pair of arms much stronger than she was. Terror exploded inside her. She panicked. Her mind became a jumble of mush. Then through the force of her own will, she brushed the panic aside. A picture came to mind. She saw the instructor from a recent class on safety. What was he doing? All of a sudden she got her right leg free. She kicked with all her might into the groin of her abductor. A male voice yelled out in pain. His grip loosened enough for her to get free. She fell to the boards below, picked herself up, and started running, calling out as she ran.

She heard waves lapping against the dock on her right and figured she had to run to the left. Holding her hands out in front to keep from running into something, she could not see her hands. She stumbled and fell but quickly picked herself up, turning to see any movement behind her.

Then out of the darkness and fog came a familiar voice, "Is that you, Alice?" She had never heard anything more welcome.

"Uncle Bill?"

"Girl, you need a good whipping. You come on here and get yourself in that car before I give it to you right here."

The threats were familiar and calming after what she had just experienced, and she could tell that Uncle Bill was glad to see her. But she was afraid to tell him or anyone about the man who had grabbed her; they would just say it was all her fault. They couldn't see her injured lips in the dark, and tomorrow she would find a way to hide them.

Falling into the backseat of the car, she was exhausted but too hyper and scared to sleep. Thoughts of her dad out in the darkness of the Mississippi raced through her mind as she cuddled up in a fetal position trying to find comfort for herself. But comfort would not come.

When the truck pulled up in front of the house, Alice jumped out and ran inside. Aunt Izzie sat at the kitchen table crying. Alice opened her mouth to speak, but nothing came out.

"They just called, Ally. He's gone."

Alice screamed and screamed, "My dad's okay; I know he is. He'll be coming back to me. You'll see." She rocked back and forth trying to shut out reality. Grabbing a pot off the stove, she threw it and searched for other things to throw. Finding none, she screamed louder, her body convulsing in anger and rage. She went on and on railing against the world and a God who would permit this to happen to her.

The loving aunt just watched and tried to protect her from herself. Finally, through her own tears, Aunt Izzie caught site of Alice's face. "Why! What on earth happened to your lip, child?"

"It doesn't matter. I don't care," she yelled and screamed some more.

Finally, Aunt Izzie took the child in her arms and rocked her until she quieted down. Then she gently cared for the broken lip. The much harder work of mending her heart would be tackled in the days and weeks to come.

Chapter 14: The Acadians

Alice was in her fourth week of grief counseling when Sister Bernadette said, "There is much you can learn about getting through the hard times from your ancestors, cher. Let me tell you a story."

Alice listened as the elderly nun looked out the window with a faraway look in her eyes. "It all started when our ancestors, the Acadians, came over from France and settled in Acadia."

Alice furrowed her brow. "The Acadians were your ancestors, too, Sister?"

The nun took the child's hand and smiled, "Yes."

"They settled there in 1604. That would be about sixteen years before the Mayflower landed on Plymouth Rock. Acadia was the first European settlement in Canada."

Alice withdrew her hand as she frowned and said, "But they were Belle's people, not mine."

"They were your people, too, little one. Now just be quiet and listen to what I have to tell you."

Alice bowed her head, "I'll do as you say, Sister. But first, tell me where Acadia is located"

"Why, Child, Acadia is located in Nova Scotia, New Brunswick, and other areas of Canada. Here, I can show it to you on this 17th century map on my wall."

Alice rose from her chair and traced the location with her finger.

"Now, cher, the Acadians had troubles like we've never seen, but they found their way, just as you must find yours." She paused, looking at the trusting child, "But I'm getting ahead of my story." She took a deep breath and continued, "Our people were happy and prosperous there for many years, with beautiful farms, orchards, vineyards, animals, and many possessions."

"What happened?"

"The British came and took control of Acadia in 1710, declaring that all the inhabitants had to pledge allegiance to the British king. That meant that the Acadians would have to renounce their Catholic faith and join the Church of England. So when the French and Indian War broke out in 1754, can you blame them for sympathizing with the French? After all, they had come from France and shared a common religion: Catholicism."

Alice nodded.

"Well, soon after the war broke out, the Acadians were expelled from their idyllic homeland by the British. Our ancestors were herded onto ships like animals, in 1755, and sent out to sea with no thought of keeping families and loved ones together."

Alice looked at her, "I always thought the British were the good guys."

"Not always, Alice." She looked around the room at her many books. "The plight of the Acadians inspired the American poet, Henry Wadsworth Longfellow, to write his epic poem, *Evangeline*. Do you know who Longfellow was?"

Alice nodded, "But I haven't read that poem."

"Well, Evangeline is a fictional Acadian maiden who was separated from her betrothed at the time of the exile or what our people called *Le Grand Derangement*. She spent the rest of her life looking for him."

Alice scrunched up her face and looked intently at the nun, "Did she ever find him?"

"You'll have to read the poem and find out, *mon petit chou*? But to get back to our story—when they left, the Acadians were allowed to take with them only what they could carry on their backs."

"But what happened to the beautiful farms and other possessions? They must have accumulated a lot in 150 years."

"Everything was burned to the ground—even the crops in the fields. And the ships our people were loaded onto were in such poor condition that half of our people died at sea. The ships wandered about from country to country. They were allowed to stop long enough to get provisions, but no one would take them in. Then in 1784, the King of Spain allowed the Acadians to settle along the coast of what is today Louisiana."

Alice looked incredulous. "They were at sea all those years?"

Yes, the French and Indian War lasted until 1763"

"I guess it took folks that long to get over their fear of causing trouble with the British."

Sister nodded. "Well, when they got to Louisiana, most of them went to New Orleans, but the French aristocracy *there* made life so difficult for them that they soon left. So our people went west and settled along the bayous of central and western Louisiana where they farmed, fished, and trapped. They ate what was available to them, and today crawfish or 'mud bugs' are one of their favorite foods."

"Ooh! Those disgusting 'mud bugs'?"

The nun sighed, "Needless to say, they had a tough life, but they were happy because they were free to live the way their consciences dictated."

"Everybody wants to be happy."

"Yes, they do. But our people worked very hard. Not to say they didn't enjoy the good times. Why a *fais-do-do* was at somebody's house every week with enough 'la la' to keep you on your feet 'til the sun came up." She cocked her ear as if listening, I can hear that fiddle and accordion now accompanied by the jure.

Alice looked puzzled, "What's jure?"

"Child, jure means clapping and stomping in time with the music, the 'la la'—kept 'em going, it did. Couldn't help joining in the fun 'cause that music come straight from the heart." She paused and looked at Alice again, "Don't look at me like that, child, I was young once, and I loved to dance."

Alice grinned, "The rub board is my favorite."

"That came later with the development of zydeco."

"But zydeco sounds so forlorn—always singing about being lonely or some lost love."

"Oh, yes, it is natural for a Cajun to sing about his troubles."

"You called them *Cajuns* for the first time. How did they get that name?"

"It's most likely a contraction of Acadians, but you will hear some negative people say that it was because the Acadians intermarried with so many other nationalities—Spanish, German, Creole, Irish, American Indians, etc. Those negative folks do not understand that national and cultural intermingling is something Acadians are proud of."

Alice nodded.

"That pride is part of our identity—just like the ability to find joy and laughter in the ordinary things in life. That ability is a powerful force in the universe."

Alice frowned in concentration, "Did all Cajuns come from Acadia?"

"No. But we are straying from the subject, my petit. We were talking about Cajuns singing about their troubles. Did you ever hear, *Les Haricots Sont Pas Sales*?"

Alice shook her head.

The nun spoke with pride in her voice, "Well, when times were so hard they couldn't buy salted meat to flavor the snap beans, they felt better when they sang about it. The song laments how the snap beans ain't got no salt. Singing and making joy about tough times is also one of our better characteristics."

"I've noticed that."

Sister smiled, "And then in 1803 we became Americans. Our people thrived on plantations until that way of life was destroyed by the War Between the States. Even that did not alter our faith and the deeply–rooted conviction that life was given to us to be lived and enjoyed. We hear it today when we say, *Laissez les Bon Temps Rouler.*"

"I hear that all the time."

"Of course you do—couldn't stay long in Louisiana without hearing it." The nun continued, "Then in 1901, oil was discovered here. Lafayette, the heart and soul of Cajun Country, became a center for oil, natural gas, refineries, and the manufacture of petrochemicals."

"Ah! Lafayette."

"So you see, my pet, the Cajun people followed their own path and found success in spite of all the hardships they suffered. And so will you if you just have faith to follow your own light."

Alice was puzzled by what she meant about following her own light. What light was she talking about? She decided not to ask because this whole discussion was pointless as far as she was concerned. After all, she did not see herself as a Cajun. *"I'm from Texas, and I want no part of Belle's people.*

As she was leaving, she remembered that Mary and Rachel were away at camp for two weeks. *I must remember to bar the bedroom door with a chair. I don't want Matt coming into my room at night again. Should I talk to Sister about this? No! They'd just find a way to blame me.*

So Alice kept on trying to get along in the world as best she could. Then came high school.

Chapter 15: Another World

Lafayette, Louisiana, 1954

The event that Alice dreaded most in high school came around faithfully every Friday afternoon: social dancing in gym. The ruminations of torture would start when she smelled fish frying in the cafeteria at lunchtime. Her fear would escalate with each image of rejection and humiliation until she was ready to give up everything and leave school.

This Friday seemed no different from all the others. Sitting alone in one corner of the gymnasium as the music started, she twisted the tissue in her hand and then used it to wipe the sweat from her palms. All of the other girls had been asked to dance, even fat Estelle, one of the few girls who was nice to her. *If an earthquake is going to strike in the near future, let it be now.*

She looked up when Mr. Harrington, her gym teacher, approached, "May I have this dance, Miss Alice?" She stood up stiffly, certain that every eye in the room was on her. She offered him her hand. He took it and began to lead her in a foxtrot as she forced a smile that came out looking like a surreal sneer. "Alice, my wife is looking for someone to help out in her dance studio. Would you be interested?"

"I might. When should I apply?" The kindness and offer were more than she had hoped for. She smiled for the first time that day.

"The sooner you apply, the better your chance of getting the position."

When class ended, Alice went to the shower room to change. She really didn't need to shower since no one else had asked her to dance, but the warm water might help wash away the feeling of gloom fighting the newly found glimpse of hope inside.

After the shower, she was bending over by her locker, searching for her shoes when she heard voices behind her. Her cousin Rachel, by now a senior, was just leaving with her best friend, Janice.

"I heard Harrington had to rescue 'the monster' in dance class. What a loser!"

Rachel turned up her nose, "Yeah, nobody likes her."

"I feel kind'a sorry for her; she's never invited to parties or sleep overs like the normal kids—just sticks her nose in a book all the time."

"Don't waste your pity, Janice. She's a nut case."

After that, Alice didn't feel up to interviewing at the Harrington Studio that day but found some comfort in remembering what Sister Bernadette had said during her last visit.

"Have you noticed that they rev up the hostility and name calling when you score 100% on a test they just failed or performed poorly on? As the old saying goes, Alice, no one beats a dead horse. Do you understand me, child? They're getting back at you for making them look bad."

The following morning, Alice stopped by the Harrington Dance Studio. Becky Harrington was a slim brunette with an oval face, large brown eyes, a straight little nose, and a cupid bow's mouth. Alice thought she was the most beautiful woman she had ever seen. Alice picked up a job application at the front desk and filled it out. Afterward, she went into Becky's small office and handed it to her. Becky looked over the simple application, made eye contact, and winked. Alice felt at ease.

She began working four days later—after school two days a week and all day Saturday. She did light cleaning, maintained financial records, ran errands, and assisted wherever needed.

Surprised to find that she liked assisting in the ballroom best of all, she went in there every chance she got—to assist one of the instructors in demonstrating a new step or to fill in when someone lost a dance partner. The instructors were more than happy to teach her a few 'tricks of the trade,' and help her smooth out her dance steps. She learned quickly, felt the rhythm deep inside, and could make her feet move in time to the rhythm.

She became their 'girl Friday.' And for Alice, the Studio became a sanctuary; and Becky Harrington, her role model and friend.

One day, Becky looked at her and said, "Alice, you have such nice features. Have you tried just a touch of liquid makeup and a dab of lipstick? You could be a beauty, you know." She took her makeup sponge and lightly brushed it over Alice's face. Then a very pale reddish-orange lipstick was added. "Let's put just a touch of blush on those high cheek bones." Becky stood back, appraising her handiwork. "Wow, girl, you've got it."

Alice looked in the mirror, but all she saw was 'Monster,' wearing makeup, lipstick, and blush. It would take years to erase the image others had placed in her mind. But she wanted more than anything to please Becky, so she agreed with her.

Becky looked pleased with her makeover, "Girl, you look so great; let's go shopping for new clothes. I know this little shop in my neighborhood where second-hand clothes are sold for next to nothing. Let's go; it'll be fun."

A few days later, they climbed into Becky's red, Ford Convertible and headed out. Frank Sinatra was crooning on the radio as Becky gradually increased her speed, and Alice threw her head back allowing the breeze to dance through her hair.

In the second-hand shop, Alice tried on several outfits before selecting a dress the color of buttercups with an empire waist; the pale yellow brought out the vibrant rose in her cheeks and glow in her pale, creamy skin. The simple lines of the dress emphasized her twenty-three inch waist and thirty-five inch bust. She walked out of the fitting room and stared at herself in the full-length mirror. 'Monster' was fading.

Becky looked her over, "That is your color, girl—brings out the natural tones of your skin and adds highlights to your hair. You need to find out what other colors work for you." She paused, eyeing the dress more carefully, "A single strand of pearls will really offset it. I have a pair you may borrow. By the way, where'd you ever find your chic taste in fashion, young lady?"

"From *Vogue, Seventeen,* and all the other fashion magazines you leave around the studio. I study every one of them."

"That's good. But don't lose sight of what's right for you." Alice wasn't quite sure what she meant by that.

They returned to the studio where Becky began one of Alice's favorite classes. "One, two cha, cha, cha. Keep those legs straight when you cha, cha, cha; the movement in the hips will follow naturally." Becky motioned to Alice, "Come dance with me and show Roberta what I mean."

Alice glided gracefully into position as Becky's partner. Her head was held high as she made eye contact with Becky and held the gaze, their bodies melting into the Latin rhythm.

"You see, Roberta, there is no need for exaggerated movement in the hips."

The music ended, and someone was clapping on the other end of the ballroom. Alice looked over to see a handsome young man with a crew cut standing there. He was over six feet tall with the broadest shoulders she'd ever seen; the rest of his body was lean and trim: the build of an athlete. He crossed the room gracefully and smiled at Roberta Hebert.

"Are you ready to do that, Mom?"

"I'm gonna try, if you promise not to watch."

He turned to go, "I'll be waiting in the car."

Alice and Becky hurried over for an introduction. Jefferson Hebert was even better looking up close. His whole face lit up when he smiled, revealing straight, white teeth and flashing, dark brown eyes that crinkled at the edges.

Attesting to his love for sports were two rather prominent scars, one beneath his lower lip and another diagonally across his forehead. Alice thought they made him more attractive and felt an almost irresistible urge to protect him, to run her fingers through his closely cropped hair and rest her head on those broad shoulders.

She was surprised to hear herself say, "Why don't you come dance with your mom?"

"Oh, no! I have two left feet when it's time to cha-cha."

"We do other dances, too, you know," she smiled.

"I'll take a rain check if you'll teach me, Bright Eyes." He winked and headed for the door, "Watch those hip sways, Mom; some Romeo might fly you away to the Mexican Riviera." He went out laughing. Alice felt her heart skip a beat.

Several days later, she was alone in the office balancing the books for an audit when the telephone rang. She mechanically picked it up and brightened when she heard, "How's the cha-cha?"

"Sorry, Jefferson, I'm the only one here."

"Well, that's convenient, 'cause you're the one I want to talk to."

She covered the mouthpiece to hide her gasp.

"I called to invite you to a dance my fraternity is giving a week from Saturday."

Removing her hand from the mouthpiece, she tried to speak, but the words were stuck in her throat. Wanting more than anything to go, she just knew she would be too nervous to dance or even talk. She'd be no fun at all.

"Is something wrong? I usually get a 'yes,' a 'no,' or 'I've gotta wash my hair.'" He laughed, "I don't know what silence means."

She looked about as if searching for an answer, finally saying, "I'll have to let you know later."

"Okay, how about if I call you tomorrow. Can't wait too long because I'd end up without a date if you turn me down."

"Tomorrow's fine."

She hung up the phone and tried to get back to the studio books, but she was much too excited to concentrate. She tried to stand, but her knees had turned to Jell-O. She was relieved to see Becky's car pull into the driveway—just the person she wanted to see. *Hope she's alone,* she thought.

Alice walked out to the car and approached the open window, "Becky, you'll never in a million years guess what just happened."

Becky listened as she watched Alice change from a flushing pink color back to normal and then pink again. The older woman let out a low whistle, "Wow, you really like this guy don't you?"

Alice did not hesitate, "He's just the most handsome thing I've ever seen. What I can't understand is why he would ask me to a dance! He could have any girl he wants, I'm sure.

I'm such a nervous ninny. I'd forget every step of the dance. Why I couldn't even talk to him today. What in the world would I do on a date? I don't have the right clothes. I'm just a mess."

"You certainly are—now just calm down. First, you take a deep breath and count to fifty. When you're calmer, we'll talk."

Alice knew that Becky was right. "Think I'll take a walk to clear my head."

"Good idea. Then come back here, and we'll talk."

Several minutes later, Alice floated back into the office to find Becky at her desk. Looking Alice in the eye, the mature woman spoke sternly, "You know who his dad is, right?"

Alice had never seen this side of Becky before and did not know quite how to respond. The girl-child twiddled her thumbs and replied naively, "Roberta is awful nice, so I suppose he's nice, too."

"I'm not talking *nice,* I'm talking *money.* Paul Hebert owns several newspapers in the state and who knows what else. The point I'm making, Alice, is that the two of you come from very different backgrounds. Can you deal with that?"

Alice's defenses went up, "Gee whiz, Becky, he didn't ask me to marry him—just to a stupid dance." *You think he's better than I am, don't you? I'll show you. I'll go to that dance just to show you and anybody else who might think I'm not good enough. Wild bobcats couldn't keep me away.*

Becky threw up her hands. "Okay, okay, my friend. Go to the dance and have a good time—just keep a close watch on your heart. I don't want to see you hurt." She shook her head before adding, "As for clothes, that yellow dress you just bought would be perfect, but you'd better check with him to be sure. Sorry, kid, I can't help you with the nerves— you gotta do that for yourself."

When he called the next day, Alice clenched that right fist and accepted—repeating to herself, over and over again, *I AM good enough. I AM good enough.*

Chapter 16: The Fraternity Party

Alice showered and then dressed slowly and carefully, using all the tricks Becky had shown her with makeup and clothes. Studying her image in the full-length mirror in Becky's office, she was shocked to see how much she resembled Belle; it seemed that she looked more like her mother every year. That knowledge made her feel good in a way, but the good feelings were tinged with fear. *What if I turn out to be just like her?*

Her long, copper-colored hair was pulled off her face and clasped behind in a single lock, leaving the rest of her luxurious mane to bounce off her shoulders as she moved. Spraying a bit of Becky's perfume, White Shoulders, into the air she walked into it—just the way Becky had shown her. Then glancing once more at the clock, she sighed, "I am ready, Mr. Hebert."

A knock on the office door announced his arrival; he was on time. Casually dressed in a brown sports jacket with matching slacks and loafers, she thought he looked good enough to bite.

He looked her over and said, "Wow! You look great, Alice." She accepted the compliment with a smile and a slight tremor of her lips.

His late model, black Corvette was parked in front of the office. Sliding into the smooth, leather seat as gracefully as she could manage, Alice breathed in the luxury of the sports car as he closed the door. She settled into the comfortable seat, feeling a bit like Cinderella heading for the ball and crossed her fingers in hope that her coach would not turn into a pumpkin.

He got in behind the steering wheel. Not wanting to appear like Cinderella in the big city, Alice looked at the speedometer and asked, "How fast will it go?"

"Wanna see," he asked with a twinkle in his eye.

"No," she laughed.

"My brother said he got her up to 85; my guess is that she'll do much better than that."

She raised her eyebrows, "You think of the car as a female?"

"Absolutely, she's fast, beautiful, and expensive to maintain."

"So that's what you think of women?"

He did not answer but kept his eyes glued to the road. Alice was surprised at how easy it was to talk with him.

That Old Black Magic was playing softly on the radio as they headed for New Orleans. Alice looked out the window and hummed along. When she glanced sideways at her escort, they both laughed.

"Are you a football player?"

"Yeah, I play a little for Hudson. You like football?"

"Sure do." She made a mental note to learn all she could about the game. "Maybe I'll get to see you play one day." Alice knew that Hudson was a prestigious private college near New Orleans, but she didn't know how well they were doing in football. She suspected that the school's focus was on scholarship—not football. "How long have you been playing?"

"Three years. This is my last one at Hudson, I hope." He looked over at her. "Didn't pass the MCAT on my first try. I'll try again later in the summer."

Her eyes opened wider, "You want to be a doctor? This is such a coincidence! I do, too."

He tapped the steering wheel, "Maybe we can practice on each other." His tone implied that he was going a bit over the line.

Alice stiffened. "Don't be fresh; I hardly know you."

He laughed.

The fraternity house was on a side street, hidden among the other old mansions in the Garden District. Jefferson had to drive around several blocks before finding a place to park.

Alice loved the Garden District—had as long as she could remember. As usual, it cast a spell over her as she walked along its broken sidewalks. She was transported to an old European city where she was free to be herself in a wonderland of fabulous gardens, statuary, and fountains. For her, it was magic, and she needed nothing more to light her imagination in this place. The trees, streetcars, shrubbery, gardens, and mansions behind wrought-iron gates were sufficient.

Three dominant styles of architecture helped create this magic: the Greek-Revival style, the Victorian, and the Italianate. Designed by leading architects of the day, the mansions dated back to the period following the Louisiana Purchase of 1803 when the Greek-Revival style dominated the landscape in New Orleans, as it did elsewhere. Residents of the Garden District were Americans, and they wanted homes socially superior to their nearby neighbors, the French. The Greek-Revival style with its magnificent columns, some of them displaying Doric, Ionic, and Corinthian orders at different levels, apparently satisfied that need. The influence of the style could also be seen in the highly decorative cornices, verandas, and enormous windows reaching from floor to ceiling. These homes looked like Greek temples of the 5th century. Fabulous gardens with semitropical plants and fragrant shrubbery surrounded most of them, often with the most interesting section of the garden in back, just outside the back door.

The white, Greek-Revival structures blended well with the two styles of architecture that dominated from 1850 to the end of the 19th century: the Victorian and the Italianate. All three styles were evident in the Garden District of the 20th century. The Victorian, developed during Queen Victoria's reign, introduced a variety of colors, gingerbread, lacey ornamentation, and the new materials and technologies produced by the Industrial Revolution. A home in the Italianate style, with its low-pitched or flat roof, resembled an Italian villa of the Renaissance.

Tonight, the fragrance of magnolia blossoms mixed with jasmine hung in the misty New Orleans night to shroud the young couple in mystery and add to the magic. Overhead the man in the moon peeked through the occasional cloud to wink at them.

As they neared the fraternity house, Alice heard jazz mingled with voices and laughter. The large, Victorian-style house appeared to shake in vibration from the noise within. It was a white frame with dark shutters and a wrap-around porch where young people sat here and there in rocking chairs or stood around holding mugs of beer.

Jefferson took her arm to guide her over a crack in the sidewalk, "I'm amazed the rocking chairs came out again. The brothers usually hide them in the basement with the old swing—Bubba does not approve of such sissified stuff."

Alice felt something hit her shoulder before falling to the walkway at her feet. She looked up at the second floor veranda where guys and girls were hanging over the wrought-iron railing. Jefferson bent over and picked up the object, placing it around her neck.

Alice frowned, "Mardi Gras beads?"

He looked at her, "Do you know what it means?"

"Ohhhh yeah! And it won't work. I'll accept the beads, but I'm not showing my boobs."

He laughed.

Duke Ellington's orchestra was playing, and couples were dancing everywhere—in the dimly lit rooms, on the porch, and in the street. Those who weren't dancing, were schmoozing, eating, drinking, or making out. Alice saw several young men apparently without dates; the odds were good for the girls.

A black cat perched on the top step of the porch arched her back at the intrusion of the newcomers and passed in front of them to scamper up the street and away from the noise.

"Why, what happened to his tail?" Alice exclaimed.

"It's not a he: That is Arabella, who got her tail bobbed by 'the brothers' last Halloween."

Alice found it hard to believe that these young men who had so many of the good things in life could act so uncivilized.

As they entered the house, a muscular young man with hair as black as coal grabbed Jefferson by the arm, "Hey, Bear, who's your friend? Looks like you been holdin' out on us, Bro."

"Alice, I wish I could think of something nice to say about our famous quarterback, but that would contradict what you read about him in the papers. I'll simply say this is Gabe Tennen, my on-again-off-again best friend."

Alice looked puzzled, "I haven't read anything bad about him in the papers."

Gabe Tennen laughed, his black eyes and matching Cajun nose leaving no doubt as to his heritage. His black hair was pulled back in what could only be called a very short pony tail. Alice had never seen a guy with a pony tail before; she found him intriguing. An inch or two shorter than Jefferson, he was taller than most Cajuns and had the build of a quarterback—muscular and yet supple enough to move quickly with agility.

Gabe looked Alice over with obvious admiration, "Never mind him, pretty one, just be sure to save a dance for me." He extended a platter of boiled crawfish toward her. "Here, have one of these 'mudbugs." Alice just looked at him.

"Can you pinch off his tail?" Alice blushed.

"Darlin', you can't be bashful and eat 'mudbugs."

Jefferson glared at his friend, "Behave, Gabe, ladies are present." Alice moved closer to her date, grateful for the rescue.

He took her hand as they strolled past the chips, dips, and sandwiches. A small tremor was travelling up her arm from his touch. Hoping that he wouldn't notice, she started talking to distract him, "He called you 'Bear."

"Hebert means bear in English." He puffed out his chest in imitation of his namesake." Want 'a hear me roar?"

She giggled. "You can keep the b-e-a-r, think I'll go for a b-e-e-r."

She surprised herself. The last alcohol she had drunk was Belle's leftover champagne, and it had made her sick. But she wanted desperately to fit in with this crowd. Most of all she wanted the approval of Jefferson Hebert.

She accepted the plastic glass of beer he offered and found a seat on a bar stool at the makeshift bar.

Crossing her legs and contemplating a sip from the foamy brew, she laughed when it tickled her nose. And although the first sip tasted kind 'a bitter, she took another. After several more, she felt her shyness and fear slipping away to be replaced by a warm, happy sensation. She felt confident and popular. Guys kept asking her to dance; Gabe Tennen, twice. For the first time in her life, she began sensing her power over guys, and this sense, mingled with the effects of alcohol, made her giddy.

The giddy feelings were dampened when she glimpsed her image in the mirror on the opposite wall. For just a twinkle of time, she saw Belle sitting there, her legs crossed, skirt hiked, head thrown back in a laugh that displayed her straight, white teeth. Alice reached down and pulled her skirt over her knees.

She looked over to see Gabe Tennen watching her from across the room. She pushed the fear away and smiled at him.

Jefferson approached, extending his hand, "Well, nice of my date to save a dance for me." Alice stared into his brown eyes and tried to read what she saw there. But he wasn't letting her in.

"Want'a dance?" As they touched, a frisson of pleasure ran through her. He seemed to sense her feelings and quickly added, "I better watch my step with you, young lady."

He took her in his arms, placing one hand low on her back. She leaned closer, enjoying the disquieting feel of his strong arms. Easing into the rhythm, they both were soon suspended in time as they allowed the music to carry them to another zone. Alice was wishing it would never end.

Later, on the way home, she snuggled next to him wanting to recapture the feeling she had found on the dance floor. She placed her head on his shoulder as romantic music played softly in the background. The man in the moon watched as they drove on through the darkness—through Baton Rouge and then over the Atchafalaya Basin.

He parked outside the modest home she shared with her adopted family, and the spell was somehow broken. He seemed to change.

"Is *this* where you live?" His question seemed a bit condescending to Alice.

"It's where my aunt and uncle live. I'll only be living here until I graduate from high school in another year."

He reached across the seat and pulled her into his arms. Gently stroking her hair, he touched her lips ever so softly. Alice cuddled against him breathing in the faint smell of his aftershave. She felt a warm glow of contentment spreading throughout her body; it was like the way she used to feel with her dad—only different.

Chapter 17: Arrogance

Lafayette, Louisiana, 1955

Alice wiped her sweaty palms against her jeans, removed a tissue from her pocket, and wiped them again. *If I'm this nervous at rehearsal, what will I do at graduation?* She was to deliver the valedictory address to all of those people— teachers, classmates, and families. *What if I should lose my voice, get a frog in my throat, or, worse yet, trip on my way to the podium? What if they laugh at me?*

A voice came from someone in line behind her. "Hey, Monster, was any college dumb enough to let you in?"

She turned to face Steve Douglas, one of her tormentors in the senior class. "How would I know? Graduation isn't until tomorrow."

"I didn't see you the day we were filling out applications."

"No kidding! Why would I bother to fill out one of those forms when the colleges will be fighting over me? Ask any of my teachers. They told me, and I believe them. Besides I was too busy studying for that chemistry final." She smirked, "Which I happened to ace." She heard a snicker or two in the crowd but ignored them. *They're just jealous. Those college reps will be at graduation, and I'll have my choice of schools.*

At the graduation ceremony, she sat patiently as the awards were given out, waiting for her name to be called. And then she heard it. Walking proudly onto the stage, she received a five hundred dollar award for scholarship.

She returned to her seat but couldn't sit still, tugging at her collar to lose some of the accumulating heat. She waited to hear her name called again for the scholarship that would pay her way through college. Waiting, waiting, waiting. It became increasingly hard to concentrate. Then the ceremony was over. She watched as if from a distance as her classmates marched out, throwing their caps in the air. *Is this for real? It can't be. A bad dream maybe. Five hundred dollars won't even pay for my books. Those books that I've been a slave to for four years. They lied to me. My teachers lied to me, telling me that the colleges would be fighting over me. I believed them. If you can't trust your teachers, who can you trust?*

It took time and many tears for her to realize that she had lived in a dream world of her own making. *That may be true, but I sure had a lot of help along the way. I must have been too busy making straight A's to see reality.*

The next day Alice went to her old elementary school to search for Sister Bernadette. The nun's office, so clean and organized with pictures of saints on the wall, never failed to bring her comfort. But there was no comfort today. Even Sister was looking at her sternly when she asked, "Did you apply for a scholarship?"

Alice couldn't look at her and began sobbing uncontrollably.

Sister got up from her desk and went to Alice, placing a hand on her shoulder. "You must put in your application, child." The nun paused, shaking her head. "I'll see what I can do, but you must complete an application." She searched the top of her desk, found the form she was looking for and handed it to Alice, giving her a steely look. "It may be too late. Life deals roughly with us for arrogance; remember *The Odyssey?*"

A bolt of terror shot through Alice, "I've been such a fool. If I can't go to college, my life is ruined." She slammed her fist on the edge of the desk. "But I wasn't the only fool. Who can you trust in this world, if you can't trust your teachers to tell you the truth?"

"Now, now, child, maybe all is not lost. Have hope. And love yourself—especially when you make stupid mistakes. And that was a stupid mistake. After all, you're only human. Forgive yourself. Beating yourself up is destructive to your self-esteem, and that will make the situation worse. And blaming others will only distract from your responsibility to correct the mistake."

It was late June before Alice received a call from Sister Bernadette's office requesting that she report the next day. Sister peered over her glasses at Alice, the dark Cajun eyes riveting the girl with direct contact, "Alice, I hope you have learned from your mistake."

"I didn't know how scholarship awards worked, and no one was there to tell me. I had it in my head that representatives from the different schools attended graduations to award the valedictorians."

"We can always rationalize our behavior—gets us off the hook. It would have been so much better for you to trust someone enough to ask them. Instead, you allowed flattery to fill your head with fantasies and the false belief that you were better than your peers. And you almost paid a terrible price."

Alice sat up straighter, perking both ears, "Almost?" *What is she saying?*

"Have you learned from this experience?"

Alice dared to grab onto hope, "Oh, boy, have I!"

"God is always ready to forgive—and relieve the suffering we bring on ourselves from our own willful misadventures." She paused, looking at Alice. "But I've said enough. The Martin Foundation has agreed to pay your college expenses for one year; you will have to prove yourself and apply for more assistance at the end of that year."

Alice had to control herself to keep from jumping like a child. She stood up and crossed the room to hug her former teacher, "Oh, Sister, I'll do anything."

The nun returned the hug before turning Alice to face her directly, "Save it for all the hard work ahead of you."

Alice floated out of the office and all the way home. Walking hurriedly along the graveled walkway through Bayou Park, she hummed a happy little tune even though the hot, humid Louisiana air was stifling. She watched the Spanish moss as it dropped in large pieces from the live oaks. Hungry for air, the epiphytic plant swirled on the surrounding grass and across her path. *Why even 'Graybeard,' our name for those rolling balls of Spanish moss, seems to be dancing to my tune.*

It's Friday. I wonder if Jefferson will call to ask me out this weekend. I bet he does. The thought made her smile as she listened to the quacking of the ducks in the pond and watched the tree limbs vibrate as squirrels jumped from one to the other.

Chapter 18: The House Party

Louisiana Countryside, 1955

Alice looked over to check the speedometer on the dashboard of the Corvette; it was registering 68 miles per hour. They were headed for a weekend party at the country estate of Jefferson's family.

"We'll slow down when we get to the turnoff from the highway—about 5 miles down the road." Jefferson spoke as if he had been reading her mind. She relaxed a bit, allowing the summer wind to whip through her hair. *The breeze feels great. Glad I didn't put a scarf on when he put the top down. But this convertible is doing a job on my hair. That's for sure.*

A brief ride on a state highway took them to the road leading to the estate, and the car slowed sufficiently for her to enjoy the view. She gazed at the flat countryside; it stretched as far as she could see, all of it enclosed by a white fence with an electric wire along the top. Inside the fence, horses of different shades of brown grazed on the rich, green grass. "I've never seen such beautiful horses," she sighed.

Jefferson nodded, "They're English running horses, fastest horse on four legs. We raise them for racing."

Brushing her hair from her face, Alice asked, "How many races have you won?"

"Took fifth place in the Derby a few years ago." He pursed his lips and added, "We'll take first place one of these days. I'll show you the stables later if you're interested."

"I'm interested." Her eyes wandered over to a horse sticking his head over the fence. "That white one is a beauty. May I pet him?"

"I don't advise it; they're all nervous and high-spirited, especially that one." Alice shrugged, grateful for the warning.

They continued for a short time in silence as Alice breathed in the beauty of the countryside and wondered just how much farther they had to go before reaching the house. Well-pruned trees along the road were now coming into view.

"Pecan trees?"

"Yes."

"What do you do with the pecans?"

"Eat them, of course. Our cook uses them in fruit cakes for Christmas, and we give some away as Christmas gifts." He glanced sideways at her, raising his eyebrows, "You like pecans?"

"Love 'em."

He was pulling up before a sprawling mansion with a circular driveway already lined with late-model cars.

"Who are all these people? You didn't tell me...." She saw Becky Harrington's face before her and heard her voice, "The two of you come from very different worlds." The voice echoed, "Very different worlds." Alice tried to stop the negative thinking, but the harder she tried to stop it, the more vivid it became.

Jefferson was saying, "Most of them are my friends—kids just like you and me. But a few old family friends will be here for lunch. They're cool, you'll see." She was having a problem focusing on his words, which were intended to comfort her.

Alice took several deep breaths and swallowed, but the air bubbles began turning flip flops in her stomach. She tried to think of other ways to calm herself. Focusing outside herself did not help: The view of her surroundings only agitated the anxiety. A well-manicured lawn girded the two-story brick colonial with its fluted columns that held up a circular veranda extending from the roof. On a side lawn, gold and orange lilies surrounded a large, white gazebo. A pathway, lined with white flowers, led from the gazebo to the stables in back.

I need to visualize a place where I have experienced peace and joy? But she was so agitated that no such place would come to mind.

Finally, she clenched that right fist, and self-will alone swept the anxiety aside with denial. More than anything she wanted to please Jefferson. That thought alone helped her focus on what needed to be done. So she painted a big grin on her face and marched behind him as he carried her overnight bag up the walkway.

He set the bag down on the porch and opened the door for her. "You okay?"

"Oh, yeah," she lied.

He said nothing.

"Where will I be staying?" she chirped with more cheer than she felt.

"You'll be sharing a room with two old friends. Annette and Sabrina are great gals—you'll love them."

I certainly hope so, she thought.

A chandelier hung above them in the foyer of the mansion. It had tiny bulbs sparkling like stars in the crystal bling surrounding them. *Very different worlds.* Alice couldn't help but stare at the fixture and walked into a large mahogany clothes tree on the side of the hallway.

She caught a glimpse of her image in a floor to ceiling mirror. A flaring multicolored skirt with sandals and a white, peasant blouse displaying a small amount of cleavage had seemed appropriate when she left home. But in this setting, her outfit seemed out of place. *Am I showing too much cleavage? Am I wearing too much makeup? I need to comb my hair—should have brought a scarf for that ride in the convertible. I feel like a fish trying to fly.*

Jefferson was saying, "The skirt and blouse will be fine until after lunch, then we'll get into our bathing suits—hope you remembered yours."

"Sure did," she chirped. "Wouldn't miss a chance to swim."

As they were ascending the circular staircase beyond the crystal chandelier, Alice turned to look back at the sunlight dancing through the many crystals, enhancing the lights from the star-like bulbs. It took her breath away. *You come from very different worlds.* She tripped but recovered her balance in time to avoid a fall. Jefferson, ahead of her, was searching for the right room and did not notice her stumble.

Alice caught up with him when he paused before a closed door at the end of the hall and knocked. It was opened by a tall, willowy blonde. He opened his arms wide, saying, "Annette, love of my life, give me a hug." The blonde threw her arms around him and kissed his cheek. They were interrupted by a slightly chubby brunette, who came from the bathroom brushing her wet hair.

"Ladies, this is Alice."

The brunette put her brush down and exclaimed, "Is that you Jefferson Hebert? You better give *me* a hug, or I'll tell your girlfriend what we kids used to call you."

Jefferson was ready for her, "Alice, the blonde is Annette, and this little piggy is Sabrina."

Sabrina narrowed her eyes in mock anger and called out, "It was 'garbage gut,' Alice. We called him 'garbage gut' because he had a habit of showing up at our homes around mealtime and eating all the leftovers."

Jefferson grinned sheepishly, "Think I'll leave, and let you ladies get acquainted," He made a quick exit, closing the door behind him.

Alice looked over her assigned roommates. Annette was busy filing her nails. Sabrina sat before the vanity intently brushing her hair. Neither of them spoke.

They were lodged in a bedroom containing one queen-sized bed with a white canopy. A nightstand on each side of the bed contained family photos, and lamps. One photo showed a smiling Jefferson with his arm around a pretty girl, who looked a lot like him. *I'm guessing that's his sister,* thought Alice. Her guess was confirmed when she saw the same girl in another photograph with Jefferson and his parents.

An antique-green chest of drawers added color to an otherwise neutral room of white and beige. On the opposite wall, a half-open door led into a spacious bathroom with a shower and a Jacuzzi. A walk-in closet opened on the right. Appearing out of place and obviously put there for the occasion, a freshly-made army cot sat beneath a bay window with a magnificent view of a very large swimming pool. Clothes were strewn everywhere.

"Sabrina and I have the bed, Alice. The cot is yours—great view of the pool." Annette said as she and Sabrina walked out, closing the door behind them. Alice was grateful to be left alone.

She unpacked slowly, hoping the familiar items would comfort her, and they did but only as long as she was able to focus on them. She hung the one dress she had brought in the closet, threw her bathing suit on the cot, and left the other things in the suitcase. Taking her cosmetic case into the bathroom, which was scented with perfume from the previous users, she paused long enough to brush her hair before the mirror. *Better get myself downstairs and join the party, or Jefferson will think I'm a stick in the mud.*

On the first floor, she followed the sound of the music and soon came upon an Olympic-size pool with clear, blue water sparkling in the perpendicular rays of the noon sun. A flagstone patio located across from the pool was filled with round tables covered by colorful umbrellas. The tables had been set for lunch.

She recognized Gabe Tennen in the crowd. His date, a gorgeous brunette with a pixie haircut, looked like one of the cheerleaders Alice had seen at a recent Hudson game.

As Jefferson held a chair for Alice, he leaned over and whispered, "Can't wait to see you in a bikini." Alice blushed.

She was seated between Jefferson and Sabrina. Starving, she grabbed a roll and some butter and placed them on a small plate to the right of her plate. Sabrina glared at her hissing condescendingly, "That is not your bread plate, Alice."

Alice turned red and could not find her voice to speak. Jefferson quietly switched the bread plates, "No real damage, Sabrina."

Lunch was served buffet style. Alice selected a hamburger from the grill attended by a young Mexican wearing an apron and a chef's hat. The table nearby contained baked potatoes in foil, an assortment of vegetables and cheeses, plus all the trimmings needed for the meal. Desserts were on a separate table—fruits, fluffy lemon meringue pies, and enough chocolate to satisfy any chocoholic.

Alice stared at her place setting. *Which fork do I use? I'll just watch what Jefferson does.* After the bread plate incident, she was afraid to try anything unless she could mimic him. He, on the other hand, made his movements rather obvious, so she guessed that he had sensed her uneasiness.

After lunch, the music from the loudspeakers changed. The smooth sounds of Nat King Cole were replaced by the Rock and Roll of Fats Domino and Little Richard. Jefferson grabbed her for a jitterbug. Slow, slow, quick, quick, slow. Alice slipped into the easy rhythm of the dance and swung. She was in her element. Anxieties faded as she focused on expressing the music with her body; the beer she'd had for lunch helped. Gabe Tennen grabbed her as that dance ended.

His whole face lit up when he smiled, "You swing good, Alice."

She returned the smile saying, "You're pretty good yourself, Gabe. And by the way, who's that gorgeous chick you're with?"

He raised his eyebrows, "Sandy? She's a cheerleader for the team."

"I thought so." Just then a tall, red-headed guy tapped him on the shoulder, so their conversation ended.

Several dances later, Alice was wet with perspiration and exhausted. She dropped into the nearest chair to catch her breath. One of her recent dance partners sat down next to her and asked, "May I get you something to drink, Miss Alice?"

"Yes. Some water would be great." She accepted the glass and swilled the ice water so rapidly that a sharp pain shot up the back of her head.

Someone was yelling, "Hey, Jeff, old man. Time for you to take a dip." She turned toward the voice and saw that Jefferson had been lifted off his feet and was being carried by several young men to the edge of the pool. Splash! Water sprayed in every direction as he hit the surface of the pool. He dived under and came up laughing. She got up and looked about for the best route to return to her room thinking, *Time for me to go, that's something I'd just as soon not experience. I can shower and take a quick nap. Oops! Better not nap, Jefferson wants to see me in my bikini.*

"I got my thrill…." She sang as the warm water streamed down her back. Lathering her body with a jasmine-scented soap, she smiled as she remembered her popularity on the dance floor. She whispered to herself, "Thanks, Becky, you taught me well."

Stepping out of the shower, she reached for one of the big, fluffy towels when she noticed that the door leading into the bathroom was partially open.

I must have left it open myself. Oh well, I'll just dry off before I close the door—don't think anyone will see me.

Before she got to close the door, she heard Annette and Sabrina talking—not bothering to keep their voices low.

"Where do you suppose Jefferson picked her up?"

"Probably some third-rate bar. She acts like she just left the farm and missed the boat after she left."

"I've seen dogs with better table manners."

"The only time she did something right was when she was mimicking Jefferson. Did you catch that?"

"And did you see how she dances?"

"Moves like she's about to have an orgasm right there on the floor."

"Well, we don't have to ask what he sees in her. Know what I mean"?

Alice retreated back into the shower and washed away her tears with the running water. She felt like yesterday's road kill and hated everything about herself. *This red hair is all wrong for me, my legs are too long, and, besides, I'm just too sexy. What I thought was popularity was only lust for what those guys saw as an easy make.*

When she finally summoned enough courage to leave the shower and walk into the bedroom, she found it empty. Falling onto the cot, she slipped under the covers, pulling them over her spinning head. *I must get out of here, but how?* It took a long time to calm down enough to think clearly. When she did, a plan began to emerge.

Minutes later, she quietly approached Jefferson complaining of a migraine headache and requesting to go home. "Mom's got plenty of pain pills around here. Let me get you something now. Don't go home. You'll spoil the weekend for both of us, not to mention the others."

She clenched her right fist for the courage to stand up to him. "I've had these before, Jefferson. The only thing I can do is get my prescription medicine at home and sleep it off."

She sensed that he was trying to cover up his irritation when he said, "Why didn't you bring the medicine with you?"

"I forgot. Please drop me at People's Drug Store on the corner from the dance studio; they have the medicine I need."

A spark of light deep within her soul, ignited by the recent events, began to illuminate a new path for her: She did not have to take the abuse of others. No one (not even she) had ever seen the light before. But the path was still too scary, and she had no clues to guide her. So the spark was nearly extinguished by distractions brought on by life and her obsessive desire to please others.

Chapter 19: Alice in Love

Baton Rouge, Louisiana, Fall of 1955

Alice threw herself into preparations for college in Baton Rouge, where she had been accepted. The busyness occupied her mind and attempted to keep thoughts of Jefferson out. But he would pop through at the most unexpected moments—riding in the car, shopping, when she awoke in the middle of the night. In social gatherings, she would do a double take whenever she saw a male with his build and hair color. Football games were the worst of all.

Even her studies could not block him out completely. She would be preparing for a test in chemistry or trying to solve a problem in differential equations when his face would appear on the page, usually frowning, as he had been the last time she saw him. The harder she tried not to think of him, the clearer and more frequently his face would show up.

She was studying in her dorm room one evening, when she was summoned to the telephone in the hall. Longing to hear the southern drawl of Jefferson, she was disappointed to hear the slight Cajun accent of Gabe Tennen. She couldn't help but wonder why he would be calling her.

"Are you and the big guy going steady or anything like that?"

"Not at all—no strings whatsoever. In fact, I haven't heard from him since the party when I last saw you."

"How about cutting a rug with me Saturday night?"

She paused, placing her index finger against her chin and screwing up her mouth, before saying, "Sounds like fun, Gabe. What time?"

"Joints in the Quarter don't get started until after ten. How about I pick you up at nine?"

"The Quarter? I've never been to the French Quarter so late."

"You haven't lived, baby."

She sighed, "Who knows? Maybe I need to learn how."

He laughed. "So, is it a date?"

"I'll be ready at nine."

"Wear your funky jeans and a tee shirt; we're goin' slummin."

She hung up the telephone, wondering whether she had done the right thing.

When he picked her up, he was eighteen minutes late. *Jefferson is always on time. I'm tempted to cancel this date, but it's about time I got out of the dorm. H*e was dressed in jeans and had his shirttail hanging out. *A little too casual,* she thought. *Jefferson would never pick me up looking like that.*

She sat stiffly on her side of the car while he sang along with the radio—apparently oblivious to her discomfort. She searched in her bag for chewing gum. Locating a new pack of spearmint, she offered him a stick. Before long, he was popping away on the stick of gum. *Giving him gum was a mistake.*

"How's the team doing this year?"

"Lost our first one; we had several injuries."

Hope Jefferson's okay. Both of them were reluctant to pierce the barrier between them. *Conversation with Jefferson is always so easy. We never have to look for something to say.*

They parked near Frenchmen Street in 'The Quarter.' Vieux Carre, the Old Square, with its 300 years of history was a different world as midnight approached. After all, it had a reputation to uphold—the birthplace of jazz as well as the blues and was located not far from the infamous Storyville. It was where *tasteful* intermingled with *tacky,* and you were never certain of the sex or race of a stranger. Inhibitions to the human spirit seemed out of place here.

The mournful wailing of a trumpet attracted the couple to one hot spot, and the lively tempo of piano music took them to still another. They guzzled beer and danced into the early morning hours. All the time, Alice was thinking, *He just isn't Jefferson—not even close.*

Shortly after 2 a.m., Alice was hungry and dragging her feet —feeling like the last lily of summer. They were headed down one of the side streets when Alice saw something that stopped her in her tracks. The sign over the door showed a large skull and crossbones in black and white; it read The Voodoo Grocer. They meandered into the strange little shop, where pictures of Marie Laveau and other voodoo priestesses stared at them from the walls. Rag dolls with pins through various parts of their anatomy and a variety of amulets were displayed for sale. Gabe picked up a stuffed spider and placed it on his date's shoulder. She frowned and shook her head, "Not funny, Gabe. This place makes my skin crawl." She was headed for the back door when she paused and sniffed. "Wait a minute. I smell fried shrimp."

Overstuffed po'boys were being served at a counter near the door; it was almost hidden by junk piled floor to ceiling. Sight of the delicious sandwich with large, fried shrimp spilling over the sides made her mouth water, so she dropped into a chair at one of the tables while her date ordered from the ghoulish looking man behind the counter.

"Yum, looks like we came to the right place for food, garcon, "Alice sighed as she tried to open her mouth wider for the fat sandwich. *Jefferson loves shrimp; he should be here.*

Alice was called to the telephone the following week. This time she heard Jefferson say, "I'm getting wheelchair fever."

Shivers were traveling up her spine but, at the same time, warming her all over. "What's wrong?"

He cleared his throat, "Injured my left leg in the last home game. Been sitting in this wheelchair ever since."

Alice felt her heart skip a beat. "Oh, no! How serious is it?"

"I'm healing—graduated to a cane for short periods." He paused clearing his throat again. "Been thinking about you a lot, kiddo." She smiled while wiping a tear or two from her eyes.

"So would you like to dine with a cripple on Saturday night?"

She heard the nervous laugh on the other end and jumped at the chance to say, "Yes."

He came without the cane on Saturday, and they ate at The House of Blues. Jefferson took a sip of the French wine, swirled it about in his mouth and nodded that it was okay. As the waiter poured a glass for Alice, Jefferson looked at her and winked.

Instead of feeling reassured, she began to doubt herself. *Do I look okay? Maybe I'd better go to the powder room to check.* She excused herself to do so and returned shortly to find menus on the table. As she read through hers, a puzzled look came over her face.

"These dishes are unfamiliar to a lot of people, but I can assure you that they're all especially delicious. Would you like for me to order for us both?"

"Please do." She sipped the wine and gazed into his eyes, unaware of the blues playing softly in the background or anything else in the elegant setting. The shrimp cocktail, one of her favorites, was served; she ate the jumbo shrimp but couldn't tell anyone how they tasted. After the appetizer, she forced down the remainder of the food Jefferson had ordered, afraid of displeasing him. The fault was not in the food or her taste buds but in her appetite, which was blunted by emotions hidden from her awareness.

Jefferson, on the other hand, cut into his fillet mignon like a half-starved man and quickly cleaned his plate. Wiping his mouth with the linen napkin, he sighed, "That steak was the best, worth every penny." Pushing his chair back a bit from the table, he swirled the wine in his glass and added, "This is the site for the world-famous Gospel Buffet. Did you know that?"

"Yes, they also offer other shows, all blues, I believe."

"But the food alone is worth coming for. Do you agree? I notice you're not eating very much."

She blushed. "Nothing wrong with the food. As a matter of fact, it's great. I'm just not very hungry." He frowned.

The dignified waiter cleared the table and looked at Alice, "Could I interest the young lady in some bread pudding with white chocolate sauce? Very delicious."

Sensing that Jefferson was *not* pleased with her, she responded with as much enthusiasm as she could muster, "Will you split it with me?"

"Sure thing. I'll have it with a cup of black coffee."

After dinner he drove to a favorite parking spot on a hillside overlooking the campus. A full moon brightened the countryside around them as Dean Martin was crooning softly on the radio, 'That's Amore.' He pulled her gently against his chest, and they sat for a long time just listening to the radio and enjoying being close to each other. Her head was swimming under the influence of the wine and his nearness, the familiar aftershave deepening her sense of intoxication. A gut feeling told her to resist his advances, but she wasn't listening. On fire with her own desires and not recognizing the desperation inside, she was powerless to stop him.

When she returned to her dorm room, she undressed for the shower. Spots of blood were on her cotton panties. That was when reality slapped her in the face. She braced herself from the tears that were starting to form. *If that's what it takes to hold him, so be it.*

Their relationship had moved to a new level, and they seemed to be addicted to each other. He started visiting her whenever he could get away. And all the time she waited for his proposal.

Chapter 20: The Letter

Baton Rouge, Louisiana, 1956

A biochemistry book lay open on her lap as Alice sat staring at the rain beating against her dorm window. The telephone in the hall rang, interrupting her daydream. She picked up the phone to hear the housemother announce that she had mail at the front desk.

Sorting through bills, ads, and a postcard reminding her to schedule her next dental appointment, she was surprised to see a letter from Jefferson. She was happy and then curious. *What in the world could this be about? Maybe he's coming this weekend after all. But he usually calls.*

She took the letter to her room to open it in privacy:

February 22, 1956
Dear Alice,

This letter is so hard to write I don't know how to begin, so I'll just report the facts. My dad has ordered me to stop seeing you. If I don't, he will cut off all funding for me and my education. As you well know, I have another year to go before graduation.

I'm sorry it had to end this way, but maybe it is the best thing for you. You will have a chance to find someone who actually deserves you. You are the best—you deserve the best.

I'll never forget you,
Jefferson

Her mind refused to register the words on the page. Then she ever so slowly jostled them about to fit some crazy puzzle that was soon blurred by her tears. She began searching her brain wildly for some plausible explanation that would bring sense to her world. Someone was trying to play a cruel joke on her. She called his dorm again and again but could not get through. Then she tried reaching him through his friends, who seemed sympathetic but unhelpful. Not daring to call his home, she finally gave up and faced the truth. He was gone. It had been a big mistake to think that she could hold him with sex.

She cried herself to sleep every night, holding her knees up against her chest in the fetal position and rocking back and forth. When Shirley, her roommate, was present, she buried her head under the covers and stuffed her nightgown in her mouth.

She had been abandoned, had lost her source of love—she'd never find another because she was unlovable. And she had to hide this great shame from the world.

Whenever she managed to fall asleep, she would wake up at dawn only to be overwhelmed with waves of depression, wondering how she could get through the day. She tried to keep up with her classes but found it almost impossible to stay focused. Her mind would wander into self-blame and imaginings about how she could have done things differently. She would pull herself out of the darkness and search for the old grit and determination that had gotten her over the bumps in her past. And somedays she actually found them. This went on for weeks. When she got on the scales one morning, she saw that she had lost eight pounds.

Her roommate noticed the profound sadness that seemed to stifle Alice's appetite and keep her tossing and turning at night. The sadness filled her eyes and radiated from her very soul. Shirley suggested counseling, but Alice refused, insisting that she was okay. *All I need is another fee to pay,* she thought.

Chapter 21: Blind Date

Baton Rouge 1956

Spring came, but Alice hardly noticed. Then one evening she was called to the telephone just before 10 p.m. Hearing the excited voice of Cecile coming through the line, she asked, more gruffly than she had intended, "What do you want, 'Cile?"

"Alice, you'll never guess what has happened."

Placing her hand to her temple, Alice said, "Tell me, 'Cile. I don't feel like playing games."

"I got a gig, girl."

Alice opened both eyes wider, "You're kidding. How did all of this happen? Where? When?"

"My guitar teacher arranged it. Ain't that the dog's bow-wow? I'll be singing and playing at a party in Lake Charles on the twenty-fifth of March. Can you believe it?"

Alice smiled as she said, "That's great, 'Cile; I'm very happy for you.

"You're gonna be there, right?"

Alice shook her head, "I don't think so, 'Cile. I'd feel funny without a date."

"Then get one, Ally. A gorgeous chick like you should have no trouble at all in that department."

"Sorry 'Cile, I just don't feel like dating right now."

"I ain't gonna let you off the hook that easy, girl. I'll get a friend of mine to pick you up."

Alice had no energy to fight back, so she stalled a bit. After attempting a few more excuses, she ended up, as usual, giving in to Cecile.

The blind date turned out to be a tall, slender redhead named Spike Jordan, who occasionally played guitar with Cecile. From the start, Alice did not like him, but Cecile was her best friend, had been her friend since second grade—at times her only friend, so she climbed into his old Plymouth and tried to make conversation.

"Are you a student, Spike?"

He laughed, "No, I work for a living."

"What do you do?"

He glanced over at her, "I tend bar at Jason's. Pay ain't all that great, and the hours are worse. But it gives me a chance to be with my friends. Left school two years ago—wasn't learning nothing useful, but I hated to give up my pals." Alice turned and looked out the window so that he could not see the side of her upper lip lifted in distaste.

Following an awkward silence, she made a few more attempts at small talk as they drove across the bayou and countryside. She was looking for common ground but finding none.

As they were nearing Lake Charles, they spotted a gigantic building that appeared to be some kind of barn. It was located in a large field, and tonight the 'barn' was surrounded by flood lights. Cars were parked in semi-organized rows all over the field. Young people walked to and from the cars or huddled in small groups near the doors of the building. Laughter could be heard occasionally above the chirping of crickets and mating calls of bullfrogs.

As they drew closer to the building, Alice could see a small red glow penetrating the darkness periodically as small puffs of smoke curled upward. She wondered about 'pot' and other drugs.

Inside, the rafters were shaking. Jimmy Sands and his Red Hot Peppers had everybody on the floor doing the jitterbug. Girls were in mid-air, sliding around and between the legs of their partners, and shimmying across the dance floor. Guys were swinging and lifting the girls in midair, 'cutting a rug,' and doing the splits.

Spike turned out to be a good dancer, so the evening was not a total loss. When they took a break, Spike disappeared for a long time, and Alice was left to fend for herself. One young man brought her an ice-cold coke, and several others asked her to dance. When Spike returned, he looked from her to her latest dance partner. His lip curled up on the left side of his face in a sneer as he said, "I see you're quite popular."

It was after midnight before Cecile came bouncing on stage with her guitar. Her feet were in constant motion as she gyrated her hips seductively, jerking her head back occasionally to swing the newly bobbed hair out of her eyes. She sang a popular Cajun song in her rich, deep Louisiana voice, and the place went wild.

Alice was debating with herself whether she wanted to dance with Spike again when he took her hand and started steering her toward the dance floor. She looked up to see Cecile watching her, so she gave in. They stayed for several dances before returning to their table. Alice was hot and exhausted, so Spike brought her a glass of punch. She was so thirsty she grabbed it and chugged. Almost immediately, the room began spinning, and she had trouble focusing.

"What's in that drink? Hit me like a thunderbolt."

Spike shrugged, "No idea. Everybody else is drinking it. Besides, beer's my drink."

She tried to stand, but her knees buckled. The floor was so crowded that no one seemed to notice. "I feel really funny—think I'd better go home." Spike encircled her with his arm as they headed for the door. She was too drowsy to think clearly—just wanted a place to lie down and sleep. She made it to the car and passed out.

She awoke the next morning soon after six and ran in the direction of the bathroom. She soon realized that she was going in the wrong direction but could not stop retching and vomiting. Punch and partially digested potato chips were spewed all the way to the front desk. A bowling ball was rolling around inside her head, striking a row of pins at random. She pulled herself together sufficiently to grab some towels from her room and wipe up the mess in the hallway. It would have to do until the dorm maid arrived. Groping her way back to the bed, she fell into it. The last thing she remembered was drinking the punch. She stayed in bed all day, alternating weak tea with aspirin.

Cecile dropped by a few days later. "On my way to New York City, cher; I'm cuttin' a record for Decca."

Alice nodded and smiled, "You were great, 'Cile. Hope it works out for you. Where'd you learn to put on a show like that?"

Cecile didn't answer—just looked at her and winked. "How'd you and Spike make out?"

Alice shrugged.

"That bad, huh?" She twirled a little jig as she reached for the door. "He's got a history with women, you know."

Chapter 22: Life

The spring rains came in April, as expected. As soon as Alice's early class was dismissed, she rushed back to her room to get her umbrella. *I won't melt, but those precious books will be ruined.* She checked the calendar again for the third time that day. April 12, the date her menstrual period had been expected, was still circled. Fighting the panic that was slowly building, she told herself, *Eight days isn't too bad. I'll just wait and see. It couldn't be pregnancy; Jefferson always used condoms. Must be something wrong with my female organs.* She looked at the calendar again. *But I just had a complete checkup. Maybe I miscalculated when my period was due."* She went back and recalculated, only to find that she had been right the first time. *My mind is in such a swirl. Can't think clearly.* She tried to remember every time she and Jefferson had had sex. Searching for any chance of an 'accident.' *I gotta get my mind off this worrying. I have a chemistry test tomorrow.*

She attended her classes, determined to concentrate on her studies. When she was successful in doing so, it was a welcome relief. But a trip to the bathroom and an agonized search for any sign of her period would throw her back into the worry whirlwind. She would return to class and imagine that her panties were wet. Only to return to the bathroom and find disappointment. Her partner in chemistry lab threatened to send her to the Okefenokee Swamp if she didn't pay attention.

And the downpour continued, saturating the dirt where flower buds or tiny blades of grass were beginning to emerge. Puddles of dirty water collected in depressed areas. A sweet, pungent zing could be felt in the nostrils—the smell of ozone. And the tree limbs that had been bare all winter were sprouting green leaves.

She would return to her dorm room as soon as her classes were over and sit in the dark pondering what to do—over and over, getting nowhere. Misery brought tears but little relief. The problem was still there. Sometimes she would force herself to study. Her grades were falling.

She thought of an old wives' tale about drinking castor oil to get the period started, but castor oil only gave her diarrhea. She knew she had to tell someone before she drove herself crazy. *But who? What will Jefferson say, what will he do?* Her shoulders sagged. *Who can I go to? Should I take something more than castor oil to get my period started? But what would I take? Abortion would be murder. I can't do that. I could never kill another human being. I'd have to live with that for the rest of my life.*

But is an embryo a human being? Some people think not. Abortions are done every day, and people go on with their lives. Just scrape out the pod and move on. But what should I do? I'm the one who has to live with my decision. She rolled her neck to work out the tension. *I don't even know where to go or who to see about an abortion.*

Chapter 23: A Friend

Friends are angels who lift us up when our wings are having trouble remembering how to fly.

Author Unknown

Alice shuffled to the kitchenette and grabbed some crackers from a canister on the counter. Tearing off the wrapper she quickly consumed them to fight off the growing nausea. It was still dark outside; she had gotten up early to catch the first Greyhound bus to Lafayette. Sister Bernadette had agreed to see her.

Wringing her hands, she went back to her room and picked up her purse, dropping her sunglasses on the floor and distractedly walking away from them. She knew what Sister would say. There would be no going back. *Have I made the right decision?*

Before long, she was watching the sun rise over the Achafalaya Basin. How beautiful! *That scene has always brought me comfort in the past.* Today, she watched an egret flap its large, white wings against the bluing sky before taking off from a bald cypress tree. The bird glided gracefully over the unruffled blue waters in search of food. *Not much comfort today. Telling Sister will be the hardest thing I've ever done in my life, but what else can I do? I can't commit murder.*

Alice turned around several times before finding the courage to knock on Sister's door. The nun studied her face when she entered the office and motioned for her to sit down. Alice sat twisting her hands in her lap, not knowing where to start.

As if in answer to the unexpressed question, Sister said, "How about starting at the beginning?"

So Alice started by telling her about the relationship with Jefferson. Sister listened carefully, interrupting only occasionally with questions. Alice spoke rapidly, at times the words jumbled and incoherent. When she finished, she sat up straight, took a deep breath, and pinched the bridge of her nose to hold back the tears. Her insides were jumping, and blood was pulsing through her ears.

But the scolding she expected, even desired, did not come. Instead, Sister got up, crossed the room and took Alice in her arms. That was when the dam broke, and Alice's tears flowed. As from a distance, she heard Sister saying, "Of course, abortion is out of the question."

Avoiding eye contact, Alice lowered her head, saying between sobs, "I know that, Sister,"

"Good!" Sister Bernadette cleared her throat and returned to her seat behind the desk. "You must see a physician, young lady. If you really are pregnant, you must tell the father as soon as possible."

Alice's mouth flew open as she shook her head, "He'll hate me, Sister; I'll be destroying his life."

"What's he doing to yours? Besides, he has a right to know. Cheer up, child, maybe it's not as bad as you imagine. I'll take you to Piccadilly for lunch. Some crawfish etouffee and carrot soufflé will turn the world around. But first, we must find out when the doctor can see you."

After dialing a number and speaking briefly into the telephone, Sister turned to Alice with a smile. "We're in luck. Dr. Johnson is a good friend and has agreed to see you this afternoon.

***

Alice sat stiffly in the doctor's office flipping through magazines, much too nervous to focus on anything but pictures. *It will be so good to get this over with, to learn that all of this worrying was for nothing. Maybe it'll teach me not to worry so much in the future. I'll have a good laugh at my silly self.*

Before too long, she entered the examining room and was given a hospital gown to wear. Her legs were then placed in stirrups with only a thin sheet to cover her most private parts.

.

164

She watched the physician, who reminded her of Uncle Bill, as he donned rubber gloves and lubricated them with K-Y Jelly. . One of the gloved hands penetrated her as the other felt her abdomen. Her face felt like it was on fire. After an eternity, he stripped off the latex gloves. A big sigh escaped her lips.

He looked at her with nothing written on his face as he said, "Get dressed, young lady, and meet me in my office."

Alice wanted to run away but knew she must stay to face the truth. Her head was hung as she entered his office a few minutes later and sat directly across from the stern physician. She tried her best to make eye contact, but her eyes kept darting to a picture on his wall.

"Alice, you are roughly 2 months pregnant."

She heard the words, but they were having trouble registering. *It cannot be. It's just a bad dream. Nothing seems real.* A choking sensation started at the back of her throat and traveled up her airways. Smothered, she stood up and headed for the door. She had to have air. As she opened the door, Sister Bernadette was saying, "I'm worried about her, Tom. She can't get in touch with her emotions. Never has been able to."

"Don't force it, Sister. She has to work that out on her own. She'll feel them when she's ready."

Their words meant nothing to her, so she dismissed them. *I have more important things to worry about.*

The next day, when the reality of her situation pierced the haze surrounding her, she thought of ending it all with a razor blade she found in the bathroom. *That would hurt too bad, and I would be taking the life of two human beings—not one.*

That night, she tossed and turned for hours, fluffing and un-fluffing her pillow. When she finally fell asleep, she had a dream. In the dream, she was in the middle of a wide, flat expanse of blue water—a deeper blue than the Louisiana sky that blended with it on the horizon. Green cypress trees bent their knobby knees in the water as if they were praying as they reached toward heaven. Here and there white egrets perched on the highest branches of those forest-green trees, their snow-white wings at times spreading out against the sky. At other times, the wings hugged the white bodies of the giant birds closer to the darkening green of the cypress trees. Then as quickly as the vivid dream had appeared, fog started moving in; the fog covered the cypress trees and everything surrounding them. But wait. There was movement in the fog. She peered closer and saw the hand of a figure reaching out to her. She awoke in a cold sweat.

Groping about for her slippers, she found them under the bed and slipped her feet into them. Putting her robe around her shoulders, she made her way to the small kitchenette down the hall. She placed 2 tablespoons of dried milk in a cup and added hot water, stirring vigorously. It didn't look very appetizing and tasted worse, but she drank it to help calm her nerves. Her problem was still there— big as life. *This is a living human being inside me. If I destroy it, I will have to live with the knowledge that I am a murderer for the rest of my life. Anything would be better than that. I'll just have to tell Jefferson and face the music. Maybe he'll marry me after all.*

On a warm and humid Sunday afternoon, Alice and Jefferson sat in his Corvette watching the ships come and go on the Mississippi. Alice had been rehearsing how she would tell him all morning, but when the time came, she couldn't open her mouth. He started drumming his fingers on the steering wheel in impatience. She sat with her hands clutched in her lap to keep from biting her nails. Staring sheepishly up at him, she was fighting the tears welling up in her eyes. After an eternity of uncomfortable silence, the words came tumbling out.

"I'm...I'm pregnant."

He jolted upright as if she had struck him. And taking a handkerchief from his pocket, he wiped sweat from his brow. "How do you know?"

"I saw the doctor."

He let his breath out slowly, "Wow, you really know how to knock a guy's socks off, don't you?"

The tears came flooding out, and she started shaking uncontrollably.

He was staring straight ahead when he asked, "Is the kid mine?"

"How can you ask such a thing?" She was screaming now. "You're the only one I've been with."

He was looking around to see if anyone was close enough to hear her. After clearing his throat, his voice trailed off as if he were searching for the right words. "I don't know what I can do, Alice. I gotta think about this—figure things out. Marriage before graduation is out of the question; my dad will cut me off without a penny."

"We don't have to tell anybody we're married."

He fixed her with a stare, "Alice, I couldn't deceive my parents like that."

"We could both get jobs."

He looked away saying, "Sweetheart, I'm barely passing as it is. A job would put my grades in a spiral downward until I was booted out of school. Give me some time. I'll try to work things out. " He looked at her. "Can you get it fixed?"

An electric shock traveled up her spine. "Jefferson! I can't commit murder."

He propped his head in both hands and leaned on the steering wheel. Both of his broad shoulders were shaking. Alice thought he was crying. She touched him gently, allowing her hand to linger. The back of her eyes were stinging from holding back more of her own tears.

"I've heard of a home in New York City… Let me do some checking, and I'll get back to you."

"But I've got no money to pay for a home."

"Don't worry about that; I'll take care of it. I'll let you know more as soon as I do a little research."

She just looked at him in disbelief. *He'll do anything to get out of marrying me.*

A few days later, he called. "As soon as you can arrange it, I'll drive you to the House of the Good Shepherd. It's a beautiful old mansion located near Central Park in New York City. No one will know you there, so we should go before you start to show." It was a pay-off, but what else could she do?

Chapter 24: House of the Good Shepherd

New York, New York, 1956-1957

The screams woke all six girls in the dorm room on the east wing of the House of the Good Shepherd. Alice grabbed the flashlight she kept under her pillow and called out to her neighbor and best friend, Carol, who slept in the bed next to hers, "What's going on?"

"Someone's in labor, and it ain't good. I'll bet it's Janet; she has preeclampsia, and that could lead to some pretty serious complications."

The two women placed robes around their swollen bellies and walked into the hallway, heading for the nurse's desk on the west wing. They were stopped midway by Sister Anna, director of the home. Holding up her hand, the nun spoke gently but firmly, "Go back to your room, ladies."

Alice held herself erect and addressed the woman she respected as much as anyone she had ever known, "But, Sister, we're all facing labor, and we need to know what to expect. We're scared." Alice was the unofficial spokesperson for the other residents.

The nun smiled but spoke firmly, "I know you're all frightened, but what's happening now will not help any of you with your own deliveries. We will keep you informed, but it is better for everyone concerned if you don't get involved tonight. Understand?"

Alice punched Carol with her elbow saying, "Of course, Sister, we'll do as you say. But is it okay if we go to the kitchen to make some tea? I don't think anyone will get much sleep tonight."

"Making tea is a great idea, but try warm milk instead."

Sister Anna was in her early fifties and ruled the House with an iron hand. The girls, whom she always referred to as 'ladies,' maintained that she wore a velvet glove over that hand. Her soulful gray eyes belied her tough demeanor. Of medium stature and weight, her power came from within. No one questioned it. She also had a wicked sense of humor and would have enjoyed a good belly laugh had she known that the girls took bets as to whether or not her head had been shaved.

Alice and Carol found their way down the back stairs to the big kitchen. Large pots and pans hung from hooks on the wall above a turn-of the century gas stove. Oversized, stainless-steel sinks lined the opposite wall surrounding a mega-sized refrigerator. In the center of the room was a long, oak table, a favorite gathering place for insomniacs—its random scratches and stains bearing witness to the past. The table, like Sister Anna, had recorded the pain as well as the joy without judgment.

The church had acquired the old mansion from Anne Simpson, an heiress in the oil industry, following her death in 1938; she had specified that it was to be used as a home for unwed mothers. No one knew exactly why the mansion had been left for this purpose. Perhaps it was her favorite charity, but some speculated that a beloved daughter had found herself in need of such help.

Antiques that had belonged to the Simpson family were scattered here and there among furnishings selected as good matches from time to time by an active board of directors. The current occupants added a "lived in" look to the former elegance.

"Any idea where I'll find a pan small enough to make milk for two, Alice?" They searched through the cupboards lining the walls on both sides and finally came up with a small saucepan.

"Put some chocolate in mine, Carol. Chocolate makes everything better."

"You find the cocoa and sugar; I'll add it."

"How about chocolate syrup? Think I saw some in the refrigerator." Carol nodded, so Alice went to the refrigerator and searched through the containers inside the door until she found the syrup. Handing it to Carol, she took a seat at the oak table and watched as Carol stirred the syrup into the warm milk. Clasping her hands behind her head, she asked, "Are you okay with the unpleasantness we just witnessed?"

Carol met her gaze, replying, "I'm okay, Alice. How about you?"

Pouring the hot chocolate into two mugs on the counter, Carol offered one to Alice and tasted the other. The rich aroma and chocolate taste put a smile on her face. "A fine cup of hot cocoa, if I do say so myself." The two friends sat opposite each other, spreading their fingers out over the warm cups and looking each other in the eye. They had met just a few months ago, but the bond between them was strong—forged by openness and the situation they shared in common. Free to be themselves, they had no reason to keep secrets from each other.

Carol cocked one eyebrow, asking, "Heard from Jefferson lately?"

Alice put down her cup and opened the palms of both hands, "He's promised to come see me as soon as he can make it to New York."

Carol narrowed her eyes, "You believe that girl? He's just stringing you along to make less trouble for himself. My unsolicited advice to you is DROP HIM."

Alice shook her head, "Easier said than done, my friend."

Carol studied Alice's face. "You still love that guy, don't you?"

Alice squeezed the bridge of her nose to hold back the tears and changed the subject. "How about George? You heard from him?"

Carol snorted in her hot chocolate. "Are you kidding? His wife won't let him out of her sight since she found out about my pregnancy."

"Seems to me you ought to take your own wise advice, dear girl. He's not going to leave his wife. You know that. Where does that leave you, not to mention your child?"

"Oh, I'm keeping the child. As for the father of that child, I don't know what he plans to do." She looked at Alice, a thoughtful expression on her face." As you said, dropping him is easier said than done." Then pursing her lips and shaking her head, she said, "Ain't we a mess? How'd we get ourselves so screwed up?"

"Love, baby, love. They say it muddles your thinking," Alice sighed. "But I don't think we're going to figure it out tonight. Let's go sleep on it."

Carol nodded, "Provided we can sleep."

The following morning, everyone was in chapel at 6:30 a.m., except Sister Anna and Janet. Morning chapel, like evening prayers, was mandatory. The sun was casting its first rays through the stained-glass window behind the altar when Sister Anna entered to lead the service. She walked swiftly and confidently to the head of the group, her fresh habit swishing slightly with each step. She began with a prayer. The girls knelt, some of them stealing searching glances at Sister's face as the brief service progressed. But Sister's face provided no clues to their unasked questions about the night before; Sister was focused on the Lord's business.

They left the chapel and walked down the hallway lined with mahogany benches and other Queen Victoria era furniture. Alice felt as though she belonged in this prestigious setting, as if she were revisiting a scene from a previous life.

They entered the dining room where several long tables were arranged to provide the best view through the open windows that reached to the ceiling. A summer breeze from Central Park enhanced the soft light in the room and brought the birdsong of dawn, interrupted at random by distant horns and other sounds of the city. Alice watched as the butterflies spread their colorful wings and flitted about from one flower to the next, inviting the tiny buds to open their beauty to the world.

Cold cereal, milk, fruit, juice, and toast with butter and jam were the usual fare, coffee and tea being the only hot foods available. The kitchen crew would not begin their work until after breakfast. But the toasters were soon put to good use, and the aroma of fresh toast warmed the air.

Sister Anna tapped her water glass with her spoon to get attention. The chatting and laughter ceased as all eyes turned toward her.

The nun paused, making certain that she had the undivided attention of her charges. "It is very important for all of you to remain calm for the sake of your babies—and, indeed, for your own welfare. What you heard last night was a young woman we knew had preeclampsia, a very serious condition that no one in this room has at this time." She paused again, searching for just the right words, "Janet was a special case. Last night she went into labor; unfortunately, she started convulsing and bleeding from an abruptio placentae, a premature separation of the placenta from the womb. The physician and Francine, our nurse, did everything possible to help her, but, unfortunately, the young woman died on her way to the hospital."

The collective gasp in the room was audible.

"I repeat; that was a special case. We don't anticipate any such complications in anyone here."

"How about her baby, Sister?"

The nun looked down and crossed herself before continuing. When she spoke, her voice was hoarse, "I'm sorry to report that we also lost the child." Several girls excused themselves and left the table. For the remainder of the week; flowers, poems, ribbons, jewelry, and other small gifts were left beside Janet's empty bed and on a nightstand nearby, displaying an unfinished pair of white booties.

After breakfast, Alice reported for her job in the formula room; she would get a head start on the day and perhaps finish the formulas before the day got so hot. The formula room could be a real hot spot once the pots began to boil. Alice rarely left her daily job without needing a shower and change of clothing.

Carol worked in the nursery, which was joined to the formula room by an open window. The tiny residents inside ranged from newborns to six months in age. Many of the girls brought their own babies home from the hospital and cared for them there. Once that happened, the children were seldom put up for adoption.

The nursery was also a foster home for other babies awaiting adoption, many had been found on door steps. All received good care around the clock under the supervision of Francine and a relief nurse.

Both the nursery and formula room were well organized and spotless.

Following a hot lunch of vegetable soup and peanut butter sandwiches, the dining room was cleaned by those with kitchen duties. The knitting class would meet there following the afternoon nap. Unless a girl had an appointment for counseling with the social worker, she attended class—sewing, knitting, cooking, balancing the budget, or another area of personal edification.

Alice was knitting a yellow sweater with matching booties. Feeling at peace among people she knew accepted and cared for her, she smiled as she felt movement within. That was life. She started calling the little kicker *Binky* and talked with him, or her, whenever she felt lonely.

"Don't forget to report to the clinic at 10 a.m. tomorrow. Dr. Thomas will be here to preach to us about our weights," Carol reminded the group. As she went back to pick up a missed stitch on the afghan she was knitting, she added, "How much have you gained this month, Alice?"

Shuddering, Alice replied, "Too much, I'm afraid. Gotta remember to take off my shoes before I get on that lying scale."

"Alice, you're in trouble, girl. I'm in trouble, too. Maybe we can burn some calories by walking to the local movie theater tomorrow afternoon."

Cocking one eyebrow, Alice asked, "Why tomorrow afternoon? Fail to see how that's gonna help me tomorrow morning."

"Clark Gable's new movie doesn't start until tomorrow."

"Oh! Tomorrow afternoon, it is."

"Exercise, diet, and Dr. Thomas will help us and our babies stay healthy."

Alice bowed her head, praying that she was right.

The next day, Alice and Carol braved the ninety-degree heat to walk to the neighborhood theater, four blocks away. After a block, Carol took a handkerchief from her purse and wiped the sweat dripping from her brow. "You sure you want to see Clark Gable bad enough to endure this torture? I can feel the heat radiating from the sidewalk."

Alice used an old newspaper to fan Carol and herself. "The theater is only another few blocks. Hang in there, girl. Think about how cool that air conditioning will feel."

It was like entering another world when they walked into the air-conditioned theater. Carol sighed and took a deep breath of the cool, refreshing air. "Can we stay in here forever?"

Alice twitched her eyebrows at her friend, "So, wasn't that short walk worth it?"

For the next two hours, the girls left all of their problems behind to become lost in the fictional world of Clark Gable, Jane Russell, and Robert Ryan in *The Tall Men.*

As they were getting up to leave, Carol asked, "Do we have to go back out into that heat?"

"It'll be cooler by now, Carol."

All of a sudden, Alice placed her purse over her face and ducked into the ladies' room. Carol followed her in and waited for her in the lounge. After 15 minutes had passed, she went back to check under the stalls for Alice's feet. Knocking on one of the stall doors, she called out, "Alice are you in there?"

A voice came from inside, "Has everyone gone?"

"The restroom is empty, if that's what you mean."

"Go check the lobby."

Carol raised her voice, "Alice, what is going on?"

"Just do it, please, I beg you."

Carol returned shortly to report that the lobby was empty, so Alice opened the door.

"What's wrong, girl? You look like you seen a ghost?"

"You're sure the theater is empty, right?"

"The only people out there are those standing in line for the next show. Now, are you going to tell me what's wrong with you?"

Alice was shaking, "I'll tell you later. First we have to get out of here as soon as possible." They left the theater and walked out into an afternoon that had just been cooled a bit by a summer shower.

Carol grabbed Alice by the shoulders and turned her to make eye contact. "Now you gonna tell me what's wrong with you?"

Alice took a few deep breaths and whispered, "I saw a girl from my chemistry class."

"Are you sure? That theater was awfully dark."

Alice fanned herself with her hand," Not sure. But I think it was."

"So what, she probably didn't even notice that you're pregnant."

Alice snorted, "As big as I am and in this pink maternity dress. I'm not kidding myself, Carol."

Chapter 25: The Decision

The dream had returned last night—the one she had had early in her pregnancy. A woman clothed in gossamer was reaching for her out of the fog. As Alice drew closer, she saw cypress trees in the background, waving their ghost-like limbs. Narrowing the slits of her eyes in an attempt to discern the identity of the woman, Alice saw only fog: The figure had vanished. She woke up again in a cold sweat.

Finishing her work, for the day, early, she went to sit by a window with her favorite view, needing to clear her head. Taking several deep breaths, she relaxed on the long, cushioned seat that was an extension of the window ledge. The broad, single-pane window provided the best view of her beloved nature, a source of comfort for her since childhood. The window was located in the room they called 'the gossip lounge,' which served as an informal living room for several dormitories on the east wing. None of the antiques from the Simpson home were located there; they had long ago been replaced by cloth-covered sofas with matching chairs. Small tables and lamps had been used to complete the informal arrangements of furniture. An old piano, donated by a former resident, sat in one corner waiting for someone to bring it to life.

'The gossip lounge' looked like a family room, and it was. It was where the girls took their shoes off, propped up their feet, and loosened the ties around their swelling bellies. They sang, played cards and other games, worked puzzles, and did whatever families do in informal settings. They had fun there and found laughter wherever they could.

Alice was not laughing today. She was gazing out the window at the leaves drifting toward the ground, many of them already beautiful shades of ocher, red, or yellow. A squirrel darted about the carpet of leaves, searching for nuts. The radio was softly playing *We'll Have these Moments to Remember.* She knew that song would awaken bitter-sweet memories in her for the rest of her life—memories of the happiness and sadness she had found at The House of the Good Shepherd.

Soon, she would be given the greatest gift any mother could receive, only to have to give it up. Signing the papers to have the child adopted was the sensible thing to do. But could she do it? The war between her heart and her head had gone on for days. A wealthy couple from the United Nations wanted her baby; they had given up on having one of their own and were desperate. Her head told her to let them adopt the child, but her heart would not let go. She had grown quite fond of Binky, her pet name for the baby. She talked with him (or her) daily. Would she regret her decision after seeing the child? She had another month or two to endure this battle before signing the papers that would relinquish her rights forever.

"They can give my child the best of everything. What do I, a single mom, have to offer?"

"A mother's love, that's what I have to offer."

"But won't his new mother love him just as much?"

"Maybe. But what if they mistreat my child?"

"The adoption agency has thoroughly investigated."

"But can that agency be trusted? I have to promise to never contact Binky once I have signed the papers. Can I do that? And what about my career? I must find a way to make a living for myself in this world."

She tried to pull her knees up to her chest, a position she loved to take when wrestling with her thoughts, but, today, her protruding abdomen got in the way.

Jefferson called regularly, and they enjoyed pleasant visits by telephone. She maintained some glimmer of hope that he would marry her and that they would raise the child together. But that dream grew fainter with each passing day. *"Am I deluding myself?"* Standing in front of a mirror and looking herself in the eye, she would ask this question during her more lucid moments, finally deciding that she probably was.

She was, in no way, ready to sign the papers. But she could not bring herself to tell the case worker that, prolonging her own mental anguish.

At the end of the week, she had a dream about herself and Binky. They were shivering in an unheated apartment, and the child was crying from hunger. The next morning she walked into the social worker's office. Holding her right hand and her head ramrod stiff, she signed the papers like a robot. *It's done. I'll not look back.*

Alice awoke close to midnight with pains in her back. It was two days before her estimated due date. *Is it time, Binky?* She switched to her left side. The pains moved to her belly and began coming regularly. She got up slowly, holding her abdomen, and donned her robe and slippers. Francine would want to know.

The nurse felt her abdomen each time she had a pain, establishing that she was indeed having contractions. "When they get to be ten minutes apart, we'll call a cab."

I'm afraid but at the same time excited that this ordeal is about to end, and I can go on with my life. She returned to her room to finish packing her suitcase.

Placing her new robe and slippers into the open suitcase, she stopped when the pain came and sat down on the bed to rest. The toothbrush and paste came next. As she added her hairbrush and makeup, she thought *Hope I remembered everything, kind a hard to concentrate when these pains keep coming.* She closed the suitcase and picked it up.

On the way back to Francine, she noticed she was dripping water on the floor. "Don't worry, child, your membranes just ruptured." Francine patted Alice's hand. "You do'in jus fine. Rest yourself in that chair while I call a cab." After the call, Francine picked up the suitcase, and they left for the hospital about 5:30 a.m.

Between pains, she watched the city wake up as the cab plowed through the darkness. Lights were gradually emerging in the darkened buildings. A new day was dawning, and her life was about to take another turn.

Francine got her admitted and turned to go. Alice looked up at her from her wheelchair fighting back the tears, "Stay with me, Francine. I'm scared."

Francine took her hand. "Sugar, you know I got to get back for the 7 a.m. feeding in the nursery. Them babies'll be screamin they heads off."

Just then the orderly approached from behind and started wheeling her through the double doors into the room next to the delivery suite. Alice turned her head and watched Francine go through the revolving door, remembering the time she had watched her father walk away from her so long ago in New Orleans; she had never seen him again. Then she doubled over with another pain.

All of a sudden the pains were coming harder and non-stop. Alice yelled.

"Oh somebody give her something to shut her up," a faceless voice shouted from the delivery suite.

Then an angel in a white uniform appeared out of nowhere and took her hand, saying, "You go ahead and yell 'cause it hurts like hell." The needle stick in her buttock brought immediate relief and sleep. She knew nothing after that until she awakened to the sound of a screaming baby.

"Alice, you have a beautiful baby boy."

Binky is a boy?...She had provided a safe journey for him into this world. *What a miracle!* Shaking herself to awaken to the new reality, she glanced over at the reddened, squirming, squealing baby vigorously kicking both feet. "Welcome to the world, Binky; it's not such a bad place."

Alice was physically and emotionally exhausted, soon falling into a deep and restful sleep. She was awakened later that morning when an aide brought Binky to her room for his first bottle. He had been bathed, dressed in diapers and a shirt, and wrapped snugly in a blue blanket. Her first action was to remove the blanket and count his fingers and toes. She couldn't believe that this perfect little human being had come from imperfect her. Her heart was aflame with love for this tiny little creature, and it caught her off guard. Placing her index finger in the small hand, she was thrilled to see him clutch it. *Of course, he knows who I am.* "Was that a smile?" The nurse said it was only gas. *The nurse was wrong.*

The small head was covered with brown fuzz, and the perfect little nose had the tiniest white spots on the end. His blue eyes were the same color as all newborns. *Who does he resemble? He looks like no one I know. He's just Binky.* She cooed and sang *Rock a Bye, Baby* to him and kissed the tiny forehead. He sucked away until the bottle was empty.

A knock on the door signaled the end of their time together.

"Can't he stay just a little longer? He makes me so happy."

They took him back to the nursery on schedule; she would just have to bear the pain of getting out of bed and walking to the nursery: She had an episiotomy with four stitches in place. And although every step was painful, she went—

returning to her room and counting the minutes until she would see him again. She had known intellectually that a mother would love her child at first sight, but she was in no way prepared emotionally for what she was experiencing.

Returning to the House of the Good Shepherd, she was unbearably sad. The emptiness and loneliness inside crept up her spine and settled around her heart like a block of ice. Binky went to a foster home to await adoption.

Carol and several other friends gathered around her in 'the gossip lounge,' trying to make her laugh. Those who weren't pregnant tied pillows around their middles and formed a chorus line, dancing the can-can and singing. "If you hate your 9-5, and you want to feel alive HAVE A BABY, HAVE A BABY." The song went on for several verses describing various situations to be resolved by having a baby. When it ended, they collapsed in laughter. Alice just stared at them. *What a silly bunch and the most idiotic song I ever heard.*

The day before she was to return to Baton Rouge, Alice took a bus to the foster home where Binky was staying. The numbness crept over her, shutting out all other reality, as she sat cuddling her baby for the last time. *Is he the only person in this world who will return my love?*

She was shocked to see the foster mother enter the room to get him about 6 p.m. *Have I really been here all day?* Alice handed the small bundle to her and walked quickly out the door. The world outside did not seem real to her. The feelings of devastating loss, loneliness, self-pity, and unworthiness were all there fighting for recognition, but she could only feel the block of ice around her heart. A passing cab driver blew his horn and yelled, "What you tryin' to do you crazy broad—kill yourself?" Alice just stared straight ahead. She had ceased to care about anything, even her own life.

She was asked to report to the dean's office upon her return to school. The older woman peered at Alice over her horned rim glasses. "Miss Hollister, the Martin Foundation has ended funding for your scholarship. We all know where you were on your recent leave of absence. You were even spotted by one of our students." The numbness, the emptiness returned.

That door was closed, but God soon opened a window when a friend told her about Mercy Hospital School of Nursing. She applied for a scholarship and got it.

Chapter 26: Starting Over

New York, New York, Fall 1957

"I will devote my life to the service of others and refrain from having sex until I have a wedding band on the third finger of my left hand," Alice muttered to herself with her right hand clenched into a fist.

Studying her new image in the full-length mirror in the center hall of her new residence, she liked what she saw–simplicity, sincerity, and a clean, natural look. Her long red hair had been pulled straight back in a chignon at the back of her head. A white cap covered the luxurious head of hair above the chignon, its starched, wide brim forming a crown on top. The calf-length, blue-striped uniform was covered with a heavily starched white apron and bib, which were set off by white stockings and gleaming white shoes.

One of her first patients, Mr. Thompson, was a middle-aged, African American who had lost his right leg to diabetes. As far as anyone could tell, the man's only pleasure, not to mention companionship, was a small radio on his bedside stand.

Having lived all of her life in the South where black people were not seen as equals, Alice was not sure how to cope with making the crumpled bed where a black man had just slept. She stood at the foot of the unmade bed, fumbling with her bandage scissors. *If my grandma Hollister can see me from heaven, she'll be shaking feathers from her angel's wings. Come to think of it, she wouldn't approve of my neighbor in the dorm either,* she thought. *Doesn't matter that she's the first black student admitted to this "prestigious" school.*

She stood staring for several minutes at Bed #7 in the twenty-bed ward, pondering what to do. Finally, the determination to succeed got the better of her, so she unfolded her arms and grabbed the foot of the iron-frame bed, pulling it away from the wall. A loud crash reverberated throughout the room. The electric cord from his radio had been wound around the top part of the frame of the bed. The plastic radio lay on the floor beside the bed, cracked and broken.

Alice was devastated. The head nurse suggested that she leave the floor to "collect herself." She made a beeline for her private room in the dorm and threw herself on the bed, crying inconsolably. *I'm just no good for anything or anybody. I can't even be a nurse. They'll expel me for sure. And then what will I do, where will I go?* The silence of the empty dormitory was her only answer.

The more she ruminated about her hopeless future, the more she cried. Finally, after the tears were all dried up, she heard a small voice deep inside. She usually ignored it, but today she felt compelled to listen. *How about that poor lonely man with one leg having to live without any companionship for the rest of his life?*

She got up, washed her face, and picked up the small radio she had received for her birthday. With that right hand clenched, she marched back to the floor. Her patient was sitting beside the still unmade bed, the stump of his right leg elevated on a chair. He did not look up when she approached him quietly and said shyly, "Mr. Thompson, I am so sorry I broke your radio."

He raised his head and looked in her direction, "Oh that ole thing—wouldn't play half the time. You done me a favor, chile. Yo' teacher done took it to the repair shop. They'll fix it better than new; you wait and' see."

She offered her own radio to use until his was repaired, but he refused her offer. "I'll make do, Miss Alice. Don't you worry." She suspected that he had been 'making do' his whole life.

Alice squared her shoulders and walked over to the bed. She mitered the corner of the bottom sheet

193

at the top and tucked it tightly under the mattress. The upper sheet was mitered neatly at the bottom of the bed, just as they had taught her in lab. She felt better.

Neither her instructor nor the School of Nursing ever mentioned a word about the incident again. And Alice experienced for the first time—the love of forgiveness.

When she returned to the floor the following week, *Rock of Ages* was softly but clearly playing at Mr. Thompson's bedside. His broad grin showed two missing front teeth, "I likes that little crack in the plastic, Miss Alice, it'll always 'mind me of you." He made eye contact with her for the first time.

Alice smiled at him and turned toward the medicine room. She needed to prepare 8 a.m. medications for Mrs. Hughes, a second patient, who was 93 years old and had been diagnosed with congestive heart failure. She entered her second patient's room and looked about at the four occupants who were all terminally ill. "Mrs. Hughes, it's time for your digoxin." No answer. She stood holding the tray in her hands and staring at the woman's chest but could detect no movement. Her mind went blank, so she just stood there gazing at the chest, afraid to reach for the identification bracelet on her wrist.

Laughter came from the doorway. She turned to see a Harvard medical student watching her. He was over six feet with an athletic build and dark brown hair cropped close to his scalp. The hazel eyes crinkled at the corners as he laughed while fingering the stethoscope slung around his neck, "What does it mean when a patient's chest is not moving? Did you feel for a pulse?"

Alice grabbed the woman's wrist. It was cold.

"That's not necessary. We pronounced her just before you came in."

Alice turned red and made a quick exit. He later found her charting in the nurses' station.

"I'm sorry I embarrassed you. Name's Chuck Haden. Could I call you sometime and try to make it up to you?"

"Not necessary to make it up, but you may call if you like. I'm in the nurses' dorm."

Later in her room; the feelings of guilt, shame, and fear lost the struggle to stay hidden. She was certain that a relationship with him would never work out. Better not to start one and risk another broken heart. *Really nice young man, high-class family and all that. Wait 'til I have to tell him I had a child out of wedlock.*

Chapter 27: The Rebels

"Alice, have you heard the news?"

"Let me get something to eat first." Sniffing the air, she added, "They must be serving chicken; I can smell it." As she searched through her pockets for her meal ticket, she said," I've had a day in clinical like you wouldn't believe, but I want to hear every luscious bit of gossip. Be right back." Her friends just looked at her.

She had found a place among several of her 33 classmates in the hospital cafeteria. They were seated around a large table, which had been hastily constructed by placing smaller tables together. Several medical students from New York University School of Medicine, one of the three affiliating medical schools, sat with them. Among them was Mark Loman, the latest heartthrob of Janie, Alice's classmate.

By the time Alice got back to the table from the serving line, the usual topics of conversation— medicine, nursing, and the gastronomically repulsive food—had been exhausted. She emptied her tray and returned it to the stack of trays in the center of the room.

Two nursing students from a hospital in Pennsylvania had stopped by to chat with Mark, who was openly flirting with the tall blond. *Have to keep an eye on them,* thought Alice. Janie sat stiffly in her chair, playing with her food, as she kept her eyes glued on Mark and the blond. Alice and her classmates exchanged knowing glances. They had handled problems like this before. Once, they had emptied the air out of the tires of a philandering medical student, as he sat in the cafeteria with his latest attraction.

Alice picked up her fork and dug into the macaroni and cheese. "Not bad for this place. I recommend the mac and cheese." She ate heartily and then paused to look around the table. The students from Pennsylvania were leaving but not before 'Blondie' gave Mark an encouraging smile. "Nothing subtle about that," Alice whispered. "She's caught on already to the games the med students play when searching for new hearts to break." Taking a swig of tea, she added, "But enough catty chatter for now. What's this hot news I missed while playing Florence Nightingale all day?"

Susan began, "The news is bad, my friend, really bad. Hope you don't have plans for the weekend."

Alice frowned. "Well don't keep me waiting."

Susan put down her knife and said, "It all began when our favorite housemother was polishing the silver this morning."

"You mean the one with the big nose for all our business? That would be Mrs. Duncan."

"Give the girl the golden apple, she got it on the first try." Rolling her eyes, Susan continued, "Well, the dear lady was polishing away when a hamster came scampering across the floor right at her feet."

Alice shook her head, "A hamster? How did that happen?"

"Hold on, Alice; we'll get there."

"Mrs. D. screamed loud enough to be heard in the Psych Building, dropped the silver teapot we use to give our little teas."

Alice clicked her tongue. "Oh what a shame!"

"Let me finish the story, Alice…. Anyway, the dear lady ran from the room in a total frenzy."

"Really?" Alice raised her eyebrows. "Sorry I missed *that*, but what's the bad news?"

"Oh there's more to the story, my dear. Just wait." Susan paused and looked at the others. "Of course, Mrs. D. made a beeline for the telephone to report it to *the* power-that-be, Mrs. Berrigan."

Alice shrugged, "She reports everything to Mrs. Berrigan. So what's new?"

"Our Director of Nursing came immediately, followed by several supervisors from the hospital. That little entourage gathered our live-in faculty, and they proceeded to search every room in the dorm for the little pet's home," Susan paused again, while she tried for a second time to cut her chicken.

Alice frowned, "Talk about making a mountain out of a mole hill. Why couldn't they just call security to take the hamster outside?"

Susan gave up on the chicken and turned to Alice, "Because, dear girl, that hamster was somebody's pet. And one of the rules for our dorm forbids pets in the residence."

"I see." Alice pushed the rest of her food to the side of the plate and waited. There was obviously more to the story.

"Well, Janie had heard the commotion in time and stashed her pet's cage in the trash outside before they got to her room."

Alice nodded, "So Janie's responsible. I should have known." She buttered her slice of bread as she gazed at the group. "But why are you guys so riled up?"

"Riled up are we? Just wait, Alice. You'll get riled, too."

Another classmate, Liz, jumped in. "Because they couldn't find anyone who'd even own up to seeing the hamster before today, Mrs. Berrigan is determined to find the owner. After all, somebody broke a House rule."

"I knew there was more to the story. So tell me the bad news." Alice looked from one to the other as she picked up her tea.

Liz frowned, "The whole class of 1960 is restricted to the dorm this weekend—no 11 pm leaves, no one o'clock leaves."

"Oh Boy! How long will that last?"

Susan shrugged her shoulders, "Who knows? Until someone gives them the information they want, I guess."

"They're holding us hostage," exclaimed Liz.

A steely look came into Alice's eyes when she said, "Well, if they want to play hardball, we'll play. They can't kick all of us out. So we stick together and don't tattle. Right?"

"Better believe it. I wouldn't squeal if they took away the nursing cap I was just awarded," Susan said as she reached for her apple pie. "This place has too many rules."

Janie looked sheepishly at the others, "I'll just go to Mrs. Berrigan and confess. I feel just awful."

Alice put her fist down on the table, "No, they'll expel you for sure, Janie" The others agreed.

The medical students were obviously trying to wipe the grins off their faces. The nursing students ignored them.

"What'll happen if some misfit should decide to tattle?" asked Alice.

"The School will do nothing; they've promised to protect her identity. What this class will do to her is quite a different story."

They all looked at each other. Alice wondered if they were secretly hoping that one of them would report the truth. But no one was coming forth. And they were far too stubborn to give in to the School. The line had been drawn in the sand, and no one dared step over it. Janie slunk down in her chair, afraid to go against group pressure.

They were challenging Carlotta Berrigan herself, and her word was law in the School of Nursing as well as in the seven other buildings that made up the complex of Mercy Hospital. If any courageous (or insane) individual thought of questioning that word, they kept their mouths shut and obeyed the law (or, at least, made a show of doing so). Still beautiful at an age no one dared to inquire about, she was a queen bee in a stiffly starched white uniform. Married to a successful surgeon, she believed strongly that her young nurses, who had come from humble origins, should be able to move about comfortably in the social circle of their choosing. The curriculum for her school consisted not only of anatomy, chemistry, physiology, psychology, and the art of nursing but also manners, etiquette, and other social graces.

A class entitled Social Adjustments, meaning adjustment to New York society, was mandatory. Each student had to host a 'high tea' and learn other social skills, including bridge etiquette, in order to pass the class and eventually nursing. In a way, the Social Adjustments class provided a balance for their self-esteem because in the clinical area they were washing the feet and personal areas of those some would label 'the dregs of society.' But they were learning to love and feel varying degrees of responsibility to help those 'dregs.'

Affiliating nursing students from eight other schools referred to Mercy as 'Mrs. Berrigan's Finishing School for Young Ladies,' a pejorative term used to show disrespect for Mercy students who were still managing two or three patients while most of them had been managing entire floors since their second year. Whenever word reached Mrs. Berrigan, she would smile and say, "Ask them what they did for their patients." She would pause and look at them over her horn-rimmed glasses before adding, "And then tell them what you did for yours." She fought many battles with administrators to ensure that the learning of her students was never sacrificed for service to the hospital. Some say she was forced into early retirement because of those battles.

If Carlotta Berrigan served as an authority figure for the students, a small black maid named Verlene was their mother. Verlene had been with the school from the beginning, and she loved every student who had ever passed through or failed out of it.

They cried on her thin shoulders when love went wrong and almost as hard when they failed a test. She always found a way to make them feel better. And when life rewarded them, she was the first to know.

The little maid was quick to turn her head the other way the times they came in from a date and signed 1 a.m. when the hands on the clock behind the desk indicated it was 1:15. Best of all, she had never developed a smell for alcohol on their breath. Without exception, they loved and respected her. When returning to the School for visits years following graduation, they invariably asked to see Verlene first.

By 7 p.m. each weekday evening, Alice was sitting at her desk studying, with the door to her room closed. Enforced study hours lasted until 9 p.m., and anyone caught outside her room during that time had better be going to the bathroom (fully dressed or in a bathrobe). If not, the offender would be given a demerit by one of the several proctors who roamed the hallways. Demerits led to forfeiture of the precious one o'clock (two per month) or eleven o'clock (one per week) leaves.

So it was shortly past nine one evening that week when Alice was called to the telephone in the hallway.

"Hi there, have you killed any more of my patients?"

"I know who this is, and you're not funny, Chuck Haden."

"Crazy how I thought you might like to drop by our local pub Friday night."

Alice was grateful for an excuse to turn him down and quickly explained that they were restricted to the dorm until the hamster perpetrator was discovered. He laughed.

On Monday, Janie went to Mrs. Berrigan and confessed that the hamster had belonged to her. The class bond had held for five days; no one had told on her. Janie had to forfeit all late leaves for two months. She was happy that she had not been expelled. It was rumored that Verlene had brokered the negotiation.

For conformists, Mercy's strict discipline and rules were paths to graduation; for nonconformists, they were red flags to be tested. And no one tested more than the class of 1960.

They passed a flagpole on their way to clinical practice each morning and quickly dubbed it 'the lonesome flagpole': It was always without a flag. One evening over dinner, they were discussing the situation and decided to do something about it. The nursing students raided the nurses' dorm for a pair of lace panties. They then accompanied a group of medical students to 'The Tower,' official residence for the docs, to find a pair of boxer shorts. The fact that 'The Tower' was off limits for student nurses only enhanced the excitement for all. Returning to the flagpole under the cover of darkness with underwear in hand, they hoisted panties and shorts into the spot reserved for *Old Glory*.

On their way to the hospital at sunrise the next morning, they rushed to the site to view their handiwork. They were greeted for the first time since their arrival by the American flag, proudly waving in the morning breeze.

One of the most sacred taboos was violated following lunch on a quiet Sunday afternoon: A male, unescorted by a housemother, went above the first floor.

In search of excitement prior to hitting the books, a group of female students had surrounded Mark Loman in the elevator and took him to the second floor. He stepped out just as Janie was sneaking out of the laundry room dressed in her panties and bra. His companions quickly covered his mouth to stifle the emerging whistle.

As orthopedic surgeons were making their rounds on Two West the next morning, the attending physician referred to Mark as 'The

Ladies' Home Companion.' The entire group laughed.

The Class of 1960 was breaking other records—like highest scores on the periodic achievement tests. Their hearts, as well as their minds, were growing as they also learned to care deeply for people of their own and other cultures. Alice was their 'golden girl,' and she loved every minute of it, never having imagined that she could actually be popular.

Chapter 28: Running Away

"The moment we begin to fear the opinions of others and hesitate to tell the truth that is in us, divine floods of light and life no longer flow into our souls."

Elizabeth Cady Stanton

"Make up your mind, Alice. Are you going with us? Just answer 'yes' or 'no.'" Liz Martin stood in the doorway of Alice's room with both hands on her hips.

Alice looked at her friend. Placing her index finger over her lips, she whispered, "Gee whiz, Liz, why don't you just broadcast that there's a party in the 'The Tower' Saturday night. We could get expelled for going, you know."

Liz walked into the room and hissed, "That's it, Alice. I'm out of here. You've been hemming and hawing all week. You're just chicken as well as a stick in the mud. A stick-in-the-mud chicken, that's you."

While closing the door to the hallway, Alice pursed her lips and made eye contact with her classmate, "I'll show you, Liz Martin. I'm in, baby."

Liz flipped her nose up with her finger, "Knew that would get you, Miss Head o' the Class. Outsmarted you, didn't I?" And with that, Liz opened the door and walked out.

Alice laughed, shaking her head, "Don't know about that girl."

As she was sitting down at her desk to study, Janie called from the hallway, "Alice you're wanted on the telephone." When she caught Alice's eye, she winked, "Sounds interesting."

It was Chuck Haden, asking her out again. She didn't hesitate when she said. "I'm so sorry, Chuck, but I have to shampoo my hair Friday night." He didn't call again.

On Saturday night, Janie packed her car with the party goers, drove off the grounds, turned around on the other side of the hill, and headed back to the parking lot behind 'The Tower.' The girls got out smoothing and checking their party dresses, breathing sighs of relief that they had not been caught. To avoid attracting the attention of hospital police, they went in twos to the back of the residence and entered through the unlocked door.

Glenn Miller's *String of Pearls* was swinging in the background of the softly lit room that had been furnished with second-hand sofas, chairs, tables, and lamps from Goodwill. Without curtains and devoid of frills and knick-knacks, it was obviously a residence for men. Looking about her, Liz commented, "This place could use a woman's touch."

"I don't think they care, Liz," replied Janie.

Alice took a deep breath to calm her nerves and tugged at her stockings for the sixth time that evening. "I need tighter garters, but I'm afraid they'd interfere with my circulation." She paused to look at her friends. "Do I look okay?"

"Like you just stepped out of a brothel," laughed Liz. "Lighten up, Alice; it's only a party; we see these people every day."

Alice searched the crowd to see who was present. In addition to the usual crowd of students, she saw several staff members from the hospital. "Do we stand for the physicians, like we do in the hospital," she asked. The others just laughed.

Liz spied Tom Whitlow, a surgical resident, at a table not far from the entrance. He was chatting with a medical student, who was gazing at him in open admiration. Making a beeline for the table and the aroma of pizza, Liz pulled Alice by the hand in that direction. Alice was waiting for an invitation to join them, but Liz took a seat directly across from Tom and motioned that Alice should take the seat beside her. Alice sat down primly and watched the others to see whether she would be welcomed. The resident slid a box of sliced pizza in their direction. Alice reached for a napkin and spread it over her lap. Since the others were eating with their fingers, she picked up a slice and brought it to her mouth. The thin crust smothered with tomato sauce, melted cheese, mushrooms, and pepperoni delighted her taste buds.

Tom wiped his mouth and grabbed another slice. Taking a large bite, he paused briefly to chew it before continuing the description of his latest surgery. "That gallbladder was starting to turn gangrenous when we got to it." He took a swig of beer from a Budweiser can and winked at Liz. "Took that sucker out, placed a Penrose in, tied off loose ends, and started suturing peritoneum and fascia." Liz watched his every move and grabbed onto his every word, all the while smiling up at him like a lovesick child.

The medical student took another bite of pizza and nodded, "No _t_ tube?"

"Naw, didn't have to enter the common bile duct."

Alice felt slightly nauseous: She had not adjusted to discussing clinical business while eating. She pushed the pizza aside. Ready to leave the table, she could feel the blood rushing to her face as she watched Liz make such an obvious play for Tom Whitlow. *This is not working for me,* she thought.

But Tom got up first, wiped his mouth again, and reached for Liz's hand. "Wanna dance, pretty lady?" Liz's face was radiant as she eagerly gave it to him. Alice watched as they shimmied onto the dance floor and started to jitterbug. When the music changed to a slow dance, she looked away, not wanting to see Liz make a fool of herself when they embraced.

Barbara Jenkins, a senior nursing student from Mercy, approached the table and sat down next to Alice. She pulled her chair up closer and whispered, "Does Liz know he's married and has two children?"

Alice's mouth flew open, "No way, Liz's got a lot of smarts. She wouldn't get mixed up with a married man. Besides, I've never seen a wedding band on his finger. Have you?"

Barbara fluttered her eyebrows. "Some people don't believe in wedding bands, especially Europeans."

"Then how do you know he's married?"

"His wife and kids were in the lobby with him one day. I spoke, and he introduced me."

"Decent of him." Alice could not keep the sarcasm from her voice as she turned to look for her friend. But the statuesque brunette was nowhere in sight. "Where'd she go?"

"Relax. You're not her keeper." Barbara swirled the contents of her paper cup and offered it to Alice. "Have some of this punch; rumor has it that they spike it with the highest proof available,"

"No thanks—think I'll wait a bit." She was scanning the room again for Liz.

"Don't know what you're missing, kid. It'll blow your sinuses open and loosen your hamstrings for dancing." Barbara winked.

Alice shoved what was left of the pizza toward her friend. "Here you better have some of this pizza with that punch; it's cold but still good." Looking about the room, she added, "And speaking of dancing, who's that good looking guy with the head nurse from Four East? He's a hunk, if I ever saw one."

Barbara took the last slice of cold pizza and leaned back in her chair. A serious look came on her face when she said, "Better stay away from him, Florence Nightingale. Remember you can still study medicine when you finish here. That guy' can mess up those plans or any others you might have. He's Ron Davis, a resident in cardiac surgery."

Alice felt her stomach flip. "And a doctor, too. What a catch!"

"Yeah." Barbara nodded, "Rumor has it that he breaks hearts faster than he can fix 'em."

Alice placed both hands on the table frowning, "Dang! Are there any good guys here?"

Her friend shrugged. "Oh sure. But just like any other place you gotta know how to find 'em."

Alice excused herself from the table and maneuvered over to the punch bowl. She picked up a plastic cup from a stack of new ones nearby. About to take a small amount for tasting, she took a closer look at the cup in the dim light; it was one of the plastic containers used to collect urine specimens in the hospital. *On second thought, think I'll have a coke to settle my stomach.*

She was searching through the nearby cooler but finding only beer. A deep, sexy voice behind her said, "More drinks are on the way."

She turned and gazed into the flashing dark eyes of Ron Davis. His blond crew cut framed a tanned face with chiseled features. He was tall, over six feet, and the outline of muscular shoulders was visible beneath his v-necked scrubs. His tanned, muscular arm was a stark contrast to the slim, effeminate hand he used to place his beer on the bar. He took her breath away.

He came closer fixing her with those eyes. "You don't drink beer?"

She tried to answer, but her voice got stuck in her throat.

He smiled. "Wanna give the dance floor a whirl while you wait for your drink?"

Her mind became muddled by confusion. A mixture of excitement, attraction, and terror were fighting to surface. In no way could she make a decision. And she didn't trust herself to dance with him. So she just stuttered, "I… I'm sorry, I just remembered something." She turned quickly and stumbled to the door, his laughter echoing behind her.

Opening the door and stepping outside, she breathed deeply of the cool, autumn air. Instead of calming her, it made her want to run. She headed downhill toward the nurses' dorm thinking only of how she wanted to be alone in the sanctuary of her room. She had to get away.

At the bottom of the hill, she heard a lot of noise and commotion on the grounds south of the dorm. Lights were flashing. She stopped and peered into the darkness. The ruckus appeared to be coming from the new Psych Building. She thought she could make out several police cars. Her first instinct was to hide. She looked about for a hiding place and spotted an old tool shed between her and the dorm. Maintenance used it to store equipment when they were mowing grass or trimming shrubbery. She ran to it and yanked on the door. It was locked. Her shoulders sagged as she looked around. *What do I do now?*

Oh calm down and think, Alice. She looked at her wrist, but it was too dark to see her watch. *Think, girl, think. The last time I looked at the clock, the time was 9:45; that couldn't have been more than 30 minutes ago. I'll just sign for an 11:00 o'clock leave, if I have to. I'm close to the dorm parking lot. If I can make it there, I'll just tell anyone who catches me that I was on a date.*

Just then a figure darted out of the darkness in front of her. His tall, muscular frame was covered by hospital pajamas, but the most noticeable things about him were his wild, shoulder-length hair and feral eyes. Her scream stuck in her throat when she caught sight of the uniformed policeman chasing him. The patient brushed past her, knocking her to the ground in his haste. She quickly picked herself up and continued running before the cop had a chance to help her, having no desire to answer his questions.

She didn't stop again until she reached the side porch of her dorm. By then her curiosity was knocking aside her fear. Climbing the steps of the porch, she looked over in the direction of all the noise and commotion. It seemed to be coming from the back of the Psych Building. Police search lights were aimed on what appeared to be a rope leading from the top floor where maximum security patients were housed.

Why those patients are dangerous criminals! The new building was supposed to reflect the latest in mental-health thinking, no bars on the windows and more freedom for patients. So much for that brilliant idea. But how'd they get a rope? Knitting her brow, she thought for a minute. *Had to be bed sheets. That's it; they tied sheets together to reach the ground.*

East of Psychiatry, she could barely make out a group of medical students sitting outside of the Obstetrics Building, obviously waiting for their patients to reach the final stage of labor. Just then another figure darted past them. He, too, was pursued by a policeman. A cheer went up; she couldn't tell whether it was for the police or the patients.

Alice heard later that all of the patients except one was caught. And bars were placed on the windows. Maximum security had enjoyed a little too much freedom.

As luck would have it, Verlene was on duty at the desk, so Alice got in by signing for an 11 o'clock leave. Calming down enough to fall asleep was another matter. After what seemed to her like hours, she drifted off into a restless sleep. But the cold-sweat dream returned. The unidentified woman was still reaching for her out of the fog. But her life was about to turn another corner. What would happen to the dream?

Chapter 29: The Contest

New York, New York, 1959

Following a vote by school children, the New York legislature selected the rose as the state flower in 1955. After that, The Hudson Valley Floral Association sponsored National Rose Week, which quickly became an annual event. No place on the planet grew this queen of all flowers more beautifully than the magnificent gardens of the Hudson Valley.

Organizations throughout New York City became involved in 'Rose Week.' School children delivered American Beauties to shut-ins and hospital patients who never otherwise received flowers. Florists threw teas, luncheons, and cocktail parties for those who were a steady source of business for them—like churches, hospitals, and funeral homes. Participants in blood drives, races, or other charitable events were awarded roses. And tour buses left regularly for the spectacular gardens of the fabulously rich, current and former residents, of the Hudson Valley. Everyone wanted to visit the gardens of the Rockefellers and the Vanderbilts. A holiday spirit, colored with elegance and brotherly love, pervaded the city and ended with a parade down Park Avenue.

Each year, the Association looked for a fresh-faced, unknown young woman, usually a nurse, to act as its queen. So area hospitals were invited to send two representatives to the International Hotel for a beauty contest during the first week of May.

When Alice was nominated by the student body of Mercy Hospital, she wanted to duck under her seat, but she dared not: Mrs. Berrigan and many of her teachers and supervisors were watching. In the back of her mind she still carried the picture of herself as 'Monster,' so it was a shock to her when she and Janie were selected to represent Mercy.

Hours before they were to leave for the International Hotel for the contest, the solarium near Alice's room was filled to capacity by those wanting to help with hair, clothes, and make-up.

Helen, a senior nursing student, brought in a pale yellow, low-cut gown borrowed for the occasion. "Try this on again, Alice; I may have to make some alterations."

Alice slid into the dress and gasped, "My boobs are hanging out."

"Shut up, Alice, and wear the dress with grace, you idiot. It seems to be a perfect fit. Here, stand on this table, and let me check it for length." Alice climbed on the table, and Helen circled her with a measuring tape, before saying, "Needs to be shortened about half an inch."

Alice scrunched up her nose, "Oh, don't bother. It'll do."

Helen glared at her and waited for her to step out of the gown.

The make-up expert, a former cosmetic saleslady at Macy's, took over. She applied make-up to emphasize Alice's best features and minimize the others, using eye make-up to match her eyes, and introducing a pale orange to her lipstick and blush to match her auburn hair.

The gown, shortened by now, was brought in, and Alice stepped into it, grumbling, "I don't know why you selected me when you know very well I never won anything my whole life."

Susan, a former hairdresser, said, "Gee, Alice, you should'a told us that before we voted for you. Now come here and let me do something with that hair." She grabbed a brush, curling iron, and some combs from her kit and motioned for Alice to sit in front of a full-length mirror.

Alice watched in awe as Susan piled her hair into a becoming French twist and used the curling iron to make becoming corkscrew curls over each ear.

"Anybody own a necklace and earrings to match this dress?" asked Helen. A pearl necklace with matching earrings soon appeared.

When they finished, Alice stared at her image, swirling with a hand mirror to get all views of the gown and her hair. 'Monster' seemed to be fading into the past. Susan took her by the shoulders and turned her to make eye contact, "Remember, Alice, your appearance is a product of all your friends at Mercy. We're counting on you." Alice looked at her friends and felt for the first time that she might actually stand a chance with all of their help.

But then she glanced over at Janie, who was receiving equal attention in the powder-blue gown that hugged the top part of her petite figure and flared out at the hips. The low-key make-up emphasized her large blue eyes that stood out in contrast to the shiny, gold color of her pageboy. *Oh, my! I'll never beat her.*

When the two girls entered the main lobby of the International Hotel, they gazed in awe at the chandelier. Hundreds of tiny lights scintillated the gigantic arrangement of flowers on the mahogany table beneath it. The fragrance of roses filled the room.

A semicircular stairway at the end of the room led to the mezzanine where young ladies in gowns of all colors were gathering; the scene looked like a gigantic floral bouquet. Alice guessed correctly that it was the place they would assemble for directions.

The judging started with dinner. Each contestant was to go to a table for ten, where one judge would be seated with guests. She would consume the first course of the meal at that table and progress to the next table with a different judge for the second course. She was being evaluated on her appearance, poise, etiquette, personality, and ability to relate with others. Alice kept in mind how well she was doing in her class on social adjustments, and the thought boosted her self-confidence.

The judge at her first table was John Reid, President of Park Avenue Bank and Trust. He was a large bear of a man whose gray suit looked tailor-made; giving him an appearance of style in spite of his size. The gray hair at his temples added to his look of distinction. With the help of his wife, Olivia, he went out of his way to put Alice at ease.

Olivia Reid, an aging beauty, fingered her water glass with a well-manicured hand. She wore an elegant, ice-blue dress that looked like the clothes Alice had seen on the cover of *Vogue* magazine. Her hair and make-up rounded out a chic look that spelled 'class' from the top of her blonde head to her dyed satin shoes.

The couple introduced her to their son, Phil, who did most of the talking. Phil Reid was tall with an athletic build, a moderate tan, and a stylish haircut. A smart, double breasted suit set off an expensive-looking shirt with a tie that matched a man's handkerchief in his breast pocket. His manicured hands displayed clean, well-trimmed nails. Everything about him spelled 'Preppy,' even his tastefully-hued gray eyes. He was attractive, but a slight overbite kept him from being what some people would consider handsome.

The beautiful people combined with the elegant setting, where the pink in the marble fireplace was echoed by the floral bouquets around the room, awakened something in Alice that she had never experienced. For the first time, she felt driven to win. She not only wanted the approval of these people, she wanted to be like them. *I'll do what I have to do to win,* she thought, clenching her right fist.

"Are you related to the Hollisters of Texas Oil?" John Reid smiled as he asked.

Alice returned the smile, saying, "I may *be* somewhere along the path in my family tree. My dad worked for Texas Oil."

Olivia raised her eyebrows, "Oh-h-h. What did he do?"

Alice looked thoughtful, "You know I'm not sure. He died when a well exploded in the Gulf of Mexico. I was very young." It wasn't entirely the truth, but it seemed to impress them. She had known most of her life that if she acted in a way to please others, a path would be cleared for her to get what she wanted eventually. Tonight it was more important than ever.

With a boost to her self-confidence from the first table, Alice moved smoothly around the room, and by the time she got to dessert, she could actually taste the cherries jubilee—the first food she could taste that evening. She relaxed and even joked during her five-minute speech before the judges.

After the speeches, the contestants took their places in the audience and awaited the decision. Ten of them were called to the stage. Janie and Alice were among them. Janie was second runner up. Alice jumped with joy and ran over to hug her friend.

"And first runner up is Amy Woodrow from River View Hospital." More whooping and clapping!

"Ladies and Gentlemen, may I introduce our Queen of Roses for 1959, Miss Alice Hollister of Mercy Hospital." Alice blinked, wondering if her ears heard correctly. *I did it. I actually did it.*

They placed the crown of roses on her head as the tears flooded her eyes and ran down both cheeks. *Pinch me. I can't believe this is real. I will wake up soon and find it was just a dream.* She was much too excited to take in her surroundings or comprehend what was happening for the remainder of the evening.

When the girls arrived back at Mercy, the entire school and much of the hospital were on the front steps of the dorm waving and shouting. A huge banner was stretched across the balustrade, 'Welcome Home, Queen Alice and Queen Janie.' A celebration was already taking place in one of the side rooms off the cafeteria. Alice was thinking, *I won that title fair and square, they should have said Princess Janie. I was the queen.*

The girls had to repeat their stories over finger sandwiches, cookies, and punch as each new group arrived on the scene. Alice shared the spotlight with Janie, saying nothing about her resentment. The others would not approve.

Carlotta Berrigan reminded both of them, "Don't lose sight of the people who made this possible for you." *Is she trying to tell us that we shouldn't let all this hoopla go to our heads? Then they should treat us fairly. They weren't fair to me.*

The resentment dissipated when a color picture of Alice wearing her crown of roses covered half the page in the women's section of the Sunday paper. Someone pinned the picture on the bulletin board near the cafeteria. During that week, Alice appeared on radio talk shows, attended luncheons and fashion shows, posed for pictures beside the buses about to leave on tours of the Hudson Valley, and presented roses to veterans, government officials, celebrities, and business leaders.

She was scheduled to open a local blood drive by being the first to donate. A camera flashed as she stepped out of the cab. After the public relations people had all of the pictures they wanted, the cab was directed to return her to school. But she insisted on staying and actually donating the pint of blood. By the time she was ready to go, neither public relations nor the media were anywhere to be seen, so she took the bus back to the dorm.

That evening she received a call from Cecile. "Saw your picture on the society page. Way to go, girl. Like to take you to lunch at The Four Seasons one day—talk over old times. How about next Thursday?"

Alice opened her eyes wide in awe, "The Four Seasons? Really? Wow! That's impressive. You must be living high on the hog, so to speak."

Cecile laughed.

"Next Thursday would be great." *Guess I'd have been better off playing guitar and goofing off like 'Cile.*

Rose Week ended with a parade down Fifth Avenue. Alice rode in a new Cadillac convertible waving and throwing roses to the crowd.

Then, faster than it had begun, all the excitement was over. Alice was still hyped up on adrenaline and found it hard to relax for days. After that, gloom sat in. When she walked past the bulletin board where her picture was posted, she noticed that someone had drawn a mustache on her face. The old paranoia rushed in, unrecognized or expressed. She was much too busy catching up with all the classes she had missed.

One evening Alice was called to the telephone to hear, "How's the busy schedule going for the rose queen?" She racked her brain to identify the voice but couldn't quite place it.

"The rose queen is rapidly fading into obscurity. Who *is* this?"

"I apologize for not identifying myself. This is Phil Reid." Alice inhaled sharply.

"Feeling let down, are you?"

She placed her hand on her chest to steady her breathing as she replied "Maybe just a little."

"I'd like to take you to dinner Friday night. Maybe we can brighten things up for the queen again."

Chapter 30: A Senior

New York, New York, December 1959 to June 1960

When the outside door of Pediatric Psychiatry
was opened by an orderly, ten-year-old Dawson
grabbed the ball out of the hand of his friend, Billy,
and threw it through the open door. Alice, their
assigned nursing student, dashed out to recover it.

Slam! The heavy door was closed and
automatically locked behind her. She waited for the
orderly to come back, but he had disappeared. Alice
stood in a foot of snow in her short-sleeved
uniform. With chattering teeth, she watched the
children waving to her and laughing.

"Our ole nurse can't get to us now."

Alice searched through her pockets with shaking
hands. Her keys were not there. After checking a
second time, she had to admit that she had just
broken one of the cardinal rules for staff in
psychiatry: she was separated from her keys. She
banged on the door with her fists. By now she was
shivering from the crown of her head to her icy
toes.

She stepped up closer to the building to get out
of the wind, but the shelter gave little relief. After
what seemed like hours, the head nurse opened the

door. She looked at Alice as if she were seeing her for the first time. "Alice, what are you doing out there? And where are your keys?"

"I forgot and left them in my locker." The stern, seasoned psychiatric nurse shook her head.

Wonder what that means. Trouble?

She struck both feet together to remove the snow and stepped inside. Spotting a radiator close by, she made a beeline for it and got as close as she could. Rubbing her aching fingers together, she watched the circulation slowly return as pain penetrated to the bone. Then she removed her shoes and placed her stockinged feet closer to the radiator; the warmth felt so...o good.

When warm enough, she returned to the chore interrupted by the incident with the ball. She had been scavenging through this year's discarded gift wraps for pieces that could be used next year. The wraps had been ripped off and forgotten, scattered all over the ward.

It was Christmas Day of Alice's senior year, and she could think of no place she'd rather be on Christmas Day. She and other staff members were occupied with attempts to distract these young patients with the screwed up minds from the obvious fact that they had no visitors on this, the most special day of the year.

For weeks, the staff and patients had been making Christmas cookies, ornaments, and gifts for each other. The ornaments decorated the skinny tree in the middle of the playroom as well as every nook and cranny with an empty space. Alice had found last year's discarded Christmas paper in the storage room to wrap the gifts donated by the Salvation Army.

Dawson came over and watched her collecting and folding the gift wraps. She kept one eye on him as she worked, never knowing what to expect.

He switched back and forth from one leg to the other before asking, "Can I help, Miss Alice?"

"You could start by apologizing to me and Billy for your behavior."

The large brown eyes, so full of mischief earlier in the day, had turned serious and angelic looking. "How do I 'pologize?"

Alice wasn't playing his game. "Oh for heaven's sake, Dawson. Just say you're sorry."

"Okay, I'm sorry. I said it—now can I eat the popcorn on the tree?"

Alice sighed, realizing that it would be useless to pursue the issue further. She looked at her young charge and said, "No, you may not eat the popcorn because it will spoil your Christmas dinner, and besides, it's a decoration."

Dawson stomped his foot. "But I strung that popcorn all by myself."

"Where were Billy, the nurse, and all the others who helped you when you were doing this?" He just looked at her like she was from another planet.

"Oh, listen, Dawson, they're singing your favorite carol. Let's go join them." She took the child by the hand and led him over to the old piano where several children were singing *Joy to the World*. When the song ended, he looked up at Alice and asked, "Why ain't my mama here?"

The Class of 1960 went to Williamsburg, Virginia for their senior trip, and while it was quite a distance to travel, they all agreed that the history lesson would be worth it. On the way back, they stopped to eat dinner in a restaurant on the side of the highway. The owner came over to tell them that the black student in the class could not be served. Looks were exchanged in the group before they stood up and very proudly walked out without ordering.

They stopped at a service station down the road where they bought sandwiches and drinks. Alice said she had never tasted a more delicious ham and cheese sandwich.

At the end of the school year, Janie was the last student in Social Adjustments to give her *high tea.* The school calendar had been filled with events as graduation approached, so her tea had to be squeezed in prior to clinical on a Thursday morning. Attendance was mandatory for her classmates, so at 6 a.m. on a Thursday, thirteen of the fourteen graduating seniors gathered in the living room with their honored guests for tea. Some sat politely nodding on the edge of their chairs as they balanced their teacups and saucers the way Miss Pittypat had taught them. Others walked about stifling yawns. Janie dozed off as she added hot water to one of the cups; of course, she flooded a small section of the table containing the dainty tea cakes.

Felicia, the black student in the class, walked past the tea table pretentiously holding the handle of a dainty china cup between her thumb and forefinger, with the other fingers extending into the air. Using a voice that matched her actions, she proclaimed, "I cahn't stahnd this dahmned tea so eerly in the morning." *No wonder I love that girl, thought Alice.* She and Felicia had become best of friends.

Then it dawned on Alice that Liz was missing. She whispered to Susan, who sat next to her, "Doesn't Liz know that she's about to fail Social

Adjustments? I better slip out and get her in here. Cover for me."

She backed out the doorway to the hall and quietly pushed the button for the elevator. Getting off the elevator, she looked around and listened. It was so quiet. The hall was usually full of life and activity as student nurses got ready for work at that hour. She walked quickly to Liz's door and knocked.

There was no answer, so she opened the door a crack and called out, "Hey, Lazy Liz, you're about to fail S A. Get your fanny in gear, girl." Getting no response, she entered the room to see that Liz was still in bed. "Liz, get up, Liz." The blankets were pulled up over her head so that only her long, black hair could be seen. *Is she cold? Doesn't seem that cold in here to me.* Alice went over to shake her but suddenly stopped, sucking in her breath. Alarm bells were going off in her head. *What do you do....*Liz was too still. The blankets were not moving at all. *Is she breathing?* Alice felt Liz's neck for a carotid pulse; it was absent. *Liz is dead!* She yanked back the covers and screamed. The bedding was covered with blood from her waistline to the area below her knees.

The class gathered in the solarium later that morning after clinical and classes were cancelled for the day. They needed to heal themselves before they would be ready to care for others. They were playing bridge, a game they had learned to help distract the psych patients from their worries. They had found that the game also worked for student nurses.

Janie spoke first, "She was pregnant, and we never knew it."

Susan nodded, "Liz kept a lot of things to herself—never talked about anything personal, especially her sex life."

Janie put down her cards to wipe the tears and blow her nose, "But why, by all that is holy, did she ever resort to abortion?"

"Must a gone to one of those back-alley clinics or tried to do it herself. Somebody said Whitlow did it."

"Don't be silly. He wouldn't risk his precious license. Well, since the powers-that-be are hushing everything up, guess we'll never know."

Janie narrowed her eyes, saying, "I suspected something was going on. She took too many overnights to stay with her Aunt in Connecticut. And all you had to do was be in the same room with her and Tom Whitlow to know they were doin' it. I should'a confronted her."

"Don't blame yourself, Janie. The only thing we can do *now* is show respect by stopping the gossip."

Alice put her cards down and walked out of the room.

On a hot day in June, the lucky thirteen received their diplomas, pins, and the all-white uniform of a registered nurse. Alice looked at her classmates with pride, thinking, *our lives were not perfect at Mercy, but could they ever be? We did learn to honestly face problems and pain, to admit mistakes, to learn from them, and to do our best to correct them. Maybe that's the best anyone can do.* She maintained throughout her career that she learned everything she needed to know about nursing in that little diploma program, wishing that the wisdom had run over into other parts of her life.

Chapter 31 Echo

New York, New York, Fall 1960

Alice answered the telephone one evening and was surprised to hear the distinctive voice of Phillip Reid. It had been a year since their date, which she thought had gone very well and had expected him to call again. After several months, she decided that he just wasn't interested.

"I'd like to see you again, Alice. Sorry it's been so long; I was in London on business."

She was thrilled to hear from him again. "So, how've you been?"

"Great. And you?"

"Fine. I'm out of school now and working."

"How about dinner Friday night?"

She bit her lower lip and nodded. *YES!* She said, "I think I can swing that."

Alice told Janie about the call the next day over lunch.

"Be careful, Alice. He may be attracted to the rose queen."

The two friends were sitting across the table from each other as they gulped their lunches between patients. The tea kettle whistled, so Janie walked over and removed it from the burner before pouring the boiling water into her bowl of dehydrated vegetables.

Alice dismissed the remark as being motivated by jealousy and wolfed down the remainder of her peanut butter and jelly sandwich. *He's one heck of a catch, No wonder my friends are jealous.*

Janie shrugged. "Don't say I didn't warn you, my friend." She took a small sip of her soup to test the temperature. "In the future, I'll just mind my own business. Isn't that what you were trying to tell me?" Alice smiled.

Glancing at her watch, Alice quickly downed her milk as she snatched up the medical records she had brought to lunch with her. *No more time for such trivia. I've got to finish this charting before 2 p.m. meds or I'll be working overtime again today.* "We may have had plenty of time to do our work as students, but we sure don't have it now," she sighed.

"You got that right," Janie nodded.

On Friday night, rain was making traffic in New York City impossible, so Phil was fifteen minutes late picking her up. Snapping open a large, black umbrella, he got out of the cab to pick her up at the door.

The taxi wove its way slowly through the city, stopping at intervals and then starting up again. Slanting against the windshield, the rain collected in a thin layer of water before being swiped away by the rhythmic motion of the wiper blades. Reflections of the yellow-white lights from the cars and street lamps merged with the reds, blues, and greens from flashing neon in the rapidly disappearing water. Alice took it all in as she listened to the rain drumming softly on the metal roof of the cab. She took a deep breath, relaxed into the soft leather of the seat, and sighed, "I love the city in the rain."

"Unless you have some place to go." Her date sat drumming his finger tips on the arm rest beside him. He looked over at her and added, "You're so easy to please; I took the freedom of making reservations at The Chinese Pavilion, that wonderful place just off Broadway? We went there before. Remember?"

"I do. The food is so—o good."

He smiled. "How about some dancing after dinner?"

"Sounds perfect."

"I knew you'd say that." He rubbed his hands together, obviously pleased with himself. Then taking a deep breath, he murmured, "I really like the perfume you're wearing. What is it?

She smiled. "White Shoulders."

He patted his knees. "Well, that shouldn't be hard to remember." Glancing over at her he could tell she was pleased.

They fell into a mode of interacting destined to become common for them: He did most of the talking. She listened and spoke often enough to keep the conversation going. Alice noticed that he had stopped tapping his fingers.

The time passed rather quickly, and before too long, they reached The Chinese Pavilion, where they were met by a doorman wearing white gloves. A host escorted them to a table by the window where Alice could look out on New Yorkers hurrying past, their colorful umbrellas pushing back the rain.

She took a deep breath, "It smells heavenly in here—a mixture of the most delicious foods I can imagine." The host smiled as he helped her remove her raincoat, held a chair, and waited for her to take a seat.

On the opposite wall, mahogany panels reflected the light from Chinese lanterns on the tables, where crystal, china, and silver sparkled on crisp white linen. The room was elegant but managed to project a feeling of coziness at the same time. Piano music was playing softly in the background.

Alice laughed. "I'm being spoiled by all of this special treatment, Phil. I could become addicted to it." He just looked at her and winked.

Phil was spreading his napkin on his lap as he asked, "Would you prefer red or white wine tonight, my dear?"

Alice was quick to imitate his action with the napkin, saying, "You pick the wine; you have such good taste. Red or white, it doesn't matter. I'm sure you'll select the perfect wine to go with our meal."

Egg rolls and wonton soup were followed by several trips to the buffet table where crab Rangoon, Moo Goo Gai Pan, Beef in Oyster Sauce, Crispy Skin Duck, and many other succulent dishes were served from heated containers. At a safe distance from the heat, another table of cold delights surrounded an ice carving of a magnificent bird.

Alice walked over to survey the table, exclaiming, "What a beautiful bird! What kind is it?"

"My guess *is* that it's a pheasant, perhaps a Mikado Pheasant. J. Fenwick Lansdowne, an artist who paints such birds, displayed his work at the Audubon House a year or two ago. He's well-known for capturing the authentic colors of birds in China."

She gazed at him in awe, "How interesting!"

"If you like Chinese art, I think there's an exhibition at the Metropolitan on Sunday. Care to go?"

"I'd love to."

"Are you ready for that dance? I think I can keep up with this." He folded his linen napkin and placed it on the table; Alice mimicked his action. After escorting her to the small dance floor, he carefully placed his right hand on her back and held her left hand out with his other. It seemed so formal. Alice pictured him learning to dance in prep school and felt so sophisticated. The romantic rendition of *Smoke Gets in Your Eyes* took over, and they allowed the rhythm to be in control in this exquisite and gracious setting.

Sunday was a crisp, fall day with plenty of sunshine for warmth and a gentle breeze to blow about the falling leaves. Alice hummed *Autumn in New York* as she carefully dressed in her periwinkle blue sheath and pearls. As she donned white gloves, she checked her image in the mirror again. She looked elegant—the effect she wanted.

Later, as they stood outside the entrance to the Metropolitan Museum of Art, Alice stared in awe, "We couldn't possibly see all of this in one day!"

"Not even three or four."

"Can we go to the Greek and Roman exhibits first? I have been fascinated by the Trojan War since I was a freshman in college. I want to see the statue of Laocoon and his sons being devoured by the gigantic serpents."

He frowned, "Afraid we'll have to go to Rome to see that, sweetie."

Alice looked thoughtful. "What a horrible price Laocoon paid for exposing the truth about the Trojan horse."

"Yeah! Even the ancient Greeks understood that."

Does he think Laocoon was wrong to tell the truth? She looked puzzled because her beliefs about *truth* did not quite match what she thought he was expressing, but she kept her mouth shut. Things were going too well. Besides, the truth was becoming a bit muddled whenever she was with him. Any doubts, like the way he looked at other women, about the relationship were stuffed. She was having too good a time. Afraid to express or even acknowledge her own thoughts or feelings— she might burst the bubble by showing that the glass slipper was, after all, a misfit. So she smiled and agreed with whatever he said.

After the Chinese exhibit, they had tea and crumpets on the terrace as Beethoven's sixth symphony played in the background. Classical music was another taste she was developing.

He began filling most of her weekends, and they were having the time of their lives. He got a kick out of introducing her to his world—the food, expensive cars, entertainment—the best that money could buy. She lapped it up and rewarded him with a shy smile.

They went to Broadway shows, operas at the Metropolitan, and shows at Radio City Music Hall. They visited museums, played tennis, and went for long walks and boat rides in Central Park. They ate at the best restaurants and enjoyed lavish parties at the homes of his friends—bankers, businessmen, politicians, and other successful people.

One evening she ran into Victoria Berrigan, director of nursing at her alma mater and now her employer. Turns out she was an old friend of the Reids. Alice couldn't help but notice a change in her behavior. *She* seems *cold. She's never acted that way to me before. Maybe she doesn't approve of my relationship with Phil.* She dismissed the thought as a figment of her nerves.

Phil felt out of place with her friends from Mercy, so they rarely joined the Mercy group. Besides, Alice was beginning to feel that they had little to offer her as did most people she was beginning to consider her social inferiors.

Believing that she had taken the right path, she tried to become what she thought he wanted her to be. She wore the 'right' clothes, used good taste in applying makeup, and frequented expensive beauty salons. Those assets combined with an obsession for proper etiquette and a good imitation of people in his social circle helped her fit into his world. She did not realize that she was building her sense of self on lies and half-truths.

One evening they sat watching the full moon as the car radio played softly in the background. *We'll Have These Moments to Remember* came on; it overwhelmed her with bitter-sweet memories. When she was able to speak, her voice was filled with emotion and barely audible, "I have something I need to tell you," she said.

"Fire away. I'm all ears."

"I have a son."

Chapter 32: Bonded

New York, New York, 1960-1961

Alice braced herself for rejection and turned to look him in the eye. He studied her for a long time and then slowly pulled her into his arms before kissing her trembling lips.

"Details?" She took a deep breath and told him her truth. When she finished, he said, "I see you've had a lot of pain." He looked away before saying, "Give me a chance to make that up to you."

She relaxed into his arms. *It feels so good to be fully known and yet accepted by the 'right' people.* It boosted her self-esteem so that she no longer felt inferior; she decided to find other ways to keep her on this plateau.

When they went to dinner the following week, he held her chair as usual. On her plate rested a small, white box tied with a blue ribbon.

She smiled at him. "What's this?"

He rocked his head back and forth, saying "Open it and see."

Her fingers trembled a bit as she untied the ribbon and opened the box. Staring up at her was the biggest emerald-cut diamond ring she had ever seen. Tilting her head toward the ceiling, she made an effort to contain the tears standing in her eyes.

He quietly whispered, "I love you, Alice. Will you marry me?"

Struggling to pull herself together from the shock, she heard herself reply, as if from a distance. "Let's wait a bit. I don't think I'm ready for marriage just yet."

Now why did I say that? I have no idea.

If he was disappointed, it didn't show when he said, "Take all the time you need. I have to go on a business trip to Italy next month, so you'll have plenty of time to sort things out."

"You're a sweetheart. I'll put on my best thinking cap."

The following Saturday afternoon they were relaxing with friends on the porch of Long Island Country Club. Having just finished a competitive game of tennis, they were pausing to calm their breathing and cool off.

"Sheesh! I'm really beat, Alice said as she wiped the sweat from her brow."

Phil's best friend, Frank, was wiping his sweaty palms down the leg of his shorts. "Alice, if you work on that back hand a bit, you could wipe Phil off the court. I'll be happy to teach you. It would be worth it to see Preppy here get his clock cleaned by a girl."

Phil grinned. "If you're so good, pal, let's see you put your money where that big opening in your face is located. You know the one, the one you're always shoveling food into."

Frank opened his mouth wider in defiance, "Give me a few more minutes with these lovely ladies, and I'll show you."

Minutes later, Phil spied an empty court. The two men grabbed their rackets and headed in that direction. The women, left to entertain each other, saw their chance to chat 'girl stuff.'

Anna, a perky brunette, belonged in this setting in all the ways that Alice did not—good family, Vassar education, social skills developed since childhood, connections. Anna had been Phil's friend since childhood, and she liked Alice. Alice sensed her acceptance, and that acceptance was another boost to her self-esteem.

After exchanging news about the latest fashions and hair styles, Anna's face and demeanor took on a more serious note. She paused and made eye contact with Alice. "So, tell me, Al, are you and Phil headed for the altar?"

Alice fiddled with her tennis racket and took some time before meeting her gaze, "Why do you ask that?"

"The guy's bonkers about you. Everybody knows that." Alice wondered whether Frank knew about the diamond. Anna appeared to know more than she was letting on.

Alice raised her eyebrows, "Who's everybody?"

Anna forgot about the question when she spotted a waiter approaching their table. Waving him down, she said, "Let's have a glass of wine while we wait."

"Think I'll wait for cocktail hour." Alice knew that alcohol would loosen her tongue—afraid that something would slip out, causing Anna to reject her.

Anna squared her shoulders, "You're *not* making me drink alone, are you?" So Alice ordered wine and sipped it ever so slowly, while guarding her tongue with great care—unable to relax.

Anna placed her hands between her knees and rocked forward, "So where do you like to shop, Ally?"

"Lord and Taylor was the favorite of my parents," she lied.

"But ' L and T' doesn't have a lot of stylish clothes for the younger set. On the other hand, the Mod on 2nd Avenue has a lot of preppy things. Wanna go next week?"

Alice was delighted to hear the invitation, "Love to. Can't think of anything I need, but I can look."

"What's need got to do with it?" Anna laughed. Alice shrugged her shoulders and laughed with her.

Taking a small sip of wine, Alice became suddenly pensive, *Seems like a miracle that I actually fit into this world. Everything and everyone seem to fall in place around me; I guess it's because they love Phil. It would be a shame to rock the boat, so to speak. One thing's for certain, I could do a lot worse with my life. Maybe I should just go ahead and accept that diamond. It'll knock a lot of eyes out around Mercy. That's for sure.*

Her attention returned to Anna, who was watching Phil and Frank on the court. "Sorry, Anna, guess I drifted a bit there for a moment."

Anna smiled. "Looks to me like Phil's winning that game. Maybe Frank will watch that tongue of his more carefully in the future."

Alice met Phil at the airport on his return from Italy and accepted his ring. Just as she expected, it attracted a lot of attention among her colleagues and former classmates. They sensed her unjustified feelings of superiority and responded coldly to her. She, in turn, sensed their hostility. Phil assured her that they were just jealous. She believed him because that belief made her feel better about herself.

One evening she picked up the telephone and was blasted back in time. She immediately recognized the lazy, southern drawl of Jefferson, her former lover.

His voice caught when he asked, "How are you, Alice?"

Her mouth flew open, and she tried to form the words. But nothing came out. Finally, she was able to mumble, "Fine."

"That's good to hear." He cleared his throat, and there was a long pause before he continued. When he did, the words came rushing out. "I'd like to see you again, Alice. I've done a little traveling, met a lot of people, done a lot of things, but I can't seem to get you out of my mind." For just a moment the years and all the resentment faded away, and she was talking to the man she loved.

But just as suddenly the hurt and bad feelings took over. *Probably just wants to get in my pants again,* she thought, so she jumped at the chance to strike back, blaming him for all of her pain. "You waited too long, Jefferson. I'm engaged to Phillip Reid. Do you know who he is?"

He was silent for a long time before saying, "No, I don't know who he is. Should I?" His voice sounded hoarse when he added, "I hope he'll be better to you than I was."

"Well, you can just read about him when the announcement of the wedding comes out in the paper. Suffice it to say for now—he could buy and sell you, baby." She hung up. That did it. Her uncertainty and self-doubt were replaced with desires to become Mrs. Phillip Reid and replace the son she had given up—the sooner the better.

They set the date for the wedding in early April of the following year He wanted to be married in his church, and Alice approved. She had not been inside a church for years.

Chapter 33: More People Pleasing

New York, New York, 1962

Alice studied her image in the mirror. *My wedding day. I'll see folks I haven't seen in years. We'll have lunch at the country club, and then Phil and I will be off to Hawaii. I should be on top of the world, but I'm not.*

Her thick, auburn hair had been piled in highlighted curls on top of her head in an elaborate hairdo. *How many nights did I slave at the hospital to pay for this hairdo, my gown, and all the other stuff.*

She poured bubble bath, Essence of Lilacs, into the tub and adjusted the hot and cold water to just the right temperature. Breathing in the fragrance of lilacs, she removed her robe and hung it on the back of the door. While turning off the water, she turned to look at Janie, who was ironing her wedding gown." Be careful, Janie, don't burn it."

Several bridesmaids came running when they heard the scream. Alice had turned the shower full force onto her upsweep.

"It'll be okay, Alice. Just take a deep breath and relax in your bath; I'll repair the damage when you're finished." Janie shook her head and whispered to Cecile, the maid of honor, "She's strung so tight, the least thing will set her off."

Cecile nodded and walked over to pick up her guitar from the corner of the room. The melody and calming lyrics to "Abide with Me" soon filled the air.

The groom arrived at the church on time but without his wedding shoes; his best man grabbed a cab, found the shoes, and got them to the church just ahead of the priest. During the ceremony, a loud crash shook the church. Everyone looked about to see what had happened. The biggest usher in the wedding party had fallen backward from the communion rail. A physician in the wedding party got up and walked to the other side of the church to examine him, honoring the cross as he passed in front. Turns out the big guy had partied too heavily the night before.

Otherwise, the wedding went smoothly. And, on the surface, it was everything brides imagine their weddings will be like.

The reception, held at the country club following the ceremony, included a sit-down dinner for two hundred. Aunt Izzie, now a widow, and Rachel, Alice's cousin, were there, appearing uncomfortable and terribly unsure about how to act. Alice tried to hide her enjoyment of their discomfort; Olivia Reid would not approve.

Aunt Izzie wore a blue, polyester dress, purchased from the rack; it was belted at the waistline with rhinestones on the buckle. Alice gazed at Rachel as they lined up for the receiving line; to her amazement, her cousin not only looked like her mother but also dressed like her.

As Alice walked past, Rachel whispered, "A Mr. Jordan has been trying to contact you—says it's very important."

Not recognizing the name and having no sympathy for her kin, Alice shrugged and answered brusquely, "Well, you have my telephone number; tell him to call me."

Don't see why they had to come anyway, but Mrs. Reid insisted I invite them. They never cared anything about me before. She paused as a picture flashed in her mind: Aunt Izzie was tenderly caring for her broken and bruised lip. *Well, maybe Aunt Izzie did, just a little, but not always.*

She looked over at her aunt, who was nervously switching from one foot to the other and wincing. Alice motioned for one of the ushers and asked him to bring a chair for her aunt. Olivia Reid smiled her approval.

The bride was busy scanning the faces of guests as they passed through the line, ready to change her behavior at the first sign of disapproval. As a result, she found it impossible to relax and enjoy herself: Others were in control.

After dinner, Alice was washing her hands at the sink in the powder room when she heard voices in the foyer. Phil's two aunts were gossiping as they refreshed their makeup before the spacious mirror.

"Did you see that horrible woman from Louisiana? She actually picked up a fork from the floor and used it. Can you believe it?"

"And that dress looks like something picked up in a yard sale two years ago. Did you see the rhinestones on the belt?" They both laughed.

Alice stepped back into one of the stalls and waited until they were gone. *They're a couple of old biddies—never done anything useful their entire lives. If they had any sense, they'd wish they were as good as my aun*t. *But I certainly don't want them talking about me like that. I'll do whatever it takes to prevent it.* And she clenched her right fist.

Following their honeymoon, Alice and her new husband returned to New York to look for a house. Phillip wanted to be on Long Island near the country club where he could swim and play tennis whenever he liked. He'd known nothing but luxury all of his life and appeared to be quite depressed when they looked at houses they could afford. Alice wanted what he wanted.

They found the 'perfect house' in Westwood, a prestigious neighborhood near the country club, but, as expected, mortgage payments would stretch their budget beyond its limits. They sat up nights working and reworking the figures, trying to find a way to make the payments fit, but they couldn't.

Finally, in desperation and without telling Phil, Alice decided to take another approach. So early Monday morning found her sitting in her father-in-law's office dressed in a navy blue suit, prim white blouse, navy blue stockings, and sensible, navy pumps with matching purse and white gloves. Her hair was pulled tightly into a chignon at the back of her head.

The receptionist looked her over and smiled in approval. Speaking in a professional tone, she said, "I'm sure Mr. Reid will want to see you as soon as he's available. Would you like some coffee?"

Alice declined, fearing that the caffeine would make her too nervous.

John Reid soon emerged from his office, reaching for Alice's hand. He smiled as he said, "To what do I owe this honor, my dear?" A successful banker, he was well known in the business world for his keen intelligence and judgment. But when it came to family, that judgment was colored by emotion. Well aware of this, Alice was hopeful that she could manipulate her father-in-law.

She followed him into his office. He closed the door and held a chair for her. She settled into the chair, crossing her legs at the ankles. He listened attentively as she filled him in on the latest details about the house hunt, ending with her description of the house in Westwood and the nights they had spent trying to figure a way they could buy it.

"Why, John, for only another $350.00 a month, we could get that house. With four bedrooms, we'd have space for our growing family within walking distance to Westwood Elementary. And you know what a good school that is."

He looked at her, narrowing his eyes, "You're thinking about your family already? Anything Olivia and I should know about?"

She lowered her head and gazed up at him, "I don't know, John. I've been feeling kind'a funny in the mornings lately."

Ten minutes later she got up to leave with a promise that he would make up the monthly $350.00 until they were 'better situated.' He smiled at her and winked. "Just leave it to me, my dear. I'll take care of everything. You just take care of yourself."

Chapter 34: Westwood

New York, New York, 1963

The house had appeared in *Homes and Gardens* a few years earlier, and Alice was determined to maintain its special status. It kept her busy all summer—painting, planting, shopping, matching colors and textures, and arranging antiques, many of them family heirlooms. The bills kept coming in—a new one almost every day. Phil showed no evidence of worrying about them. He told Alice over and over that this Dutch colonial home, the essence of charm and good taste in one of the better neighborhoods, would pay for itself in just a few years. With the connections and advantages it would bring, his career would be zooming in no time at all. He believed that and Alice bought it, so she kept herself busy preparing for the house warming in early fall, shoving the nagging little worries into the background.

The home was set on a beautifully landscaped lot that echoed the charm of the house, both providing a lovely setting for the open house in late September. On the big night, the English garden, highlighted by the setting sun, was redolent with the fragrance of sweet autumn clematis. A mourning dove could be heard in the distance, its call adding a homey feeling to the otherwise very sophisticated ambiance.

Guests mingled by the Tiki torches on the two-tiered flagstone patio. Others gathered in small groups on the first floor and around the full service bar in the basement. A uniformed maid circulated among them delivering hors d'oeuvres and drinks as classical guitar music played in the background. The bartender, dressed in a white jacket, mixed drinks at the temporary bar on the side porch.

A tall blonde, svelte and beautiful, had Phil totally engaged in front of the bay window facing onto the patio. Alice had seen her on a recent visit to Phil's office but had hardly noticed the unremarkable secretary in a navy-blue business suit and thick glasses. Tonight, she looked striking in a red cocktail dress that flattered her figure and showed more cleavage than Alice thought to be in good taste.

Swiping her long, blonde hair from her eyes with a slender, manicured hand, she gazed adoringly up at Phil while sipping her gin and tonic. He was gazing into her eyes and hanging on her every word, his face reflecting excitement in the flickering candlelight from the dining room. *I'll have to keep an eye on her,* thought Alice. *But I have to be smart about it. A put down would only drive him into her arms.*

Inside the dining room, candlelight sparkled on gleaming crystal and silver, set on white-linen-covered tables laden with shrimp, Swedish meatballs, smoked salmon, caviar on toast, cheeses, cold cuts, and several beautiful relish dishes. The aroma of wine and spirits wafted into the living room where it mingled with the smell of fresh coffee. Yellow-blue flames in the fireplace licked away the evening chill, inviting guests to linger for a fruit tart or chocolate mousse to end their evening. The basement was open for those who wanted to mix their own drinks or take a swing on the polished dance floor.

Alice wore a low-cut, black cocktail dress displaying a 'fashionable' amount of cleavage. The guys were knocking each other out of the way to get a better look, as their wives glared daggers in their direction. She had few female friends, and that dress wasn't gaining any new ones for her. Phil told her it was because other women were jealous. She accepted his explanation because it fed her ego and protected her from looking at herself—to admit that she didn't know the first thing about being a friend. It was much easier to think that other women just couldn't be trusted. *They are conniving and manipulative—better to avoid them.* And she unknowingly sought opinions that would reinforce that delusion about her relationship with half of the world's population.

"Hey, Alice, when you gonna ditch that husband of yours for a real man?"

"And who might that be?" She batted her eye lashes sweetly at one of her husband's competitors.

He winked at her, "Why me, of course."

She flipped her hair out of her face and walked away, saying "When you make more money than he does, sugar." Her small crowd of admirers laughed.

She saw Phil headed her way, accompanied by a young man she did not recognize, "Alice, I want you to meet Jim Williams, an old college buddy."

"Hello, Jim Williams. Your glass is empty; let me fill it for you."

He did not smile when he said, "No thank you. One's enough."

She sensed his disapproval as his glance swept quickly over her cleavage. She made a mental note to wear conservative clothes and to act prim and proper in future encounters with him while secretly hoping that those encounters would be few and far between.

He looks like a guy from my chemistry class in high school. I could feel his disapproval. Could he be the same guy? What if he heard the stories they circulated about me and my pregnancy? If that word got out, it could ruin everything.

Quickly brushing aside the negative thinking, she entered the living room to join John and Olivia by the fireplace. They sat next to end tables where they rested their plates periodically as they chatted with a couple Alice had just met.

Placing her plate on the coffee table, Alice took a deep breath and warmed her hands a bit before the fire. It was the first chance she'd had to relax all evening. Returning to her food, she plopped a big, juicy shrimp dripping with hot sauce into her mouth. Her taste buds tingled as she bit into the succulent shrimp. Olivia gave her the old familiar smile, a gentle reminder that she was being monitored. "Have you checked the food in the basement lately, Alice?"

"Glad you mentioned that, Olivia. I'd better go see." She put her plate down and headed for the stairs to the basement.

"Oh, finish your dinner first, Alice," John barked.

But Alice was already descending the stairs. At the bottom of the steps, a conga line was forming. She yelled to the dancers, "Wait for me, Folks, while I check on the food."

As she passed the bar, Cecile's date approached her with an unusual-looking bottle clearly labelled 'the anything bottle.' Alice laughed, "Oh no, my friend, don't use that for anything you plan to drink."

He looked at her in dismay, "Why? What's in it?"

She placed her right hand over her chest, saying "Let me put it this way—it's properly labelled. As bottles of alcohol are emptied, the remnants go in there—bourbon, Scotch, tequila, vodka, you name it. Drink that, and I can't promise what will happen to you."

"Really? Sounds interesting." He held the bottle up for closer inspection but did not drink.

Alice did a quick check of the food before remembering she had left an unfinished plate upstairs. The conga would have to wait. As she passed the basement bedroom, she noticed that several of the guys had found a football game on the television. They had moved their food and drinks into the room and sat intently watching, their feet propped on the table in front of the lounge. She did not disturb them.

When the last guest had gone, Alice sat down on the patio with Phil; they were having a nightcap and reliving the excitement of the party. Alice swirled the liquid in her glass and took a deep breath. "Whew! It sure is peaceful and quiet for a change— not a sound." She picked up a cigarette from the table beside her and placed it in her mouth. Phil leaned over to light it as he inhaled deeply on his own.

Blowing smoke into the air, he grinned. "It was a success, Alice. You outdid yourself."

She shrugged, "I think everyone had a good time. Your dad sure knows how to cut a rug; we had a great time with the 'lindy,' as he calls it." She paused to swat at a bug before continuing, "I spoke too soon—looks like this bug will give us some excitement."

"Blow smoke on him."

Alice grinned, "I'd like to have blown smoke on Anne Duncan. Did you notice that awful dress she wore to *my* party?" Shaking her head, she said, "The woman has absolutely no sense of fashion."

He looked in the direction of the red glow from her cigarette, "Alice, my darling, I hate to tell you this, but you have a habit of seeing the negative in other people. A lot of my business associates like and respect her, so do me a big favor and look for the positive things, please."

She jiggled her glass again as she lifted her eyebrows, "Like what?'

"I don't know. I'm a lot like you, but I hear she's a good wife and mother. People seem to like her for some reason. Oh, they say she has a killer smile. Maybe that's it."

"I wouldn't know about that because I've never seen her smile."

He flicked the ashes from his cigarette. "I believe you."

Alice kicked off her heels, "I get along okay with people I want to get along with." She turned toward him, her tone of voice becoming more serious, "And how would you know about my social skills? You're out working every night, and I'm not really close to anyone in your family." She shrugged her shoulders. "Other women just don't like me. Guess I'm a threat to their precious little worlds." Taking a drag from her cigarette, she smiled. "The guys like me fine, but I can't hang out with them all the time: I'll get a reputation."

He dropped his cigarette on the flagstone and squashed it with his heel. "I didn't mean to pick a fight at the end of such a nice evening. Come sit in my lap, and Daddy will make the booboos go away."

She stood and hiked her skirt above her black bikini panties, exposing her gartered black stockings. Breathing in her heady perfume, he reached for her, pulling her into his lap as she straddled him. It didn't take long for this argument to end like most of their others.

Chapter 35: Settling In

Alice awoke the next day with a drum roll in her head and surging nausea. Turning away from the slit of sunlight filtering through the blinds, she covered both ears to shut out sounds of the fire engine outside. It was obviously going to a four-alarm fire. Soon realizing that it was not a fire engine but the doorbell ringing, she forced herself to turn and face the clock. Blinking, she thought, *Is it really 12:42 p.m.?* Flipping back the satin sheets and covers and reaching for her robe, she put it on inside-out and then pitched a fit because she couldn't find the belt. Feeling around on the thick carpet for her slippers, she soon gave up and descended the stairs in her bare feet. Peering through the peephole in the door, she saw Anne Duncan standing there, holding a large box. *Oh great—just makes my day.* With her left hand pressed to her temple, she opened the door with her right.

"Good morning, Alice." Anne paused and took a better look at her neighbor. "You look like death warmed over."

Alice squinted at her, replying, "I'm okay, Anne. What's up?" *How can anyone be this cheerful so early in the morning?*

Anne tapped her foot on the porch floor, "Did you forget that you're supposed to drop off the forms for the ballots at the community center?"

"No," she lied.

Anne's face said she didn't believe her, but she said nothing. "Well, be sure to get them there an hour before the meeting starts, so folks can vote; I'll be a little late—have to pick up the kids." She paused, "Aren't you excited? We're going to have a whole set of new officers in our homeowners' association."

Alice started to nod her head but stopped suddenly: Pain was threatening to blow her forehead off. "Exciting," she mumbled.

Two Alka Seltzers and three cups of coffee later, Alice started to feel alive again, only to hear the telephone ringing. She picked it up to stop the noise. "Is this Ms. Alice Hollister?" She did not recognize the male voice, but the slight Cajun accent put her on guard.

"Alice Hollister Reid," she replied.

"You're married?"

"That's right."

"Well, Miss Alice, my name is Henry Jordan. You don't know me, but my son, Spike, took you out on a date some years ago."

Alice felt a sliver of fear traveling up her spinal cord as her eyes opened in surprise. "So, why are you calling me?"

He paused as if searching for the right words. "My bizness is of a rather personal nature." Another pause. "Maybe I should write it to you in a letter."

"Tell me now, Mr. Jordan, or you may never have the opportunity again. In other words, quit beating around the bush and just say what you have to say."

"Yes, ma'am." Another pause. Just as Alice was getting ready to hang up, he started again. "Well my boy, the only famly I got—make that *had.*"

Alice was tapping her fingers on the telephone table, "Get on with it, Mr. Jordan!"

"I'm tryin to, Miss. This, as I said, is of a rather delicate nature." Alice sighed, but something kept her glued to the telephone—a vague shadow of a memory. A struggle in the front seat of a car. She quickly brushed the shadow away.

"Anyways, Spike he done got kilt coupla years ago—ridin' that ole motorcycle o' his'n. I tole him not to git the durn thing. But would he listen?"

Alice stomped her foot. "Mr. Jordan, you have five minutes to state your case before I hang up."

"Well, 'fore he died, he tole me thet he slip somepin in yo' drink on that blind date." His voice caught when he said, "My son won't no angel,

268

Miss." Another long pause and some coughing. Then very rapid speech, his words jamming into each other. "To make a long story short—that chile you went away to have could'a been his'n."

Alice was fully awake now. She shouted into the telephone, "That's impossible. First of all, I never had a child. And if I had, there's no way I could have had one with your son."

"Word gits around, Miss. And my son say that chile could'a been his. Ya'll do some heavy…what young folks call pettin?"

"Certainly not," she realized she was screaming.

"Miss Alice, my son wuz dying. You think he lie to me on he death bed? No more'n I'd lie to you, Miss. I'm an old man. I could die tomorrow. An' all I wants is to see my only kin 'fore I stands afore my Maker."

Alice slammed the telephone down. "Crazy ole Coot… I can't remember a thing after I blacked out, but I'm not about to tell him that. I need a drink—bad. Better make it vodka, so they can't smell my breath at that community center." Her hands trembled as she descended the stairs to the bar. After knocking over a bottle of bourbon, she finally located a bottle of vodka in back of the liquor supply. She poured herself half a glass and gulped it. "Now I have to clean up the mess I made with the bourbon."

Oddly enough, she actually got the forms to their destination only ten minutes late. And if anyone noticed the alcohol on her breath, they said nothing. The vodka had calmed her sufficiently for her to stay for the meeting.

She was putting on her sweater to leave, when she was approached by the chair of the nominating committee. "You can't leave yet, Alice. We need you to help us count the ballots."

Alice bit her lower lip. "Sorry, I forgot."

She reluctantly joined the other members of the nominating committee, who were sipping tea and chatting around a table in the kitchen.

Susie Frawley sat down next to Alice and began opening the sealed envelopes with a small kitchen knife before passing the ballots to the others. Susie was the neighborhood gossip. Alice guessed that her main reason for being there was to carry out what everyone recognized as her self-appointed duty: to spread the news (according to Susie).

Susie swept her reddish-orange bangs away from her squinting eyes and took a deep breath through her narrow nose. As she pushed her horn-rimmed glasses closer to her eyes, everyone knew that a spicy tale was about to unfold. Some would have liked to leave the room, but others, including Alice, relaxed and perked up their ears for a juicy story.

"Did you hear? Albert Stuart and that long-legged secretary of his were seen at the airport Friday night."

Jane Hampton, who was sitting next to Anne Duncan, frowned, "Maybe they had business there, Susie. Who knows? People go on business trips all the time; they even take their secretaries along. Would you believe it?" She looked at Anne for support.

Anne nodded. "That's right, Susie, happens all the time. Let's concentrate on these ballots, so we can get out of here without too many errors."

Susie narrowed her lips and twisted her mouth to the side, peering at her audience. She spoke as if she were making a final pronouncement on the situation. "They were each carrying an overnight bag."

"Let's talk about something else. Surely we have better ways to spend our time—like focusing on these ballots."

Anne twirled her tea bag in the hot water and chimed in immediately, "Oh yes, get this out of the way, and we can go home."

Susie, more determined than ever to prop up her story, shook her index finger at the group and said emphatically, "Just stay alert for the next couple heading for divorce court. And remember who saw it coming."

After that, they were able to finish counting in a relatively short time. Anne gathered up the cups and saucers for Jane, who was washing them in the sink.

"Grab a tea towel out of that second drawer, Anne. I know it's better to let these dishes air dry, but they'll be full of dust before they're used again." She handed a cup to Anne, commenting, "Pat Davis's party is only a week from next Saturday. Are you going?"

Anne smiled, excitement written on her face. "Wouldn't miss it for the world; she throws the best parties in town." Placing the dish she was drying in the cupboard, she added, "Don't you think so?"

"Without a doubt. Wonder what she'll do to top last year's party of the year."

"Don't know, but I can hardly wait." They turned to see Alice standing in the doorway, helping Susie Frawley with her sweater. Anne and Jane exchanged glances as Alice fumed inside. *Nobody even mentioned my party. Guess my spread wasn't good enough for them.*

The following Saturday morning, Phil and Alice were enjoying a leisurely breakfast in their sunny breakfast nook. Phil bit into a slice of whole-grain toast as he read the morning paper. "Hmm, this bread is delicious, Alice, I love that nutty taste. You'll have to buy more of it." He placed another

272

slice of bread in the toaster and returned to reading his paper. "Here's something you should know about." He flapped the paper with both hands and turned to his wife. "The health department closed Royster's Market due to an outbreak of salmonella. You didn't get this bread there, did you?"

"No--oo. Besides, I don't think you get salmonella from bread."

"It says here that you can get it from anything contaminated with animal feces."

"Really?" She took another sip of black coffee. "That's a real shame about the market. They have the best meats in town. But food poisoning is very serious and can prove fatal for some."

Phil looked at his watch, "Uh-oh, didn't realize it was so late. I'll miss the tee off." He gulped the rest of his coffee, pecked Alice on the forehead and headed for the door. As he closed the door behind him, the telephone rang. Alice picked up the receiver to hear Susie Frawley's high-pitched voice. They exchanged pleasantries and Susie got right down to business, "Alice, have you heard about Royster's Market?"

"We were just reading about it, Susie." Alice reached for her coffee, suspecting that more was coming.

There was a pause on the other end of the line before Susie continued. "Well--ll" She took a deep breath and talked very slowly as if she were savoring every word. "I heard from a very reliable source that Pat Davis buys all of her meats there."

"I don't doubt that for one minute, Susie. Where else would she buy them? She always has to have the best of everything."

"Well, if you ask me, anybody going to that party next Saturday night is just asking for trouble."

"I couldn't agree more, Susie. Thanks for letting us know. I'll do what I can to pass the word around." Alice smiled and hung up the telephone.

Phil returned home a few hours later. He washed his hands at the kitchen sink and splashed a bit of water on his face before grabbing the dish towel to wipe his hands. As he took a beer from the refrigerator, he saw Alice standing in the doorway frowning. "Phil, that towel is for drying dishes. And kitchen sinks should not be used for bathing."

He slammed the refrigerator door and looked at her. "Damn it, Alice, a man needs to be able to relax in his own home. You care more about this mausoleum of antiques than you care about me."

Although feeling that she was right, she backed down, hoping to avoid a fight. "Okay, sugar, I hear you. I'll talk to your mom and see what we can do to make you more comfortable around here."

He scratched his head. "What's my mother got to do with this? Alice, you can't change the color of your lipstick without my mother's approval." He took a swig of beer and went outside, slamming the door behind him.

Shrugging her shoulders, she thought, *He'll get over it.* She went to her room, carefully removed the bedspread and folded it prior to placing it in its special place in the closet. She took two aspirins, stretched out on the bed, and closed her eyes. Her head was swirling. *What should I do? If I please Olivia, Phil's unhappy and if I please Phil, Olivia's unhappy. It makes my head swim. My thinking is getting more muddled every day, and I used to think so clearly. Maybe a nap will help me put things in order.*

She fell into a restless sleep, and the dream about the phantom woman reaching for her returned. As usual, she woke up in a cold sweat. Bending over the bed as she tried to find her slippers, she fell onto the floor with a loud crash.

"What happened?" Phil stood in the doorway, breathless, his face flushed from his flight up the stairs.

She looked perplexed. "Just a dizzy spell, I guess."

"I want you to make an appointment with Dr. Thompson first thing Monday morning, young lady.

Do you understand? Alice nodded in agreement. She had to wait a couple of weeks before the doctor could see her.

The evening following her appointment, Phil arrived home to find a pitcher of martinis waiting— dry just the way he liked them. The aroma of prime rib wafted from the oven, and a deep-dish apple pie sat on the kitchen counter.

She appeared in the doorway with an apron covering his favorite, blue dress. She smiled as he bent to kiss her and wipe a smudge of white flour from her cheek. "Is that roast beef I smell?"

She answered by handing him a martini. He took a sip and smacked his lips. "Um--mm…dry, just the way I like them." He looked around the kitchen, "Is that a deep-dish apple pie? What's the occasion?"

She grinned as she took his hand, "I saw the doctor today."

He looked at her, raising his eyebrows. "And?"

She moved her feet in a happy little dance before hugging him. "Congratulations! You're going to be a father."

The look on his face told her that he was shocked and overwhelmed, but he quickly took hold of himself and laughed, saying "Why that's wonderful, simply wonderful. But shouldn't you be in bed or something. Sit down, and let me finish dinner."

"No, silly, I'm fine. Women have been having babies for thousands of years."

As they lingered by the fireplace after dinner, Phil finished his second serving of apple pie, placed the plate on the side table, and sighed. "That was some dinner, Alice. Couldn't eat another bite, but I will have just a little more of that delicious coffee."

She poured him half a cup and went over to relax in her favorite recliner. Picking up one of several magazines she had purchased on her way home from the doctor, she was soon lost in the world of babies: cribs, baby clothes, wallpaper for the nursery, and stuffed teddy bears.

As Phil got up to stoke the fire, he looked over at his wife. Her face was radiant and serene in the firelight. He had never seen her so happy. "By the way, good thing we missed the Davis's party. Heard it was a dud."

Alice lifted the magazine she was reading to hide the smile on her face. Everything seemed to be going her way: rich husband, beautiful home, and a replacement for the child she had given up. Why even Pat Davis's party was a flop.

Chapter 36: Shadows

New York, New York, 1963, 1964

Alice and Phil were sitting by the fireplace a few weeks later, when the telephone rang in the hall. Phil put down his martini and went to get it. "It's for you, babe." Covering the mouthpiece, he whispered, "It's Pat Davis. Wonder why she wants to talk to you?"

Alice averted his gaze. "Well, I don't want to talk to her.'

"Alice, you have to. Jack Davis is one of our clients."

Alice shrugged her shoulders and went to pick up the telephone. "Hello, Pat, what can I do for you?"

She paused to listen as her hand gripped the telephone a little too tightly, "No, Pat, I don't know anything about a rumor that you shopped at Royster's Market. Besides that market was open again for business last time I went by there. Sorry, I have something in the oven. Talk to ya later."

Phil looked at her when she returned to the fireplace, "What was that all about?"

Alice pouted, "Oh, she's trying to find someone to blame for her failed party. You'd think she'd have gotten over it by now." She primped up the back of her hair, rotating her shoulder in the opposite direction, mimicking a glamor queen. "Oh, no—not Miss Arrogance herself. If every party she gives isn't the best in Westwood, she's destroyed. What an ego!" Phil raised his eyebrows but said nothing.

Walking over to the bar, he poured himself another glass of wine. Pointing the bottle toward her, he asked, "Would you like more wine?"

She shook her head. "No more for me, babe; I'll have juice instead. No one has told me, but I suspect that too much alcohol may not be good for the baby."

He looked at her. "Orange juice okay?"

She smiled at him. "Perfect."

He went to the kitchen and soon returned with a glass of orange juice.

Alice studied his face as he approached. "You look a little sad. Is something wrong?"

"I was just thinking that maybe we should go out tonight. Our lives will never be the same once the baby gets here."

Using her toes, Alice flipped off her slippers. "That's for sure, but we still have a few weeks of freedom, Phil. Let's enjoy each day and take life as it comes. I just want to relax before this warm fire." She searched his face once more as she asked, "Are you happy about the baby?"

He was tapping his fingers on the arm of the chair and did not look at her. "Sure, I'm happy. Guess we can get Mom to baby sit, so we won't be tied down too much."

Alice grabbed a jar of olives Phil had left on the coffee table and poured half of them into an empty bowl beside her. "How about your dad? Never seen such a proud expectant grandpa." She plopped one olive after another into her mouth and then added, "I'm hungry."

He laughed, "You're always hungry."

"Goes with my condition, dear. Know what I'm craving right now? A big, fat, banana split smothered in whipped cream."

He looked at her incredulously, "With olives and orange juice?" She grinned, patting her swollen abdomen.

Shaking his head, he added, "What's with you pregnant women? I think you just want to hold it over the heads of us poor slobs that you can have babies, and we can't." He shrugged as he picked up his car keys from the coffee table, "I'll go look for 'a big fat, banana split."

She nodded before adding, "Smothered in whipped cream."

He raised his eyebrows at her. "Can your weight stand all those calories? I don't want a fatso for a wife when this is all over." She laughed.

When Alice was six months into her pregnancy, Phil came home one evening to find her bent over the stair rail sobbing. A puddle of water was collecting on the stairs. She cried out in a voice filled with hysteria, "Call the doctor. My membranes just ruptured."

The doctor placed her on bedrest in hopes that the membranes would seal over. Olivia came to stay with them, taking charge of Alice, Phil, and the home. She planned the menus, did the cooking, and went shopping with Phil for groceries and supplies. She selected Alice's reading material, and taught her how to do needlepoint to fill her time. Olivia took over everything including supervision of household cleaning, which was done once a week by her maid.

One evening, Alice overheard her say to Phil, "Alice has requested that we have dessert with our meals; you know how she loves sweets—developed that bad habit during her childhood."

"Dessert isn't good for any of us, so let's forget about the sugar; she'll go along with whatever you fix, Mom. She won't make a fuss, believe me."

Alice felt like she couldn't breathe but did not make a fuss. When she fell asleep, the dream returned. Only this time she was in quicksand as the figure reached for her. She woke up in that same cold sweat just as she was about to sink into the quicksand.

John Phillip Reid III (a.k.a. Bubbie) remained in his mother's womb until one month prior to his due date; he came into the world weighing just under five pounds. Doctors said he could make it. The entire family was ecstatic, no one more than Alice. She felt that she had been forgiven for former indiscretions and that she and her family could look forward to a happy future.

Bubbie was to remain in the hospital until he was more mature and his weight reached at least five pounds. Alice went home to recover and paint the nursery blue. John established a trust fund, and Olivia promised a lifetime of baby-sitting services. They visited Bubbie as a family daily and marked each hospital day off the calendar in anticipation of his homecoming.

The day finally arrived when the pediatrician called to say they could pick him up the next day. Alice's elation deflated when she heard the physician say, "Mrs. Reid we have picked up a small heart murmur." Alice never even heard the last part of the conversation, the part that said he would probably outgrow it but that it would need to be followed. Her emotions were swirling in the spiral of shame she had carried since childhood.

The shame called out to her that because she was defective, Bubbie's heart was defective. How could she have dared to hope that such a defective person could produce a perfect child?

Lowering her head to the table and burying it in both arms, she sobbed. She cried until her attention was drawn to something bright red flying past the window. Getting up to investigate, she saw a male cardinal on the ground next to the patio, busily searching for food. As a child, she had believed that blowing a kiss to the 'redbird' would make a wish come true. She placed three fingers over her mouth, kissed them, and blew the kiss toward the bird. If that wish came true, Bubbie would be whole again.

The action was enough to pull her out of her funk. *I better get busy doing my best to make that wish come true.* She paused. *But what do I do if his little heart stops beating.* She was well aware that health professionals often became paralyzed with fear when the patient is a loved one. One of her classmates from Mercy had reacted that way when her baby choked.

That night the dream returned. As she tried to discern the figure in the fog, it backed away and was lost in the mist.

Chapter 37: Bubbie

New York, New York, 1964-1971

The outside world was covered in white the day
Bubbie came home. And just as the snow
highlighted the beauty in the world, the family
maintained a cheerful chatter about the wonderful
bundle of joy and heir.

As family members drifted away one by one,
Alice was left by the fireplace to feed the tiny infant
his formula. She clutched the bottle nervously
before remembering that an anxious mother was not
good for the baby's health, so she tried to relax by
thinking about a fishing trip she had taken with her
dad into the Louisiana swamps. She had been free
to be herself on that trip, knowing that she was
loved no matter what, and that freedom had brought
peace and joy. She wanted to relive that experience
and calm herself for the baby's sake.

If she had been able to discuss the heart murmur
openly with others, she might have felt less
overwhelmed. But Phil's family seemed to see the
defect as a shame, not to be shared with others.
Added to that mistaken belief was another: that
discussing negative things only brought them into
reality. So Alice was left to face her fears alone.

The tiny infant had to be fed every three hours around the clock. She was surprised to find that when the busyness left no time for her to think about herself, she found a deep, inner peace. It was welcomed.

One day as she was feeding him by the fireplace, she turned her head toward a dripping sound outside the window. The melting icicles were sparkling with a brilliance that seemed to illuminate the important things in her inner world. The ice on nearby trees, transformed into diamonds in the sunlight, aided that illumination. She felt the warmth of the fire. She sniffed the fragrance of pine cones drifting in from the hallway and snuggled in the soft blanket wrapped about her shoulders, holding the child closer. She felt peace.

The sun's rays were parallel with the snow's surface by the time half the formula was gone. She carefully placed the baby on her padded shoulder for a burp, and most of the formula, emitting a sour smell, returned with the burp. The pediatrician later adjusted the formula, but it did little good. She finally resigned herself to wearing blouses that could be removed easily and thrown in the washer. A feeding without a soiled blouse became a cause for celebration. From the beginning of their marriage, Phil had insisted that his wife not work. Now she was grateful to be a stay-at-home mom.

Sleep was rare, but *the dream* came less frequently. Alice guessed that she was not getting enough REM sleep, that phase of deep sleep when dreaming occurs.

The parents were reluctant to leave the child with anyone other than Olivia, who asked to wait until he was a bit older before assuming her baby-sitting duties. So Alice was house bound for many months, but she didn't mind. She loved being with the precious tiny infant.

Other mothers would drop by with their healthy children, and Alice would feel bad. She soon learned that the bad feelings could be avoided by not comparing Bubbie with other children. But that didn't stop her from watching neighborhood children riding their bikes or playing ball and wondering whether Bubbie would ever be able to join them.

She vowed to herself, fist clenched in the old determination, that she would do everything in her power to help this child grow up as normally as possible. And he was well on his way. When he became tired, he would squat to get his breath; otherwise, he was active and curious about the world around him. He was accepted by neighborhood children, who seemed to know intuitively that he should be protected. The little boy loved people and would climb into the lap of anyone who invited him. When folks said he never met a stranger, Alice would fear for his safety.

He took the school-readiness exam before kindergarten and ranked in the 99th percentile in the country. The teachers thought he was a genius and treated him as such. By the time he finished first grade, he had read 16 books and pushed himself much harder over the following summer when another child his age was catching up. Alice recognized the competitive streak, so much a part of her own personality. She tried to slow him down by saying, "Be happy with what you *can* do, Bubbie, and don't push yourself beyond your limits." When her nagging appeared to cause him more stress, she left him alone.

He got off the school bus one day and ran toward his mother, clutching something in his hand. Alice lifted her eyebrows saying, "What you got there, tiger?"

His large, brown eyes looked up at her, saying, "A snake."

She clutched her chest. "Really? Let me see, baby."

Frowning, Bubbie pursed his lips in determination, "I'm not a baby, mother."

Alice reached to pry his fist open, but he obediently opened it. A small semi-squished worm crawled out.

"Bubbie, that's a worm. I'll show you what a snake looks like the next time we go to the zoo. It's very important to know the difference between a snake and a worm. Snakes will hurt you."

The story was passed around the family, and all were amazed. "All boy," they agreed—"bet he'll be a surgeon."

"No, an entomologist," laughed Grandpa John.

Time passed pleasantly enough. But as Alice feared, Bubbie did not outgrow the heart murmur. And one day on a routine visit to the pediatric cardiologist, the physician met afterward with the parents in his office. "He's beginning to get changes in his lungs that we cannot correct. It's time for him to have that hole in his heart repaired." Neither Alice nor Phil felt ready for this but knew it was the best thing to do for the child.

Dr. Turrow, a surgeon in a nearby state, was having the best results with ventricular septal repairs, so he was selected for the job. Bubbie would have a cardiac catheterization as soon as it could be arranged.

Alice focused on doing everything perfectly, believing that if she were just perfect enough, the surgery would be successful. She locked herself into that mindset—would not even consider or talk to anyone about anything else.

The mindset kept her from looking at her own faults, so she believed that she was a paragon of the virtues and white as the driven snow. She was so pure that sex became dirty and repulsive to her. To make matters worse, she refused to talk to Phil when he approached her saying that he had a 'bad feeling' about the surgery. She answered him by saying, "The best experts in the field have told me this is the right time (the only time), and we have the best surgeon in the world. We stick to the plan. God will take care of the rest. If I just have enough faith and do the right things, everything will be okay."

The old dream returned; it came more frequently and by now had morphed into a nightmare. She was always in a swamp—at times trapped in quicksand. She couldn't free herself, no matter how she tried. At other times she was in a small boat rowing through heavy fog, and the harder she rowed the more the fog would thicken. The figure was always there, reaching out to her.

Phil was left on his own to handle the stress and emptiness inside. He took quite a different approach. He drank heavily and rarely came home before midnight. On more than one occasion, the telephone would ring late at night. A strange female voice would ask for him and hang up when Alice asked who was calling. She confronted Phil. He responded that some thief was probably calling to see if anyone was at home. Alice did not believe him, and an argument followed, ending in his knocking her across the room. That was the first time he hit her. She was afraid to confront him again.

Then one day Alice was doing laundry when she discovered lipstick on his boxer shorts. She clenched that right fist and tried even harder to hold the marriage together until after the surgery. Bubbie was all that mattered to her now.

For a long time, she had felt a dissonance between the beliefs of Phil and his family and her own values. She had dismissed the dissonance as soon as it appeared, not realizing that it came because she had allowed the Reids to define who she was. And now she did not have the time or energy to figure it out: She was fully occupied, trying to make things work for Bubbie, having no idea who Alice Hollister Reid was.

One snowy Friday afternoon she was reading to Bubbie, who was recovering from pneumonia following a cardiac catheterization. Pausing for a moment, she looked about his bedroom. The paint was starting to peel from running the humidifier continuously. *We'll have to paint this room as soon as he gets well.* Her thoughts were interrupted by the ringing of the telephone. *Who could be calling so close to dinner time?* Placing a bookmarker in the book, she got up and walked toward the telephone.

Bubbie called out, "Don't stop now, Mom, this is the best part."

Placing her index finger over her lips to shush him, she picked up the phone and was surprised to hear Phil's voice.

"Where are you? Dinner is just about ready."

"Alice, I won't be home for dinner." She heard him clear his throat. "I'm going away for the weekend—going to see an old army buddy in 'Philly.' You remember Gordon, don't you? Tall redhead at the wedding?"

"Just a minute, Phil. I'll take this call downstairs."

Signaling Bubbie to stay put, she put down the phone and descended the stairs, holding onto the railing for support. *I can't believe the nerve of this guy. I don't buy that story for one minute. But I have to try to hold things together until after Bubbie's surgery* Squaring her shoulders with that right fist clenched, she spoke firmly into the telephone, "But I need to do some shopping for Christmas. You promised to stay with Bubbie."

His voice caught when he said, "I can't, Alice. I just can't take it anymore."

Her lips trembled when she replied, "How about Bubbie and me?" He said nothing. Anger boiled up inside her as she said through clenched teeth, "This is the last straw, Phil. I'll have a nervous breakdown if I let you abuse me like this." She sucked in her breath before continuing. "If you don't come home tonight, don't ever come back." She slammed the phone down and stared for a long time at the wall in front of her, but it offered no help.

Sinking into her old habit of self-doubt, she asked, *Have I done the right thing?* Then answering her own question, she thought, *If I fall apart, who will take care of Bubbie? Who would keep his spirits high—assuring him that he's going to be okay? He just has to have a positive attitude when he goes into that surgical suite. His attitude will affect the outcome. As for Phil, I stopped caring about him a long time ago.*

She slumped down on a nearby couch, placing her head into her hands. But the tears refused to come. She had too much to do. "Now, it's all up to me. I have to find solutions to all the problems on my own. I don't know how or when, but I'll do it".

Then, pulling herself up, she went to the foot of the stairs. Calling out to her son, she yelled, "I'll finish the story later, sweetie." Returning to the telephone, she called her next-door neighbor, asking

292

her to stay with the child while she shopped for his Christmas presents.

When she took his dinner up to Bubbie, the child took one look at her face and said nothing.

Alice put as much cheer into her voice as she could muster when she said, "Daddy has to go away for the weekend, champ. But Mrs. Thorpe from next door will be over to take care of you while Mommie finishes her Christmas shopping. Won't it be nice to visit with Mrs. Thorpe? Maybe she'll finish the story for you. I'll just bet she does."

Bubbie rubbed nervously on his teddy bear.

New locks were put on the doors to keep Phil out. And the week after Christmas, Alice contacted a divorce attorney.

Chapter 38: The Operation

Boston, Massachusetts, 1971

The icy, New England wind whipped Alice's breath away as she stood on the street corner waiting for the light to change. She was between the wind and Bubbie, who looked like a large round ball in his snowsuit and layers of clothing. Afraid that he would topple over, she picked him up and held his face against her chest. They had come to Boston from their home in New York to have Dr. Turrow do the surgery. He was Bubbie's best chance.

Struggling with the weight of the child, she found her way to the entrance of the hospital. Luckily the walkway had been cleared of snow, so she was able to enter the warmth of the building in a short time. The smell of ether and antiseptics hit her as she put Bubbie down to walk on his own. He ran over to the elevator and pushed the button to go up after looking at Alice for her approval.

Once on the right floor, Bubbie made a beeline for a playroom on their left. Alice watched as he approached an African-American boy, who appeared to be about seven, the same age as Bubbie. The young man was constructing a fort with Legos. Before long, Bubbie was helping him.

When Alice completed the admission procedure, she found them seated side by side on a child's bench. Bubbie was reading to his new friend, whom he introduced as Spiderman.

"That bear is just plain stupid, if you ask me," said Spiderman.

Bubbie took the hand of his friend and looked him in the eye, "Spider, that's Winnie the Pooh, and he certainly is *not* stupid."

Spider met his gaze and stood his ground, "Sticking his paw into something too small for it. He should'a knowed better."

The dispute was interrupted by the entrance of Dr. Turrow, Bubbie's surgeon. Alice caught a glimpse of the fear in her son's eyes when he saw the man in green scrubs. Pain shot through her heart like lightning when she realized that he must have picked up the fear during the cardiac catheterization.

The surgeon placed a hand on Alice's shoulder, saying, "Mrs. Reid, I'm sorry to inform you that we have to postpone the surgery for a day: We're still awaiting results from his last cardiac catheterization."

"Will he stay here in the hospital?"

"Oh, yes. We have some more work to do to get him ready."

Alice nodded, and then smiled, realizing that she would get another day to spend with Bubbie.

The surgeon paused to grin at the two boys, "And, by the way, could I put in a good word for the Pooh Bear?" Both boys looked up in awe at this distinguished man as he said, "He certainly is not stupid. You'll see, young man." As he walked away, he high-fived Spiderman.

"That's your doctor? He's okay, man." Bubbie looked away.

A nurse came over and introduced herself as Bubbie's nurse, Angie. "Bubbie, I have something to show you. Can you and your mom meet me in the conference room across the hall in a few minutes?" Bubbie nodded.

In the conference room, Angie said, "Bubbie, I hear you like Winnie the Pooh." Bubbie gave her a puzzled look. Angie handed him a bear, having a strong resemblance to the Pooh bear. The bear was used for a demonstration of how the surgery would be done as she gently explained what Bubbie should expect. She was upbeat and encouraging as she watched his face for signs of fear. She paused occasionally, asking "Do you have any questions? If I don't know the answer, I'll bet Winnie does."

Bubbie took his thumb out of his mouth and looked at her. "Will it hurt?" Alice thought he had given up sucking his thumb years ago.

"You'll be asleep during the operation, Bubbie. You may have some pain when it's all over, but we'll be right here to give you medicine for it." She finished and studied him carefully. "Are you scared, Bubbie?"

He looked at Alice for support before replying, "A little." Alice smiled and winked at him. He was relieved to see that his mother was okay.

Angie picked up on Bubbie's response, "It's good to say we're scared when we are. Your mother will be here with the rest of us after the operation, and you can bet we'll all take very good care of you."

Alice nodded. "Your dad will be here, too. He's flying in tomorrow night. I'm sorry Grammie and Grandpa can't come. Grandpa is sick, and Grammie has to be there to take care of him."

The child literally jumped for joy as he eagerly said, "Dad's coming!" Alice tilted her head toward the ceiling in an effort to contain the tears in her eyes.

Mother and child spent the next day just enjoying each other's company and getting to know Spiderman. They watched a rerun of *Lassie Comes Home* on television, read to each other, worked on picture puzzles, listened to music, and ate the chocolate-chip cookies and fudge Alice had brought from home.

As the day was coming to an end, Alice sat in the chair by her son's bed, watching the sunset. The bare limbs and trunks of trees were outlined against the crimson sky, which was slowly turning purple. Venus was lighting the way for a half-moon moving in its direction. The world beneath it was all white. Alice sighed, *Such a peaceful day. Will I feel this way tomorrow at this time?*

All of a sudden, Bubbie jumped out of bed yelling, "Daddy, Daddy."

She looked up to see Phil standing in the doorway with a gigantic panda under one arm. Bubbie ran to him grabbing him around both legs. Alice left the room, telling herself that she was doing it for them. She returned a little later and joined them for a family dinner in the cafeteria.

The following morning, Alice and Phil, putting on a brave front, eyed each other over the stretcher holding their son. He was lying so still under the blankets and sheet. Each bent to kiss the small form dwarfed by the hospital gown. Groggy from medication, he entwined both arms around his parents before the orderlies came and wheeled him away. Alice was numb and disoriented. A gigantic blockade was protecting her from feeling anything. She walked beside the stretcher until they reached the doors of the operating suite. When the doors closed behind the stretcher, she no longer had to hide her tears. They flowed freely as she murmured to herself, "I pray I made the right decision."

She felt the arms of someone embracing her from behind. Turning, she collapsed into the arms of Angie, who was saying, "Mrs. Reid, you and your husband may wait in the waiting room for the Surgical Intensive Care Unit; they will contact you there if they need you. The surgery will take from four to six hours. He's in the best of hands. I must leave you now, but let someone know if you need me."

Alice picked up a magazine in the waiting room but could not focus enough to read. Phil was pacing the hallway; he came in occasionally to see whether she wanted anything. She had thumbed through all of the magazines just looking at the pictures and glancing at the clock whose hands were moving in slow motion when Dr. Turrow entered the room about 3 p.m. Afraid to look at him, she sat wringing her hands and staring at the floor. He placed one of his hands on her shoulder and said, "The surgery was successful."

She just looked at him, trying to register what he was saying. "Over, it's really over." Her lips trembled as she uttered, "Oh thank God; it's over." Her shoulders were shaking in huge sobs of relief.

The surgeon embraced her, quickly adding, "The next 24 hours are critical. The worst part *is* over, but we're not out of the woods yet." By then, Alice was so elated she didn't even hear his last words.

Phil squared his shoulders and offered his hand to the surgeon as he asked, "When can we see him?"

Dr. Turrow removed his scrub cap and replied, "They'll let you in for ten minutes every hour on the hour."

An hour later they walked into the room filled with the in-and-out sounds of the respirator and beeping of the monitors. Alice wondered how anyone could sleep with all that noise. She hardly recognized her baby—so little of him was showing. He was strapped to IVs, tubes, and machines. She longed to pick him up and hold him, to love him until his natural color returned: His skin had a bluish tinge. But she dared not touch him in fear that she would do harm. The nurse indicated that she could hold his hand. She wrapped her fingers around the small hand. It felt like an icicle.

He was in a semi-conscious state—not aware of his surroundings and far from being able to recognize anyone around him. A mumbling sound came from the blue lips, "I'm firsty."

His nurse placed a straw between his lips and allowed him to sip a small amount of water; fluid balance was critical to his survival, so she withdrew the straw after a sip or two. The parents lingered for ten precious minutes before returning to the waiting room.

They had been there for only a few minutes when Phil approached Alice, "If all goes well, I'll be leaving on an early flight tomorrow morning. I have to get back to the office." She nodded.

He left as planned. And Alice was left to face the world on her own again.

It was 3:43 the next day when Dr. Turrow reappeared in the waiting room door. Sadness seemed to emanate from every pore. The usual spring in his step had morphed into the slow shuffle of an older man; he looked as if he had aged 10 years. Alice knew something was wrong.

He spoke slowly, choosing his words carefully, "Mrs. Reid, he's in congestive heart failure." His voice broke as he added, "fighting for his life." And then as if looking desperately for some sort of explanation, some way to comfort her, he commented, "Sometimes these little hearts just can't make the adjustment after being fixed."

Alice started screaming, trying to turn reality around with her cries. "No, it can't be. Go back and examine him again." Two nurses grabbed and held her. She shook them off and started pacing. The physician returned to Bubbie's cubicle. More than anything she wanted to go with him, to her son, to comfort her baby, to be with him. But wild horses could not drag her into that room. A barricade she could not see blocked her way. *When he sees my face, he'll know he's going to die—that I alone led him down this path to his death.* She could not face it, could not face him.

When they told her he was dying, she went crazy—picking up a lamp from a nearby table and throwing it. The magazines scattered about the waiting room followed the path of the lamp, hitting the wall, one by one. She was out of control, but the insanity was better than going into that room and looking Bubbie in the eye—knowing that she had failed him. He was going to pay with his life. It would be months before she would be able to look another human being in the eye—years before she would be comfortable with people. The shame was too overwhelming.

A protestant chaplain entered the room and tried to comfort her—finally telling her that he was dead. When he left, a Roman Catholic priest came to sit with her. He gave the only words of comfort she could find in this topsy-turvy nightmare. "God gave you a helpless little baby. You gave him back a beautiful child." She would remember those words for the rest of her life.

And then a knife sliced into the boil of her pain—just at the time when she thought it couldn't get any worse. A female resident approached her. With eyes as cold as ice and hands to match, she grabbed Alice's elbow, "Mrs. Reid, we need permission for an autopsy." Alice had witnessed an autopsy as a student nurse. She had seen how they removed the corpse's heart and slung it on the morgue table like a piece of meat.

"No, you can't do that to Bubbie," she screamed.

"Think of how much we will learn to improve future surgeries. Picture all the children whose lives will be saved."

"I don't give a damn about your future surgeries," she yelled. "I need Bubbie to be whole." She collapsed again in bitter sobbing.

But the resident would not give in and brought on reinforcements from other staff members. Alice could not stand up to them, so she gave her consent for the autopsy. That was when she decided that she would be cremated.

Chapter 39: Juliet's Lament

New York, New York, 1971

On the day of his funeral, Alice was still in a daze. Her eyes still red from the dried up well of tears, she embraced her black mourning clothes, hoping they would swallow her. She wore no makeup. And like a robot, she interacted with the many people in attendance. They weren't registering in her mind. There were no connections. Life had lost its meaning. She had believed that if she led a good life like the Good Book told her, that a benevolent heavenly Father would look after her and Bubbie. She had even been encouraged to think like that by the church they had been attending. She had found out that it was all a lie. A big fat lie.

The only thing she remembered from the funeral was a passage from Romeo and Juliet by William Shakespeare:

Take him and cut him out in little stars,
And he will make the face of heaven so fine
That all the world will be in love with night
And pay no worship to the garish sun....

She had requested that it be read. Today, she felt like she would never love anyone again because it hurt too much to lose them. But the loneliness and deep, relentless pain could be anesthetized with alcohol.

Chapter 40: Fear

New York, New York, 1972

Fear became Alice's compass in life. It hung over her like a dark cloud, coloring everything and directing her away from the light. What she feared most was making eye contact with people, so the fear multiplied each time she avoided the dreaded action. Alcohol and Valium became her saviors. The nightmares were more frequent and more frightening. By now the quicksand was up to her neck, and the figure had been swallowed by the fog.

Even the thought of interacting with another human being brought on the stress reaction. If she sensed that the person did not approve of her, it turned into a panic attack. If someone smiled at her, they had an ulterior motive. She fought with everyone, especially herself. The fabric of her soul had been torn, and she couldn't fix it. The struggle for existence had defeated her. She trusted no one—not even herself. Relieving the suffering of her patients became her only bond with the rest of humanity.

At 10 p.m. one night in late fall, the alarm clock screamed its wakeup call. Alice wanted to shut it off, but she needed her job at the hospital to survive. Phil's alimony payments were barely enough to take care of the mortgage. The medical and hospital bills had wiped them out financially, and they could no longer count on his parents for help. John's bank had failed. She had considered looking for a housemate but, like everything else in her life, had not gotten around to it. She was depressed, so everything moved in slow motion.

It's a lousy time to be going to work, she thought, *but at least I don't have to put up with all the mayhem on day shift.* She dressed as quickly as she could and sat at her kitchen table for a peanut butter and grape jelly sandwich, which was washed down with plenty of strong, black coffee.

When her car started right away, she sighed in relief. *I hate going to a garage—hate hassling with those mechanics—they can tell right away that I know zilch about cars. I'm sure they steal me blind.*

Alice tried to shove aside the discomfort she often felt in this upscale neighborhood. But she needed to wait until the market improved to sell the house. The discomfort was trying to come through tonight as she drove past the lovely homes, all darkened for the night. *Guess my snooty neighbors are sleeping or getting ready to. Wonder what they think of a poor night nurse.* She tapped the steering wheel with her fingers, thinking *Oh well, can't think about that now. Have to get myself together for my patients.*

She took the interstate for five miles or so and got off in a very different neighborhood: Most of the small homes were in need of paint or repair with abandoned cars in many of the yards. She usually went another way, but tonight she was running late and took a shortcut. As she turned a corner, she felt the car swerve to the left. *Should I stop or keep going to a safer place?* Then she thought, *if it's a tire, I'll ruin it. Better get out and see.* Reaching under the seat, she grabbed a large flashlight. Her worst fears were realized: The left rear tire lay flat on the asphalt. *What will I do now? Never changed a tire in my life.* Her mind was about to take a dive into her usual swirl of panic, when she pulled herself out of the whirlwind by thinking of one of her patients. *Mrs. Carson is scheduled to start chemo at 7:30 a. m.; she needs me there now.*

A dog was barking nearby. A hoot owl answered from a distance as a late model Cadillac pulled up behind her and turned off the lights. Feet apart and standing erect, she held the flashlight in her right hand like a club, ready to attack. Her other hand was on the door to the car.

Before she could get back in the car and lock the doors, she heard the voice of an angel calling out, "Can I help you, Miss?" She directed the light of her flashlight on a greying African American man slowly getting out of the car. Of medium build, he steadied himself before walking with a limp in her direction. She decided to trust him.

Sizing up the situation and scratching his head, he said, "See you gotta flat."

"Can you help me?"

"No problem."

Alice felt a surge of gratitude and hope. "I'll be happy to pay you whatever you charge."

He did not reply but went to work removing his jacket and folding it neatly, hanging it over the seat in his car. Rolling up his shirt sleeves, he opened the trunk of her car and removed the jack and the spare, placing them on the ground next to the flat tire. After jacking the car up, he expertly removed the flat and replaced it with the spare, carefully tightening the lug nuts. After checking the pressure in the spare, he brushed his hands together before returning the flat and the jack to her trunk. It had taken only minutes. Alice watched in awe, trying to print the procedure on her mind.

"Looks like you picked up a nail."

"May I write you a check? Don't carry a lot of cash with me."

He turned away to retrieve his jacket and get back in his car. Looking at her uniform, he smiled and said, "Just pass the favor on to your patients."

She felt an inner glow of real happiness for the first time in years. The glow went with her to work and lasted most of the night. She wondered why she felt so good inside. Later, as she sat reviewing charts, she wondered what had brought on the warm glow. Then it dawned on her: She had discovered that there were people in this world who helped others without expecting anything in return. It was an eye opener.

About 3 a.m. the dim silence of the ward was broken by a scream. Alice put down the chart she was working on and went to investigate. It was coming from Room 627 where a thirteen year-old-girl was located. Alice entered the room with her flashlight to find the girl standing in the middle of her bed and screaming uncontrollably while pointing at a corner of the room. Bessie, the nurse's aide, entered the room behind Alice and turned on the overhead lights, revealing a small white mouse in the corner frantically trying to climb the wall to escape the mayhem.

"Bessie." Alice turned to give the aide instructions only to find that she had disappeared. Returning to the patient, Alice found her slippers, helped her out of bed, and walked her to the nurses' station, all of the time whispering soothing words of comfort.

"It's' okay, Jennifer; we'll transfer you to another room, and security will take care of the mouse."

By now, every patient on the floor was awake, most of them crowding into the hallway. Alice made her way through the conglomeration of hospital gowns and pajamas to the desk. Mrs. Glimmer in Room 625 had grabbed the bag of urine attached to her bed and dislodged the connection. Urine was running down the hall and collecting in a puddle in front of the nurses' station. Alice turned to her aide saying, "Bessie, mop up this urine before somebody falls." The aide quickly obeyed.

Alice went to the telephone and dialed security. A sleepy voice came over the phone, "Throw a trash can over the mouse, and I'll be up there to return the little critter to Dr. Dobson's lab."

Alice hung up the telephone with a deep sigh. "Oh great!" Wrinkling her brow, she went into the hallway to find the aide. "Bessie, will you, please, get an empty trash can and throw it over that mouse. Security will be up to get him, assuming he can stay awake long enough."

The aide placed both hands on her hips and looked at Alice, her large soulful eyes pleading. "Ms. Reid, I'd do anything for you, but I just can't go in that room with that mouse. You can have me fired if'n you wants, but I just can't do it."

Alice looked at her and started laughing. "Okay, you get housekeeping up here to clean up the rest of this mess." Bessie nodded.

Shaking her head, Alice went to the utility room and soon located a large, metal trash can that was empty. She picked up the can and headed for Room 627, mumbling to herself, "Of all the rooms that mouse could have gone into, it had to be the room of a thirteen year-old girl." Several towels from the bathroom helped her corner the hysterical mouse, who was promptly imprisoned with the trash can. *They never taught us how to handle hysterical mice in nursing school.*

With the help of several sleeping pills, the floor gradually returned to normal. Bessie gave Mrs. Brown, the patient in Room 623, a soothing warm bath and glass of warm milk. Afterward, Alice sat at the patient's bedside holding the old lady's hand and listening. She understood that the lady was facing death and needed someone to face it with her. The family kept telling her that everything would be okay. Alice thought long and carefully, searching for the right words to be truthful and yet comforting.

"Yes, Mrs. Brown, you are getting ready to enter a new phase of life."

Relief was written on her face, wrinkled by years of living and the wisdom that living had brought. "Alice, it's such a great comfort to have another human being face this with me; the doctors tell me that I'm dying. But they don't have the time to sit with me."

"We're all here for you, dear Mrs. Brown. Just talk about anything you wish; we'll listen." And like any good nurse, she refused to think about the many less important things she had to do before leaving work.

It was still dark at 6 a.m. when they started preparing the patients for doctors' rounds, various tests, and other business of the day. Bessie was busy on one end of the hall taking vital signs and weighing patients. Alice entered the medicine room and picked up the bottle of Valium. Carefully removing five of them, she placed them in a secret compartment of her purse; they would make a good addition to her supply at home. By now, she needed that sweet little pill whenever she had to deal with the outside world.

The eastern sky was turning red when she finished passing medicines to her patients. The world outside was waking up. She was ready to finish charting, give report to the day shift, and go home. When she finished all of her chores, she noticed that she was late signing out, as usual. Walking down the front steps of the hospital, she noticed the sun's rays bouncing off the gathering clouds.

Patches of blue were peeking through here and there in a threatening sky when she opened the front door of her home and slumped wearily onto the bench in the hall. Looking around, she saw through half-opened eyes the staircase that Bubbie used to slide down to greet her when she opened the door. The mantelpiece where his Christmas stocking had hung every Christmas was collecting dust mites. And the house was deadly quiet, no longer ringing with a child's voice or his laughter. The world was such an empty place without his laughter.

She thought some eggs and bacon might cheer her up, but after she made them, she just sat at the kitchen table staring at the untouched food. She couldn't bear to use the dining room anymore: His place at the table was so empty. After several minutes she took a bottle of vodka from a kitchen cabinet and poured half a glass into her orange juice. *It'll help me get to sleep.*

Chapter 41: Easing the Pain

The following midnight found Alice back on the west wing of the sixth floor. It was time to make her rounds. After removing a flashlight from the desk drawer, she went to the first room on that end of the hall and quietly opened the door. Some cowboy was aiming his rifle at an Indian on the television set. She turned it off and went to check the IV. The IV was running on time, and the insertion site appeared to be free of redness, heat, and swelling. Quiet snoring assured her that the patient was sleeping.

When she entered the next room she found Mrs. Carson sitting by the window, the night light on over her bed. Alice went over and took her hand. "What's wrong, lady, can't sleep?"

The patient patted Alice's hand as she looked at her. "My head's spinning with worries, Alice. It's not bad enough I lost my breast in surgery, now I'm to start chemotherapy, and I'll lose my hair. How do I hang onto my husband with no breast and no hair? He's my rod, Alice. I can't do without him." The patient shook her head, mumbling, "Our kids aren't much help; they just keep smiling and telling me that I'm going to be okay, when I know damned well what I'm facing." She paused. "The next idiot appearing in that doorway with a cheerful expression painted on his face is going to get the underside of my shoe." Her voice rose as she said, "Why can't they allow me my own reality?"

"Take it easy, Mrs. C.; it's their way of coping—assuring themselves that they're cheering you up." Alice pulled up the other chair at the bedside. "And you, my dear, are having a classic case of AWFULitis. Let's see what we can do to scare that devil away. How about a hot bath or a back rub?"

The patient got up to return to her bed. "Let's skip the bath, but a massage sounds good."

"You got it Mrs. C., but first let me straighten the bed for you. Nothing like a nice, refreshed bed to bring on Mr. Sandman." The patient watched as Alice tightened the draw sheet and straightened the top sheet and blanket.

Alice searched in the bedside stand for some lotion and carefully warmed it in her hands in preparation for the massage. The patient climbed back in bed and exposed her back. Alice began kneading and massaging, keeping up a continuous chatter about pleasant things. "Seems to me Mr. Carson was very supportive during your surgery. Appeared to me that he loves you a great deal. I got the impression he doesn't care what you look like." She paused, "How long you been married?"

"Thirty-eight years in June."

Alice nodded, "After all you've been through together; you think he's going to leave when you temporarily lose your hair?"

Mrs. Carson raised her head, "Temporarily? No one told me it was temporary."

"You see what AWFULitis does to you? It makes you shut out all the good and only allows the bad things in. Why you can get a wig when your hair falls out, and then one day you'll get a beautiful new crop of your own. Why I knew one patient with mousey brown hair; when her hair came back, it was flaming red."

The patient laughed. "I don't think I want flaming red hair."

Alice finished the backrub with some long, smooth strokes down the patient's back. "Why I know a flaming redhead who had her breast removed twelve years ago. She just married a man ten years her junior."

Mrs. Carson shook her head. "Oh, Alice, you big fibber."

Alice returned to the nurses' station to look for an order for a sleeping pill for Mrs. C. Finding none, she called the resident on call.

He yelled over the phone, "You wake me up for a sleeping pill. The other night nurse lets me sleep all night."

Alice clenched that right fist and spoke ever so slowly, "Dr. Ellis, when I think a patient needs your help, I'm going to call you. If that makes me unpopular with the medical staff, so be it." She got her order and hung up.

Returning to Mrs. Carson with a sleeping pill, Alice was filling the patient's glass with water when she noticed the small figure of a beautiful bird on the nightstand. Not much bigger than a charm, it was silver with piercing blue eyes. The eyes drew her to it like a magnet. She picked it up for closer inspection, turning it over in her hand to get a better look at the hypnotizing blue eyes. A master craftsman had arranged them so that they conveyed a sense of hope as she stared at them.

"What a beautiful bird, Mrs. C. Is it a phoenix?"

"Oh, yes. The mythical bird that rises from its own ashes."

Alice nodded. "How many cultures have embraced that myth?"

The patient placed the sleeping pill in her mouth and drank a full glass of water before replying, "Hebrew, Greek, and more, I guess.

"Where did you get this replica of the phoenix? The eyes are so unusual; I would call them spellbinding."

"It was a gift from my husband. The eyes are sapphires, you know. The Greeks believe that blue

318

eyes bring good luck. I think he found it in Athens." She paused to pull the covers over her shoulders. "He was there many years ago."

Raising her eyebrows, Alice placed her tray down on the nightstand and looked at the bird again. "They're real sapphires?" The patient nodded.

"Well, that bird should not be out here where it could be stolen. Let me lock it in the medicine cabinet for you."

The patient sat up in bed. "Oh, please, don't take it away. I find so much comfort every time I look at it. When the going gets rough, it reminds me that everything will be okay, no matter what happens."

Alice placed her index finger against her chin. "Will you, at least, let me wrap it and hide it in the drawer?"

The lady complied.

"Don't let the head nurse or supervisor see it, or it will be locked away for sure." Alice caught the patient's eye and winked.

As she continued on her rounds, Alice heard muffled laughter coming from Room 635. She jerked the door open and saw scrambling under the covers. "Ms. Langford, is your boyfriend in bed with you?" She closed the door and turned on the overhead lights. Broadening her stance and placing both hands on her hips, she said, "He'll have to leave the hospital. NOW!" She turned briskly and walked to the telephone to call security. The young man was escorted off the grounds.

Returning to her desk, she poured a cup of black coffee. "All in a night's work," she sighed.

At 5 a.m. she went into the medicine room to prepare her medicines for passing at 6. Seeing that the bottle of Valium was almost full, she walked back to the desk and removed an envelope. Returning to the medicine room, she carefully poured four tablets into the envelope, sealed it, and slipped the envelope into her pocket.

As she did, a voice from the doorway startled her, "We've been watching you, Mrs. Reid."

She turned to see the night supervisor glaring at her.

"I'll get someone to replace you. I want you to leave the hospital as soon as possible. But first give me the pills you just put in that envelope. You're fired."

Alice was in shock as she dragged herself to her locker and emptied it. She stuffed her lunch box, a thermos, a pair of extra shoes, an old notebook, and an extra uniform into a plastic trash bag. Tying the ends of the bag together, she dragged it to the entrance of the hospital and walked down the steps as if in a dream. The eastern sky was beginning to lighten, its reddening clouds promising bad weather.

She tried three times to open the door to her car before realizing that she was turning the key in the wrong direction. When she finally got it open, she slouched to the rear of the car, opened the trunk, and threw the trash bag inside before wearily falling into the driver's seat. Her on-again, off-again state of confusion had morphed into a full-blown daze. As she slumped over the steering wheel, someone tapped on the window. She lifted her head and stared into the face of Earle, an orderly who had been sent to her floor when the regular man had failed to report for duty.

"I got somethin' make you feel a lot better, Miz Reid." He took a syringe from the bag slung over his left shoulder. She just looked at him—too tired, too weary, too depressed to resist. She held out her arm. The feeling of euphoria hit as soon as the drug reached her bloodstream. The man watched, nodding his head. Then quickly slipping his card into her purse, Earle walked away.

The "high" exploded throughout her body like fireworks igniting frissons of pleasure all over. Her eyes popped open, and she saw a rainbow of colors lifting her spirits into the stratosphere. This lasted less than an hour. After that she just felt good and ready to take on the world. Looking down at the key she had placed in the ignition; she turned it and drove out of the parking lot.

By the time she reached the front door of her home, the 'good' feelings were fading. And all she could think of, all she wanted was to experience that intense euphoria again. Whatever it took, she had to have it.

Walking past the sink full of dirty dishes, she made her way through the clutter in the hallway to the stairs. And although she felt giddy and woozy, she climbed them by hanging onto the rail. She entered her bedroom and didn't even notice the unmade bed or clothes strewn in every direction. Giggling, she sketched her initials in the dust on her dresser and grabbed a pile of dirty uniforms from her bed. She threw them on the floor and crawled in bed, pulling the expensive bedspread over her head.

Her drug dealer called the next day. And she started seeing him regularly.

The final check from the hospital arrived 3 weeks after her dismissal; it was accompanied by a small package. Curious, she shone a flashlight through it before turning the package all around and listening carefully. She shook it. It appeared to be harmless enough, so she removed the outer wrapping and examined the small cardboard box inside. It was sealed with masking tape. She carefully removed the tape and opened the box. Something was wrapped in several layers of tissue paper. Unwrapping one layer at a time, she finally reached the last one before gazing in surprise into the sapphire eyes of the phoenix. A glimmer of hope pierced the darkness of her soul: Somehow, someway—everything would be okay. A note lay under the bird:

Dear Mrs. Reid,

Our precious Mabel passed last Thursday. One of her last requests was that you should receive the phoenix you admired so much. Thank you for the comfort you brought to my wife in her last days. May this bird do the same for you!

Sincerely,
Wayne Carson

She had the bird made into a charm, which was attached to her charm bracelet. And although a bit cumbersome, it gave her comfort whenever she looked at it.

Several days later Alice shoved aside her bad feelings and reluctance to face some of her old coworkers and went back to her former nursing unit. There were a few people she wanted to say goodbye to, but most of all, she wanted to know what had happened to Mrs. Carson. She was in luck. Joy Atkins, one of the few people in the world with whom she retained a modicum of trust was on duty. Pity was etched on Joy's face as she smiled at her old friend. "I don't have much time, Alice."

"I won't keep you, Joy, but I would like to say goodbye and find out what happened to Mrs. Carson."

"Well, all I can say is that she went steadily downhill soon after you left. When she went into cardiac arrest, the family would not let go—wanted to do everything possible to save her." She paused and looked about her to see if anyone was in hearing distance. "But old Dr. NO happened to be on call; he persuaded Dr. Sinclair, her physician, that they should do a 'slow code.' In the end, Dr. Sinclair was persuaded that the quality of her life would not justify the extended pain for the patient and her family."

Alice looked at her in amazement, "What is a 'slow code'?"

Joy shook her head and drew closer to whisper in her ear, "Alice, you are so naïve." Joy paused again to look about her before continuing, "Although it was 3 a.m., family members were hovering about us like hawks, so we put on a convincing show of doing everything we could to save her. Actually, we did all we could to make her comfortable. She slipped away free of pain and was surrounded by her family."

Nausea clutched at Alice's throat. She was relieved that she would not be coming back.

Chapter 42: Doorway to Hell

The Bowery, New York City, 1973

In 1973, everything in the Bowery was cheap—
cheap movie houses; stores selling cheap junk;
cheap, all-night, diners; and saloons on every
corner. Even the rent was cheap, so artists often
lived there in loft apartments. Brothels and
flophouses were thrown in here and there. Graffiti
was everywhere, as was the odor of stale beer and
urine. The 'do-gooders' had also left their marks:
soup kitchens to feed the body and missions to feed
the soul.

Alice stood in an alley near a corner infamous as
a meeting place for prostitutes and 'johns.' Since
losing her job, she had moved on to cocaine as her
drug of choice, a habit that, even in its infancy, was
rapidly depleting what savings she had. She had to
find a way to pay for that next fix, the only thing
she cared about these days.

Her high-heeled leather boots reached mid-thigh,
ending just below a skin-tight miniskirt. The
peasant blouse opened at the front to show ample
cleavage. Eyes, heavy with shadow, mascara, and
eyeliner, peered from beneath arching eyebrows.
The fire-engine red lipstick and matching rouge
added to her cheap appearance. She bore little

resemblance to the woman who had been Phillip Reid's wife and the mother of Bubbie. But she was surviving.

The Third Avenue El thundered overhead as she ambled into the street, swaying her hips. The movement brought back the memory of a young girl following her hip-swinging mother out of a saloon. Although she had fought the thought all her life, she was now ready to accept it. *I'm just like her. Might as well accept my fate.*

A car approached. Its window on the passenger side was being lowered. Alice backed into the alley behind her, stumbling over something blocking the entrance. *What is it? A body? Tramps love to sleep in these alleys.* Upon closer inspection, she saw it was a plastic bag filled with garbage; the smell of rotten food confirmed it. Peering around the corner of the building, she saw the car move on very slowly down the street.

Hiding in the shadows and too afraid to move, she watched as a pickup truck cruised by, maintaining the same slow speed. A bleached blonde in pants that fit like her skin stepped out of the shadows and approached the open window. Pulling her low-cut blouse down farther, she leaned into the truck so that the occupant, who was discussing something with her, could have a better view of her cleavage. Alice could not make out what they were saying: She had been distracted by a noise in the alley behind her. *Were those footsteps I heard?* She stood very still and listened. *Must a' been my nerves. I don't hear anything now.*

Out on the street, the blonde and the driver seemed to be haggling. Alice guessed it was over price.

I hear something; it's in this alley with me. A low hissing sound came from behind her. Something soft brushed against her legs and then crossed her path before scampering out into the street. It stopped at the feet of the blonde long enough to rub its nose against her white boots. *It's a black cat.* The blonde kicked at it with her boot before tugging at her tight pants and climbing into the cab of the truck. The truck drove away, and all was quiet again—deathly quiet. The cat moved over to the curb across the road, its green eyes piercing the darkness as it watched.

But the footsteps were still there, picking up their pace. Alice hurriedly walked out into the middle of the road and found the nearest street light. The El rumbled overhead again, setting her surroundings in vibration. Broadening her stance to maintain balance, she stood still and waited for the train to pass. Another car drove by; the driver hung his head out of the window, "Get out'o the street you dumb broad." She moved aside and started to run. But the boots were not made for running, and it wasn't long before she felt the pain of a blister forming on her left heel. Stopping under a streetlight, she slid the boot down, folded a piece of tissue, and cushioned the heel. She looked back at the entrance to the alley. A tramp was rummaging through the bag of garbage. *Was it his footsteps I heard?*

Ahead of her, a dim light was shining from one of the buildings, so she headed in that direction. But it wasn't long before both feet were killing her. She removed the boots and carried them in her hands. The asphalt felt hard and cold beneath her bare feet. She looked about her. *What do I do now?*

Out of nowhere a late model black Lincoln pulled up beside her. "Want a ride, honey?"

The single occupant was a heavy-set man in casual dress with well-trimmed hair that was graying at the temples. His gloved hands clutched the steering wheel as he leaned forward to peer at her through horn-rimmed glasses.

Alice opened the door and climbed in. It felt so good to get off her feet that she relaxed for a minute and reached to pull her skirt down before quickly jerking her hands back. Leaning toward the driver she exposed more cleavage, imitating the woman she had spied on from the alley.

The driver looked confused but reached over to adjust the radio; it had been blaring Ravel's *Bolero*. She could feel him undressing her with his eyes. "You ever done this before, sweetheart?" She didn't answer. "Cat got your tongue, Dahling?"

He's as phony as that accent, thought Alice. He reached for her knee. She backed away getting as close to the door as possible, "Not, not so fast," she stuttered. "We—we haven't agreed on a price yet."

He sneered. She took a closer look at her client. *Probably in his late fifties-early sixties,* she thought. A diagonal scar cut across his left cheek. The scar and muscular body build belied the ridiculous act of sophistication he was putting on.

His gloved hand returned to the steering wheel as he sighed, "Okay-ay, what is your price, and what you got to offer?"

Alice eyed the bulge under his jacket and wondered whether it was a gun, "I charge $200.00." The words came gushing out like a reluctant spigot that had just been turned on.

They were crossing the Hudson River Bridge—looked like he was heading for the harbor.

It will be even harder to get help down there. And even if I got someone's attention, who'd rescue a prostitute from a 'john'? I'd better think of something. But her mind was in a swirl.

"Damn, bitch—I can get a high-class broad for that kind'a money. I ought'a throw you out right here."

She opened her purse, searching for something to defend herself with—a nail file, something heavy, any kind of spray. He grabbed her hand as she was digging through the contents of her purse. Her charm bracelet, keys, and lipstick spilled out and onto the seat between them. The car was picking up speed and starting to swerve. Through the windshield she saw the railing of the bridge; they were headed for it.

All of a sudden the car started slowing down.

"What is that?" He was eyeing the phoenix with the sapphire eyes attached to her charm bracelet. Where'd you get that?"

None of your business, you son of a bitch. But Alice was too scared to say that to him. Instead, she clutched the bird in her hand and meekly mumbled, "A patient gave it to me; it…it was a gift from her family." Alice sensed that something was changing, so she bit her lower lip, deciding to play along.

"What was the patient's name?"

"Carson, her name was Carson."

He flinched. The name obviously meant something to him. Was he a relative of her former patient?

"Why'd she give it to you?"

Alice knew she was onto something, so she continued with as much calmness as she could muster. "For making her laugh when she needed it the most—for just listening to her and allowing her to have her own reality."

"Where was her family? How come they couldn't do that for her?"

"They couldn't face her impending death. Many people are like that. They use denial to hide things they can't cope with."

By now, they were on the docks of New York City, an unsafe place to be at any hour. She felt the panic returning and could not focus, could not think. She was powerless. Then the reality of that moment pierced her mental haze. The car was turning around. They were headed back to the bridge. Still frozen in fear, she sat like a zombie and dared not open her mouth.

They drove for what seemed like hours before the car stopped. He did not look at her but just shouted, "Get out! You heard me, get out!"

At first, she thought her ears were deceiving her. When his words finally penetrated her confusion, she grabbed the door handle and jumped out. Taking several deep breaths of the refreshing air, she thought, *Freedom has never tasted this good before.* The elation even provided anesthesia for the pain in her aching, blistered feet.

Chapter 43: A Light

She was somewhere in New York City—exactly where she wasn't sure. It appeared to be the same street where the Lincoln had picked her up. But was it? She was disoriented and confused. What was worse, her feet had started to hurt again. Realizing that her shoes were missing, she looked around for them. The boots lay in the middle of the street behind her. *The 'john' must have thrown them out after I left the car.* At first, she decided to leave them there, quickly changed her mind and went back to pick them up. Carrying the boots in her hand, she saw on her right what appeared to be an all-night bar. *I need something more than a drink after all that.* She walked past it, attracted to the flickering light beyond. The light came from a rustic lantern above a wooden cross. *It must be a mission of some kind—dozens of those in the Bowery. Maybe that's where I am. These missions seem to be all over the slums of New York, reaching out to the homeless, the drunks, the addicts.*

The door beneath the cross was open, so she walked in. It was a small chapel—couldn't possibly seat more than 20-30 people. The nave of the tiny church led to a small altar where several candles were burning. The familiar cross beyond the altar brought a feeling of safety. Genuflecting, more from relief and habit than feelings of reverence, she entered one of the pews and knelt. As she crossed herself, the tears started. The flood gates had opened, and there was no holding them back. Audible sobs were shaking her body when she turned to see a priest standing at the entrance to the pew.

Looking down at her outfit, she felt shame. She was *not* dressed for church.

He didn't seem to notice. "Would you like to come back to my office, my child?" She thought of all the lewd stories she had heard about priests and wondered whether he was like them. *What the hell,* she thought. *What have I got to lose?*

He handed her a box of tissues, which she used to wipe her face and blow her nose. He waited as she was deciding what to do next.

"If you would like to freshen up a bit, there is a bathroom near the office."

She got up slowly and followed him down the aisle, turning left in front of the altar.

He pointed to a small door on the right, saying, "That's the restroom. Do you want something to drink? I can offer you water or some warmed-over coffee."

"Coffee sounds good."

Entering the restroom, she stopped to stare at her image in the small mirror. Most of the heavy makeup had been washed away by her tears. She removed the rest with warm water and combed her hair. She felt better.

Walking back to the office in her bare feet, she pulled her blouse up to provide better coverage and tugged on her tight skirt. She had left the boots in the chapel. The priest was seated at a table near his desk. Dominating the room was a large, rustic cross on the wall behind the desk. He motioned for her to take a seat across from him at the table. She tugged at her skirt again and sat down. Sipping the strong, black coffee in front of her, she was surprised to find that it actually tasted good.

The light provided a better view of her companion. Probably in his late twenties, he was tall with an athletic build. He smiled often, the smile lighting up his entire face. But it was his eyes that drew her attention; they radiated strength and inner peace. *I want what he has* she thought as she struggled to hold back the shame she felt from doubting his character. *Why one look into those eyes would tell anyone who he is and that he respects who they are. A view into his soul.*

He extended his hand, saying, "I'm Tim Norton, Associate Rector of Saint Paul's Episcopal Church and sometimes volunteer for this chapel. Would you like to tell me who you are?"

Alice had assumed he was Roman Catholic, but it didn't *really* matter. She liked him and was beginning to feel something she had not felt for years—a connection and the sense that he was someone she could trust. She took his hand, knowing that she could finally be herself.

Twisting her hands in her lap, she furrowed her brow. "Who am I? I don't know. I can only tell you about my life."

He smiled, "Tell me about your life."

Listening attentively, he allowed her to express her own reality. The soulful, brown eyes showed emotions appropriately, but she could detect no sign that he was judging her or her actions. He asked questions for clarification but, otherwise, allowed the words to tumble out one over the other, expressing feelings that had been locked inside all her life. Finally, after the well of tears had run dry and all her words, spoken, she gave a big sigh of relief. Pulling on her favorite strand of hair, an action she had not taken in years, she sat twiddling her toes.

He offered her more coffee before pouring a cup for himself. Looking at her, he asked, "Do you have an immediate need?'

She rubbed her hands together before speaking, "The nightmares. I hate to go to sleep because I know they will come."

He looked pensive, "I can't be sure yet, but from what you've told me, I'd say that there is something in your life that you don't want to face. Be patient. It will take time and therapy to uncover it. You must face it when you do." He paused, "But let's not get the cart before the horse, so to speak. First, we need to get you clean and dried out. I recommend the Lakewood Rehabilitation Center. When ready, you will start a program of rehabilitation, which includes therapy."

Alice looked down at her hands, "But I don't have any money and no job."

"I'll contact the social worker for financial assistance tomorrow. But right now, I'll take you home. You need to rest."

Chapter 44: Recovery Begins

New York, New York, 1973

If light is in your heart you will find your way home.
Jallaludin Rumi

It took four months to get most of the alcohol and cocaine out of Alice's system. That time passed in a haze of tremors, nausea, vomiting, sweating, delirium tremens, and nightmares. Then one morning she woke up and noticed the sun shimmering on the lake under a cloudless blue sky. She stretched her arms over her head and actually felt alive for the first time in years: Medications were easing the anxiety and depression. She was ready for rehabilitation.

Following the humiliating attempt at prostitution, she had embraced this program with everything she had. On some days more than others. But the night she attended her first AA meeting, she was filled with self-doubt. *There's no way I'm going to stand up in front of all of those people and say I'm an alcoholic. I just can't do it.* When the time came, she forced herself to stand. Wringing both sweaty palms, she looked out on the sea of faces, holding tightly to her sponsor's hand. She started to sit back down, but her sponsor gave her a little push. She opened her dry mouth and spoke so quietly that it came out barely more than a whisper, "Hi, I'm Alice…I'm an alc…alcoholic and… drug addict." But they weren't rejecting her. As a matter of fact they were greeting her with open arms.

"Hi, Alice. Welcome!" She took a deep breath, relief flooding her whole body. *Why I belong here. They like me just as I am.* She would discover in the years to come that some member of AA would be there for her whenever she needed them. It was part of their own healing. And it would be hers.

When attending meetings of Adult Children of Alcoholics (ACAs), she learned that ACAs have the disease of alcoholism even if they never touch a drink of alcohol. And if they do, they become addicted more easily.

Most helpful of all were her sessions with Dr. Benson, her therapist. She saw him in closed sessions when necessary but mostly in group therapy. He took advantage of her experience in nursing and soon made her his assistant. Of course, she still had a lot of work to do on herself-- recognizing and dealing with her own character defects, one at a time. And she still had an occasional craving for cocaine.

In group session one morning, Alice repeated something she had heard from another AA member: "The world is full of nuts, and it is our business to get along with each and every one of them."

Jeannie Fordham, who was new to the group, stood up and dressed her down, "You're so full of bullshit, Dope Head. There're people in this f…ing world that don't deserve to live, much less get along with others." With that Jeannie turned her back on them and walked out. She could still see, feel, smell, and hear every detail of the scene that had occurred about a year ago on that lonely country road.

"I was fifteen years old the day I climbed into the backseat of Jake's old jalopy. He and Gertie, his wife, were driving me to catch the bus back to the orphanage. Another foster home had kicked me out. "So what's new," I asked myself. It had been the fourth one in five years. Folks said I was maturing into a beauty. And maybe that had something to do with it. How should I know? All I knew was that things just didn't seem to work out for me.

I was furious at my latest foster parents: They hadn't even had the decency to take me to the bus station themselves. Instead, they had pawned me off on their friends, Jake and Gertie, who just happened to be going in that direction. I knew I didn't want to go with that couple 'cause I didn't like the way Jake looked at me with his shifty eyes. But what choice did I have? I'd just report all of them to the orphanage when I got back, maybe they'd all be in big trouble.

Jake was giving me that look today through the rear view mirror whenever he could catch my eye. I scowled and tried to focus on pleasant things, so my mind was a million miles away from that smelly car and the creep with the unshaven face and filthy ring around his collar. My nose started running, so I rubbed snot across my dirty face, hoping it would make me even more repulsive.

Gertie, his wife, never moved from the passenger seat where she had been playing a game with their young son, who was sharing the back seat with me. The two of them had been counting houses—she on the right side of the road while he counted the left.

"Looks like you won, Son; I only got 12 on my side," she chuckled as she took her fat arm from the back of the seat to search for peanut butter and crackers in the bag at her side.

"I want a drink, Mamma," the boy said.

Gertie crammed a spoonful of peanut butter in her mouth and mumbled, "Hold on a minute, Son." Brushing her bleached hair from her eyes, she searched in the paper bag for an orange drink, his favorite.

Gertie, a woman in her early fifties, appeared to be content with the extra weight she was carrying around. She would occasionally pat her protruding abdomen in self-satisfaction as she laughed. "Shakes like a bowl full o' jelly," The heavy makeup and bleached hair were the only signs that she cared about how she looked.

The popping sound, made as the drink was opened, jolted me back to reality, but no one seemed to notice.

"It's not cold, Son, but it'll quench ya thirst," Gertie handed the opened drink to her son.

Jake pulled over to the side of the road under a grove of pines. Pulling the baseball cap lower over his balding head, he opened the door. His beer-guzzling middle had him pretty well pinned under the steering wheel, so he forcefully pushed his seat back, hitting his son's knees in the process. The boy started to cry.

"Stop whining 'fore I give you something to whine about." Jake said as he got out of the car. He stretched his arms above his head and then rubbed the small of his back. "I'm gonna stretch my legs a bit. Come on, Jeannie, walk with me."

"I'm fine, I don't want to walk."

Gertie lowered her head as she spoke, "Oh go on with him, so we can get going, or we'll sit here for the rest o' the day."

The group assured Alice that she had done nothing wrong. But she was still shaking when the session ended. So she went to look for her friend, John. *I always feel better after talking things over with him.*

John Stewart was working on his PhD in psychology at a local university and working part-time as a counselor at the center. His research focused on identity, so he spent a lot of time with Alice, who was struggling to find hers. But dedicated, as he was, to that research and his profession, he made a special effort to see that his other patients got equal time and attention.

John was tall and attractive, in a geeky sort of way. The horned rim glasses, which he removed and shook to emphasize a point, gave him the appearance of being an intellectual. An appearance belied by his frequent episodes of playfulness. He took neither himself nor life too seriously.

Today, Alice was unable to find John but ran into her roommate, Marci, who was having coffee in the lounge next to the porch. Marci motioned to her. "Come join me, roomie." Alice was grateful to see a friendly face, so she got a cup of coffee from the nearby kitchen and walked over to join her.

"What's up, Alice? You look upset."

Alice pinched the bridge of her nose as she shrugged, "Oh it's nothing really. I just had a run in with Jeannie Fordham in group this morning."

Marci raised her eyebrows. "Why, what happened?" Alice told her.

"Oh, Alice, you're overreacting. Jeannie is full of anger and has a lot of work to do in therapy. Don't blame yourself." She paused as she stirred half a packet of sugar into her coffee. "And speaking of therapy, how's yours coming along? I see you're doing quite a bit of work with John Stewart."

"Well, that's because his research is related to identity. That's a major issue for me, you know."

"Word around here is that he's sweet on you."

Alice jerked her head around, "Says who? I'm nothing to him but an object of his precious research. Besides, Marci, I have to fix myself before I'm ready for a romantic relationship."

"Have you told him that?"

"Don't have to. He's well aware of that. Besides, it would be unethical of him to have a romantic relationship with a patient. He could never be unethical—it's just not in him."

Marci made a clicking sound with her tongue and teeth. "Me thinks she objects too loudly."

Alice shrugged, "Okay, think what you like."

"Don't get mad, Alice, I'm just teasing. But speak of the devil, look who's about to join us for coffee." Marci stood to leave. "See you later." She gave a little wave with her fingers, grinning as she walked away.

"May I join you?" John Stewart sat down across from Alice before adding two jiggers of creams to his coffee.

She offered him the sugar. As he stirred a packet into the rich coffee, she asked, "Aren't you afraid of getting fat?"

Shrugging, he replied, "All the time."

Alice rolled her eyes. "By the way, I've been meaning to ask you something"

"Okay ay."

"How do I give Belle back the shame I got from her by osmosis?"

He removed his glasses and held them in his right hand. "You may use any of several techniques. The best way may be to write her a letter telling her exactly how you felt as a child." He shook the glasses. "Of course, some folks just meditate, picturing their abuser sitting across from them, listening to everything that needs to be said."

"I see."

With that, he gulped the rest of his coffee, got up, and quickly walked away.

Chapter 45: Relationships

"Character cannot be developed in ease and quiet. Only through experience of trial and suffering can the soul be strengthened, vision cleared, ambition inspired, and success achieved."

Helen Keller

As Alice progressed through the program, she recorded the highlights in her diary. Each new insight seemed to break another tie that had her bound to an unhappy life.

July 25, 1973

We often stray from the true self in order to get the love and acceptance of others. But when we do, we lose that part of ourselves that we are rejecting or failing to validate—often the part that needs our acceptance the most. We add to that un-validated self in a myriad of other ways—with something as simple as an exaggeration. The rejected self with all of its baggage forms a shame core inside us. John says the emotions in those hidden parts of me have collected, like food rotting in a refrigerator around that shame core. My job now is find and deal with each of those emotions, one at a time.

Like many people raised in dysfunctional families, I muddled my way through the world by pleasing others or, at least, I thought I was. It never occurred to me (until now) to ask what I wanted or even what I thought. It was as though I didn't exist. And never having formed an identity of my own, I had no boundaries between me and other people. If someone called me 'monster' (and they did), that was my reality. I got lost in whatever crowd I happened to be in—swirling from one reality to another in a haze.

Overwhelmed with confusion and uncertainty, I struggled to gain some sense of control by trying to control the world outside. Of course, that didn't work; it only caused problems for me and everyone around me.

July 28, 1973

Marci reminded me today, "There is a center to the universe, and it ain't you." I was so self-centered that I became the center of *my* universe, and the actions of others were interpreted from that center: If a friend chose to ride a bike to school one day, it was because he did not want to walk with me. I could not see beyond that. Could not fathom that my friend might be riding a bike because he needed to get there faster, had an injury, or simply enjoyed riding a bicycle. Everything was all about me.

After I lost my dad, I had no one to tell me "I see your little light, and it's just precious." How was I to know it was there if no one had ever seen it? If I had found that light and trusted it to guide me to maturity, my life would have been very different. But I became an emotional orphan always looking for a place to fit in, a place where I could feel like I belonged. In order to get there, I tried to control the world outside, including others. My program has helped me turn to my Higher Power as a source of Light in the world and to gradually, day by day, focus on that reflected light inside myself."

It has been said that alcoholism is death of the soul. If that is true, what does it say about children of alcoholics who get this soul-killing disease through no fault of their own? We don't even have to touch alcohol. No one knows whether the origin of the disease is genetic, learned behavior, or a combination of the two. I suspect the last.

July 31, 1973

I shouldn't have been so critical of Jeannie. The bond of humanity runs through us all. And whether we realize it or not, we have many characteristics in common. We are often most critical of faults in others that we hide from ourselves. And criticizing them empowers the self-critic within so that when we make a similar mistake, the empowered self-critic does a job on us.

August 1, 1973

I'm really trying to get along with everyone here. I know now that relationships and the environment we create for ourselves, partly through them, are as important as achievements. We need to surround ourselves with positive people but, also, to understand that excluding others often deepens our own feelings of alienation.

Genuine love for others creates a nourishing environment. And we show genuine love best by accepting others just as they are. In doing so, we validate their inner most self. When we do this, we are most likely to receive love in return and, thus, find it easier to navigate in the world. It has been said that one who is physically blind will find that navigation easier than one who is spiritually blind. And our self-esteem comes from the belief that we can cope with the world.

Of course, genuine charm helps smooth the way for us. John defines charm as putting others at ease and helping them feel good about themselves.

I can tell this program is working by the way I'm relating with others. I feel a connection, a bond that wasn't there before. I used to feel that others were avoiding me, and they probably were, to be honest. Now, folks seem to seek my company. I think they're attracted to this light within me. Why even Jeannie Fordham and I are getting along. Kind of. We tease each other in a good-hearted kind a way. And I'm actually beginning to enjoy being around her.

Alice put her diary aside and went out on the porch of Lakewood. The summer breeze felt good against her skin. Sitting down in a wooden rocker, she sipped hot coffee and gazed at the scenic waterfall in the distance. Flowing from one of the encircling mountains, it emptied its clear, blue water into the lake below. The Mountain Laurel surrounding the lake was fading, dropping its white and pink blossoms into a sea of green. *Places that draw us closer to the heart of God. How much longer will I be here to enjoy its beauty? The answer is: I'll be here as long as it takes. Guess I grew up all wrong, and now I have to undo all the old habits and learn new ways of doing things— following that light within, my guiding star. I'm so glad I finally found it.*

My companions keep telling me the program works if I work it.' And I'm surely working it. Some days I feel like I know who I am, like the day I looked in the mirror and saw a whole person for the first time in my life .Other days, I get lost in the fog again. But my friends say that progress is two steps forward and one back. She crossed her fingers, hoping they were right.

With a big sigh she got up to water the yellow and purple pansies surrounding the porch. *These pansies are so pretty and dainty and yet so tough, withstanding winter's cold and frost. Hope I'm like them. It's easy to relax and live in the moment here—so calm and peaceful. But what will happen when I return to the hustle and bustle of distractions in the real world? Will I be able to stand up to the pressures of everyday life, staying tough like these pansies?*

She looked down at the rubber band on her wrist and flipped it to stop the worry. She needed a positive thought to take its place. Turning to the scenery surrounding her, she found it in the beauty of the mountains.

Unlike the surrounding foliage, the mountains do not change, standing guard throughout the ages and promising to be here in ages to come. Their stable, steadfastness offers comfort to those who have come here to get their lives back on track. People like me. We need a replacement for the things that have filled the emptiness in our lives temporarily but destructively—alcohol, drugs, sex, or other addictions. Today, like every day since my arrival, I need the comfort of the mountains to feel grounded in something permanent.

Chapter 46: Making Amends

New York
Lafayette and Baton Rouge, Louisiana
1973

As part of her healing, Alice had to make a list of anyone she had harmed throughout her life. The list was then discussed with her sponsor in preparation for making the proper amends.

The voice of an old man, Mr. Jordan, came to mind. *Could he have been telling the truth?* Her system of denial had hidden the truth from her for so long that she wondered whether she would recognize reality if it slapped her in the face. But she was determined to keep trying: Her life did not work the way it had been.

She argued with herself. *But I am sure that Jefferson Hebert was the only man I ever made love to before my pregnancy. Or was he? I was totally out of it after that dance I went to with the old man's son.* She pulled herself erect and looked about for something to do. *I better find something to keep me busy. I'll never heal—doubting myself like this.*

But the voice would not go away. No matter how busy she made herself, it would return as soon as she relaxed. So she finally decided that she had to deal with it. *Could there be some truth in what Mr. Jordan said? Did his son, Spike, rape me? Surely I would have known. Was I so filled with shame that I couldn't see past it? I have to know the truth, no matter how painful that may be.*

Her research was thorough. After many hours, she ran across a case history of a young woman who claimed to have become pregnant without being aware of it because she had been intoxicated. She asked a friend at the 'rehab' center to verify the possibility with a physician. The answer came back to her several days later that it was possible.

"The doc says there are cases of girls becoming pregnant when doing nothing more than heavy petting."

Alice searched through some old textbooks she had owned since her break with Jefferson Hebert and found the note that had broken her heart—a 'Dear John' from Jefferson. The date read February 22, 1956.

Then she remembered that Cecile had a habit of keeping scrapbooks, so she got in touch with her old friend, who was in London. "Hey, 'Cile, do you happen to know the date of your first concert?"

"Gee, Alice. And how are you?"

"I'm sorry, 'Cile. How are you?"

"Still kicking, Ally. But I can see that date is really important to you." She paused. "I'm pretty sure I saved a flyer. I'll look around first chance I get. If I find one, I'll send you a copy."

Two weeks later, Alice received a large envelope from London. Her hands trembled as she tore into it. The concert had occurred on April 25, 1956. That meant that the blind date with Spike had occurred on April 25, 1956—42 weeks, almost to the day, prior to the birth of her first son. Forty-two weeks was the period for normal gestation. Jefferson had broken off with her long before then.

She finally had to face the truth. *Jefferson could not possibly be the father of my first child. Then it had to be Spike.* She shuddered. *That means I have to make amends to Spike's father, not to mention Jefferson. What a mess I made of everything. I told Jefferson he was the father. And he believed me— even paid my expenses at the House of the Good Shepherd. Well, I created this mess, so now I have to fix it.* She paused, nodding her head, *or, at least, try to.*

A member of AA drove her to Lafayette, where Alice stayed with a friend, another AA member. Henry Jordan was found in the Lagniappe Hospice, located near Bayou St. John.

Approaching the young Cajun woman at the desk, Alice squelched the last-minute hope that she had gotten there too late to see him. Clenching her right fist, she announced in a voice louder than she had intended, "I'm here to see Mr. Henry Jordan."

The young woman looked her over. "You family?"

"No, but I know he wants to see me. I'm Alice Hollister Reid. I spoke with him by telephone not too long ago."

The woman studied her face and evidently decided to trust her. She got up from the desk and started down the hall, saying, "Follow me."

The elderly man was sleeping when Alice entered the room, the white covers pulled up to his blue lips as if he were cold. She turned and was about to leave when he opened his eyes as though he had sensed her presence. "Who are you?" His raspy voice strained to make the sounds intelligible.

Alice reached for the blanket at the foot of the bed to cover him, but he waved her away. She offered him her hand as she faced him directly so that he could read her lips. "Mr. Jordan, I am Alice Hollister Reid. You called me some time ago in regard to your son, Spike."

A look of anger flashed in his eyes as he said, "You hung up on me."

Alice steadied herself, saying, "I came to apologize for that and to tell you that I now realize that Spike could be the father of my first-born child, a son." The look of joy on his face broke her heart.

She paused, rubbing her hands together before looking into the old man's eyes, "I gave him up for adoption, Mr. Jordan. I had to sign papers that I would never try to contact him." Disappointment shown on his face.

"But I want you to know that he was adopted by a family who has the resources to give him everything he will ever need. I am convinced that he will make a positive contribution to mankind." Her voice caught. "I'm so sorry." She stiffened her upper lip as her eyes flooded. "So very sorry that you won't have a chance to see him ... get to know him."

He slowly reached for the hand she had offered him. "I understands, Miss. Guess that was the best you could do."

He smiled, his sense of peace radiating out to her. She was glad that she had come.

Jefferson was harder to find, but she remained in Louisiana until she located his father, Paul, through one of his newspapers. Paul refused to give her Jefferson's telephone number at first but relented when he learned the nature of her call. Seems her former lover was living and working in Baton Rouge.

Needless to say, he was shocked to hear from Alice after so many years. But, for some reason, he agreed to meet her for lunch at La Maison, a popular restaurant in Baton Rouge.

She arrived early and was seated at a table near the window. She wanted to see him first.

Then, right on time, he appeared. She recognized his stance and purposeful strides, noticing that he still had a slight limp, resulting from that old football injury to his left leg. The expensive business suit spoke volumes about his success. The crew cut had been replaced by a stylish short haircut, and he had put on some extra pounds, mostly around the middle. She remembered how he loved beer.

He looked about, and his face lit up when he recognized her. As he drew closer, she noticed the touches of gray in his hair, giving him a distinguished, mature look. He was even more attractive than she remembered.

He extended his hand, "Nice to see you, Alice. I must say, you're more beautiful than ever."

She looked to see whether he was pulling at his ear, a sure sign that he was lying. He wasn't.

He motioned to the waiter as he sat down. "I'm working, so I'm afraid this will have to be a dry lunch." He ordered unsweetened tea. When it came, she raised her glass of water laced with lemon in a toast. He reciprocated.

As he reached for the menus, she noticed the gold band on his left ring finger.

Scrunching up her features to avoid showing emotion, she said, "I see you're married." He nodded.

"Children?"

He smiled. "Yeah, two great kids." He pulled his wallet out to display pictures of a smiling boy and girl before adding, "How about you?"

"Divorced. No children." She couldn't bear the thought of discussing Bubbie with him, so she had taken the easy way out. A look of sadness flashed across his face but was quickly wiped away. She sensed that he knew that pity would drive her out of the restaurant. They both ordered Shrimp Etouffee, the house specialty.

She clasped her hands in her lap to keep them from shaking before speaking, "There's something I have to tell you." She sighed and took a deep swig of her water, wondering where she would find the strength to go on. That strength came slowly from deep inside. He was watching her.

She paused, waiting for another surge of strength. "I wronged you, and I must make amends. I truly believed that you were the father of my first child. Do you believe that?"

He nodded.

"I even allowed you to pay all of my expenses." She paused again, taking a deep breath. "I now realize that you couldn't have been the father." She looked down at her hands and spoke so softly he could hardly hear her. "I… I was a victim of date rape." She was expecting shock or at least surprise as her story unfolded. Instead, he just sat there watching her and nodding. She ended by saying rapidly, "I'll repay you every penny I owe you."

He scrutinized her face as he said, "You owe me nothing."

It was her turn to be surprised. "What do you mean? You paid all of my expenses at the House of the Good Shepherd."

"Your expenses were paid by the church. My mother had all but established that home. The church repaid her for her services by taking care of you."

More surprise registered on her face. "Roberta knew?"

"My whole family knew. And, Alice, we can figure due dates as well as you can."

She looked at him incredulously, "And you're not angry?"

"No one's angry. My family rescued me after I told my brother that I wanted to commit suicide."

She brought the fingers of her right hand up to cover her lips. "When did that happen?"

"Soon after you left. I couldn't give you up, and I couldn't leave school."

"Were you in love with me?" she searched his face for the truth.

He looked down before answering,

"Yes."

She looked at the ceiling to hold back the tears that were burning the backs of her eyes. "Why didn't you ever ask me to marry you? I waited and waited."

He shrugged his shoulders, "I was waiting for you to grow up."

Her sense of peace deepened when she realized that she could now love him as a friend.

Chapter 47: Voodoo Revisited

New Orleans, 1973

Alice was not ready to leave Louisiana just yet. All during recovery, her mind had been flitting from one scene to another... her father's face when she told him of Belle's affairs...blood on the front porch steps...a miniature coffin nearby...the priest telling her that there was something in her past she could not face. And then there were the nightmares; they bothered her most of all. As she was preparing for bed one evening, she confided in her new AA friend, who suggested a séance in New Orleans. In some mysterious way, voodoo held a key to her healing and the nightmares. So Alice returned to New Orleans, the city where it had all begun.

The half-moon darted behind a cloud just as she located the address she had been given for the séance. The Quarter was unusually quiet for midnight. A lone trumpet wailed the blues from a bar down the street as she placed a foot on the first step of the creaking stairway. The stairway led to the veranda located off the second floor of the building. She toyed briefly with the notion that the rickety stairway might not support her weight but decided that the wrought-iron railing on the side was strong enough to help her make it safely. *The séance should be located behind one of those closed doors facing onto the street,* she thought.

She made it to the top step leaning on the rail and soon located what turned out to be the right door. Two heavy knocks followed by three quick ones and then another heavy bang were soon answered by a voice from within.

"Nelda sent me," she called out.

She was debating whether she should turn and leave when the door swung open. A tall, muscular black man, dressed only in pants that reached to his knees, stood with his legs apart and arms folded. He must have been close to seven feet tall. He didn't say a word but just stood there looking at her.

A young black woman soon appeared at his side. She was wearing a red and white checkered cloth tied about her head and knotted at the back of her neck. She resembled pictures Alice had seen of Marie Laveau, the iconic priestess of voodoo. The girl spoke, "Why you come?" Her black eyes seemed to pierce Alice's soul.

"I'm troubled by a nightmare that I can't quite seem to shake."

The woman blocked her from entering; the man stood behind the woman. "And Nelda say we can help you?"

Alice backed away. "She said you could try."

"What the name of the spirit you wish to call up?" Alice gave her father's name and passed the woman a bill. The woman, in turn, nodded to the man, who stepped aside, allowing Alice to pass into a room lit only by candles and smelling of incense and mold.

In a corner near the entrance sat a crate covered with a black cloth. But no one appeared to notice it. All eyes were focused on an older woman in the center of the room. She, too, wore a cloth tied about her head; it appeared to be identical to the one worn by Alice's greeter. The older woman sat at a round table with several people near her.

Others stood about in the shadows. They were a microcosm of the citizenry of New Orleans—Hispanic, Creole, Oriental, Caucasian, and African American.

The table, like the crate, was covered with a black cloth reaching to the floor. The old woman's hands embraced a large crystal ball in front of her. Reflected lights from the candles flickered like tiny stars in the crystal. The priestess was calling on the spirits of the dead; followers of voodoo believed they walked among the living. The spirits were being asked to help those who had brought their problems to her, the priestess of voodoo.

Manuel, a small Mexican man, was trying to contact the spirit of his grandfather to request help in bringing his family to be with him in the United States. He was told to continue to work hard at his job and save every penny he could and that one day he would have enough money to send for them. If he did this and believed every day that a way would be found, he would receive help.

Alice distanced herself from the crate. *Did I hear movement inside that thing?* It appeared to be moving. Or was it the flickering of the candles?

Hilda, an obese, middle-aged woman, was next to address the priestess, "There has been no peace in my family since my sister-in-law came to live with us. She steals my grocery money and all the time she is fussing at my kids. But my husband does not believe his baby sister can do nothing bad. No peace. No peace. I don't care how you do it—just get rid of her."

The priestess stood and faced Hilda. In a loud voice, she announced, "Voodoo not used for evil. Never for evil. But there's always them who use it for their own gain. We believe that the spirits of the dead walk among us and that their wisdom can be used to help the living—never to hurt them." The woman was sent away without help.

The candles had burned to within an inch of the holders when Alice heard her father's name, "Tom Hollister, spirit of the dead, I implore you to come into this room. You are needed to set this woman free from her nightmares."

A wind swept through the room blowing out all but one of the candles. The crate crashed to the floor. Alice turned to look in the direction of the crash but was immediately reprimanded by the old woman, "Do not take your eyes from the crystal ball." Alice obeyed, keeping her eyes glued to the crystal orb. A weird screeching sounded in a room out back, like someone was opening an old chest that had been sealed for years by rust. Alice shuddered. *Is it my imagination, or is something crawling over my feet?* She didn't dare look down but kept her eyes glued hypnotically on the crystal ball.

"He is here in this room with us. I can feel his presence." The repetitive chant went on and on.

As Alice watched, the image in the crystal appeared to be changing. *Is that a face? Will I see my dad's face from the grave?* She wanted to run away but used all her strength to stand there and keep her eyes fixed on the crystal ball. Somewhere a ticking sound could be heard. Alice hoped that it was a clock. She heard the minutes ticking slowly by. She listened. After what seemed like hours, she could make out a metronome behind the priestess. *She's timing me* thought Alice. The thought grounded her sufficiently so that she could see the crystal ball more clearly. It was just that—nothing more than a crystal ball. The image wasn't even there. *Why it was nothing but my own fears that created the image as well as the change. Did I also imagine something crawling around my ankles?* She paused, placing her index finger against her left temple. *Amazing what fear can do to you. But look it squarely in the eye, and it has a tendency to disappear.*

Did I cause Dad to put a curse on Belle by telling him the truth? If so, then I, too, am responsible for her death. Is that what I've been running away from? What I couldn't admit-- even to myself? I'll stop running and open my eyes to the truth. And she prayed to find that truth.

It seems to me that voodoo is not really as scary as I used to think. The priestess calls upon the spirits of those who have passed on to give wisdom to the living. When solutions are found for their problems, people remember how they were helped and forget the other times. It's all in the mind.

Before leaving New Orleans, Alice stopped by her favorite restaurant for their legendary turtle soup. Although heavily laced with sherry, the cooking process had removed the alcohol, so it was okay for her to have it. The soup was served with freshly-baked French bread in an elegant dining room with silver, candles, and a sea of white table cloths and napkins. The soup was just the right temperature as it caressed her taste buds with a subtle flare of seafood and sherry. It was so-o good. She broke off a piece of bread, slowly buttered it, and bit into the crusty morsel. She took her time, enjoying every mouthful of the food, not knowing when, if ever, she would have it again. *This soup alone is worth a trip to New Orleans,* she thought.

A woman was smiling at her from across the room. Her face looked familiar, but her name was eluding Alice at that moment. The woman got up, crossed the room and stood next to Alice, waiting to be acknowledged.

She spoke with a slight Cajun accent. "You don't remember me, do you?"

Alice thought for a minute before asking, "Is your name Noelle?" The woman smiled showing a row of straight, white teeth. Alice stood up, nodding slightly, "Ah hah! You lived next door to me and Belle. We used to cut paper dolls out of the Sears and Roebuck catalogue. Of course, I remember you. Won't you have a seat?"

"I will, but first I want to give you a big hug."

The two women embraced, patting each other on the back. Noelle seated herself across from Alice as she waved the waiter away.

They studied each other for some time before Alice asked, "What are you doing with yourself these days, Noelle?"

"I'll tell you in just a minute, but first you must eat your soup before it gets cold." Alice gladly complied. Noelle watched her a bit before continuing, "I'm working nights in Medical Records at Charity Hospital. Pay ain't so good, but the hours are worse." They both laughed.

Alice frowned. "Belle died there, you know."

"Yes, I followed the story of her death in the daily newspaper. But what ever happened to your dad?" Alice filled her in on the details of his death. Alice read pity in her face and quickly shifted the conversation back to Belle.

"I'm still confused about the cause of Belle's death. If I knew, it might clear up a few things for me."

Noelle twisted her mouth to the side before saying, "I don't remember the details, been so long ago. Tell you what—if you drop by Medical Records one night, I may be able to show you her chart. But you can't tell anyone; I could get fired for doing it." She shook her head, "Big deal!"

"A pair of pliers couldn't open my sealed lips. I'll be there tonight. What time?"

Noelle looked thoughtful for a moment before saying, "Three a.m. is the best time. I'll pull the chart and leave it on the table; no one will ever know the better."

"Thanks, Noelle. I owe you big time." The two women stood, embracing each other, and Noelle walked away.

The dimly lit Medical Records department gave the impression of a musty-smelling morgue when Alice arrived at 3 a.m. Noelle was waiting for her. Alice handed her a brown paper bag as she said, "Here, I brought you an oyster po'boy, just in case anyone gets nosey about why I'm here."

Noelle accepted the bag, saying, "Thanks, I was about to take a lunch break. I'd invite you to join me, but I'm sure you understand why I can't." Alice nodded.

Noelle placed the bag on the table before leading her friend through dark corridors to an even darker room in back. The overhead light bulb in the room was switched on to reveal rows and rows of filing cabinets against the walls on both sides. A scarred wooden table and some chairs occupied what was left of the space in the room. A thick folder lay open on the table; it was labelled 'Charity Hospital'. The name, Belle Hollister, had been written in ink at the top of the chart.

Alice sat down at the table, her hand trembling as she reached for the document.

"Shhh!"

The overhead light went out. Alice looked for Noelle but could only see the light from her flashlight. Footsteps were coming from the main corridor. Alice sat very still, hardly daring to move, as Noelle left the room. A few minutes later, Noelle's voice could be heard, talking to someone in the hallway.

"No problem, Officer, just have to retrieve an old chart for some anal retentive doc over at Tulane—wants to know family history back to the Civil War. You know how that is."

Alice was still frozen in place when her friend returned.

Noelle whispered, "The guard saw the light and came to investigate. It's okay. I covered for us. But he'll be back this way in about 20 minutes."

Alice thumbed through the thick chart. Belle had been treated with several antibiotics but was not responding to any of them. She had died of pelvic inflammatory disease soon after Alice had gone to Lafayette to live with her aunt and uncle.

She closed the chart, giving a big sigh of relief, feeling that a great weight had been lifted from her soul. *So it was venereal disease that killed Belle. Why the knot I created for myself is continuing to unravel. On some deep level that even I did not know about, I guess I was ashamed of the person my fears led me to believe I was. So I used denial to hide that shameful self from the world. The nightmares were about breaking through all the denial to find the real person inside.* She was just beginning the journey, and the nightmares were fading.

It was such a coincidence—running into Noelle right after the séance? Did voodoo have anything to do with that? No! Voodoo only helped me face the fear so that I could open my eyes and search for the truth.

Chapter 48: A Healing Place

New York, New York, 1973

"Our birth is but a sleep and a forgetting:
The soul that rises with us, our life's star;
Hath had elsewhere its setting,
And cometh from afar:
Not in entire forgetfulness..."

William Wordsworth
(as cited in Breathnach, 1998)

Returning to Lakewood Rehabilitation Center, Alice continued with her diary.

September 3, 1973

Truth is what I perceive with my five senses, realizing that I may see only part of it; others may see the same situation quite differently. If I try to manipulate the truth as I see it, my soul starts down a slippery slope. If I lie, I must spend a lot of psychic energy defending that lie. And the one I lie to, owns me. Above all, I must never lie to myself for I can get so far off the right track that I can no longer perceive the truth.

When I exaggerate or understate, I am not telling the whole truth. And in doing so, I rob myself and others of reality. If I am aware of some knowledge but fail to report it, it is a lie of omission.

Living by the truth I know (allowing the chips to fall at random) may be the best way to find peace and joy. And personal power comes from aligning thoughts and actions with the soul (mind, emotions, and will).

September 5, 1973

We have humility when we are honest about our strengths and weaknesses. Groveling is false modesty.

September 6, 1973

In searching for the positive in every situation—in myself and others, I find a better life. Norman Vincent Peele wrote a book, The Power of Positive Thinking. In it, he claimed that expecting the best releases a magnetic force that by the law of attraction brings the best to us. Might the opposite also be true? Could expecting the worst attract the worst to us?

September 8, 1973

Faith means letting go of worry and fear (when action will not solve the problem)—believing that life will be okay. Fear is the opposite of faith; it leads our imaginations down dark paths where we are apt to follow. But letting go of worry and fear takes practice; it is like sweeping water out of a basement. The water just collects again in deeper places. Finally, after sweeping it out for the fiftieth time, it does not return.

One of the deepest fears, common to most of us, is that of abandonment. We fear that we are not good enough to fit into the tribe, so the tribe will abandon us for rubbish. Trying to prove that we are good enough can become an obsession, turning us into work-o-holics or worse.

Alice sat reading her daily meditation on the porch of Lakewood. Below her, the lake was shimmering in the autumn sunlight, surrounded by trees just beginning to display touches of yellow, orange, and red. A flock of wild geese flew overhead, honking to each other as they headed south. *Yes, it's easy to find peace here. It quiets my soul.*

"Meditating, Ally?"

She looked behind her to see John Stewart, who had been reading over her shoulder.

She frowned, "You're invading my personal space, John."

"Oh my, my, my! Someone's developing boundaries." He laughed as he pulled up a chair beside her. "Is your twelve-step program helping you find what you need, Ally?"

"Absolutely." She paused. "For me, God is that something greater than myself to believe in. I trust Him as my Light, my Inner Compass, and that Light descends to my very soul."

He lifted his eyebrows, saying, "Oh? How's that?"

"As I follow His guidance, I'm learning who He is and in the process who I am. Why when I discern and try to do His will, the path ahead of me becomes clear."

"How do you discern His will?"

"I search my heart and soul and, when necessary, I consult the Bible or people I trust. As I walk along the path that I have discerned, things just seem to fall in place if it is His will. If they don't, I return to the discernment step."

"How does that help you find out who you are?"

"To use an extreme example, if the thought of killing someone fills me with horror, I know I'm not a killer. In other words, emotions I experience from my thoughts help me to know who I am. The insight brings acceptance or motivation for change."

He looked at her, nodding his approval.

She beamed, wondering why his approval was so important to her.

They sat—looking into each other's eyes for one brief moment. A question was asked but unanswered. All of a sudden, he interrupted this exchange of intimacy by turning his head toward the woods. "Is that a white-crowned sparrow I see?"

"A what?"

"A white-crowned sparrow."

"Wow! You really know your birds, don't you?"

He looked at her, "You like birds?"

"Of course. Who doesn't? Wish I knew more about them."

He looked thoughtful for several minutes before saying, "My bird club hikes once a month to hunt for them."

"Your *bird* club?" She laughed a little disdainfully.

He shrugged, "So much for that idea."

"What?"

"I was going to invite you to go along on one of our hikes, but if you're going to make fun of us...." He chuckled and never had a chance to finish his sentence.

"Give me a date, and I'll check my calendar?" He gave a sly little smile causing her to wonder whether she had just told him too much.

He stood up. "We're hiking next Saturday. Be ready at 6:30 a.m. if you want to go." Pausing, he rubbed his chin. "It's not a date, simply therapeutic for both of us." Then, giving a little wave, he walked away.

Alice scratched her head. *What did he mean by that—therapeutic for both of us? So why am I getting all aflutter?* She didn't know the answer to her own question. She had been trying to get in touch with her feelings but found them really scary. John was a big puzzle and the scariest of all.

She had learned that recognizing and acting on feelings were the way to develop trust and, eventually, respect for herself. She wanted to respect and believe in herself. But dealing with feelings was not an easy task for someone who, until recently, didn't even know she had any. Her first attempts had been pathetic. She would think of an emotion and then try to force herself to feel it. Of course, that didn't work—the harder she tried, the more the feeling would elude her. Then one day she was on the basketball court when one of the older boys slammed her in the back with the ball. It knocked her breath out. She fell to the hard surface on her face, blood spurting from her nose and down the front of her favorite shirt. She felt anger, and she knew it. After that, new feelings seemed to pop up rather frequently. She had been progressing nicely. So why was it so hard with John?

Her thoughts were interrupted by Jeannie Fordham, who was ascending the steps to the porch. "Uh-huh, flirting with Dr. Stewart again, weren't you?"

"I was not *flirting* with John Stewart!"

"Oh yeah, then why are you blushing?"

"I'm not blushing." They both laughed, and Alice realized that she and Jeannie Fordham were actually bonding.

October 3, 1973

Gratitude brings joy; the joy springs from being grateful for who we are and what we have. Ever notice that people admire those who have the courage to be themselves—not the person who is trying to win their admiration.

October 5, 1973

Actions have consequences; when we lose sight of this law of the universe, we're in for a lot of pain.

When we can find joy and/or laughter in the ordinary things of life, we tap into the Most Powerful Force in the universe.

October 7, 1973

Attempting to be perfect may be what the Greeks meant when they said that the greatest sin is trying to be godlike. Just take what you got, and do what you can.

That afternoon, Alice entered the small library at Lakewood. *Guess I'll see what I can find out about birds.*

Chapter 49: Birding

New York, New York, 1973

"It's almost seven o'clock. John said he'd be here at 6:30." Alice picked up the telephone and dialed his number. There was no answer. *What now? Guess Dr. Stewart is too busy finishing his doctoral degree to remember his 'non-date' with little old me. He got me all interested in birds and then forgot about me. Oh well, maybe I'll go on my own in the near future. Who needs a man anyway?*

She slammed the receiver back on the hook and glanced out the window. There was sufficient daylight for her morning jog.

As she was heading out the door, the telephone rang. "I'm sorry, Alice, I overslept, but I think we can catch up with the others at the Ramble. Give me a few minutes to check with some friends, and I'll pick you up at 7:30. Okay?"

Alice was skeptical. "I called your number but got no answer."

"I had the phone unplugged for the night....Sorry about that."

"I was just going for a jog." She paused, taking a deep breath. "I'll meet you at the entrance to Lakewood in thirty minutes."

The sun had risen, its rays awakening the autumn leaves on the side of the road, as Alice climbed into John's Jeep. Looking him over, she struggled to hold onto the last bit of anger she felt. But it soon dissipated when she noticed his appearance: His sweat shirt was inside out with a large manufacturer's tag, which should have been hidden at the back of his neck, showing below his Adam's apple. His rumpled head of hair obviously had not seen a comb since yesterday. He looked like a mischievous school boy. With a jerk of her head, she reminded herself to focus on making conversation. "What a beautiful day!" He nodded as he concentrated on his driving.

They rode for a while in silence before she found the nerve to say, "I don't know where we're headed. Can you tell me more about the Ramble?"

"It's in Central Park."

"Central Park?" She blinked in surprise. "You mean to tell me we're going into the heart of New York City to see birds?"

"Yep. It's one of the largest bird sanctuaries in the U.S., and people come here from all over the world to watch our feathered friends. Central Park is located in a valley that was created by moving glaciers over 15,000 years ago; it provides a very attractive terrain for birds that stay here year round as well as the migrators in spring and fall." He glanced sideways at her before returning his attention to the road. "More than 300 bird species have been sighted in its reedy salt marshes, brackish ponds, and the Ramble, among the oak trees and grasses."

Alice was fumbling with a button on her sweater as she asked, "Don't we need binoculars to see them?"

He nodded. "All taken care of. I have my own, and my friend, Janice, has rented a pair for you. "

Alice adjusted her gloves.

He stole a quick glance in her direction again. "If you're cold, turn the heat on."

"I'm fine for now. But how should I be dressed for the hike? You didn't tell me. Am I okay?" *Why am I asking him? Can't imagine that dressing appropriately for the occasion is high on his list of priorities.*

He shrugged. "You look fine to me. Dress in layers and wear comfortable, supportive shoes." She lifted her running shoes for him to see.

"Don't distract me when I'm driving in traffic, Alice." There was a harshness in his voice she had not heard before.

"Sorry." She folded her hands in her lap and waited for an opportune time to extract more information from him. When the traffic slowed down a few minutes later, she asked, "Do I dare inquire about how long the hike will last?"

He chuckled. "Usually takes about three hours, but we missed part of it." Nodding his head back and forth as though calculating the time, he added," Probably take us about two today—that is unless you get so excited you want to stay longer."

She gave a slight grin and rolled her eyes. "Think I'll probably be happy with two."

When they arrived at the Ramble, the 'birders' were taking a break. Spread about in random fashion, they were sitting wherever a large rock or log could accommodate them. They drank steaming cups of liquid from thermos bottles, while carefully protecting the binoculars hanging about their necks. "We're waiting for you, John," someone called as several waved.

The new arrivals joined a nearby couple who were seated on a large boulder at the edge of a wooded area. "I'm sorry I didn't have time to bring coffee, Alice. Did you bring any?"

"No." He scrunched up his features to show disappointment as he drank water from his canteen.

"I see you're a coffee person."

"Yeah, love my java in the morning. You remembered to bring water and food?" Alice nodded. "Good girl. Better hydrate yourself while we have a chance. The hikers don't pause a lot once they get going."

When the break ended, the 'birders' fanned out in single file or doubles to follow a well-worn path through the woods. John stood up and brushed the dirt off the seat of his jeans before offering a hand to help Alice up.

As they were leaving, an attractive brunette came up to John. Hooking her arm through his, she purred. "You missed the best part of the hike, John; we spotted a Scarlet Tanager and a cardinal on their way South."

"Males?" he asked.

"Both of them," she smiled as she looked him over from head to toe, allowing her gaze to linger on his face. "Isn't it a shame that the males in so many species get all the looks?"

He laughed. "That's because we're the ones most anxious to attract a mate." Reaching down to retie a loose shoe string, he freed his arm. "Sandi, I'd like you to meet my friend, Alice Hollister." The two girls looked each other over as they exchanged greetings.

John gave a slight cough and turned to Alice. "Think I'll see if I can find Janice. You'll need those binoculars when we stop. You're in a good position in the group, so you go on. I'll get the binoculars and catch up with you."

Alice continued along the narrow path, following the others in single file. A cool breeze brought the songs of birds from the surrounding woods, adding to the pleasure of the hike.

It wasn't long before the trail crossed a small stream where several rather large rocks formed a bridge across the rapidly flowing water. The first stone was stable, giving Alice a bit of confidence in her ability to cross without getting her feet wet, a worthy endeavor since the air temperature was in the 40's. The second stone surprised her by rocking as she stepped onto it. Her foot slid into the cold water. She shivered as she continued toward shore, trying to keep the other foot dry but soon deciding that it was a hopeless cause.

"Get your feet wet?" asked a voice behind her.

"I was thinking of going swimming," she replied.

He laughed. "Too cold for you, huh?"

"You might say that." She turned around to take a better look at the person asking such asinine questions. Dressed in red sneakers and old clothes that had long ago lost all semblance of style, he was tall and skinny with thick-lensed glasses and graying hair that reached to his shoulders and surrounded his unshaven face.

About to turn her back to this dork, she remembered that she was not supposed to judge people, so, instead, she *looked* him squarely in the eye. He smiled. The smile was both genuine and enchanting. "I carry an extra pair of socks for such mishaps. I'll be happy to let you wear them home." She felt like kissing him.

"There you are, Alice. I've been looking for you." John was successfully navigating the stream. He reached the shore shortly after Alice and her new acquaintance.

"John, I'd like you to meet my new friend. What's your name, Friend?"

"Frank White," he replied as he extended his hand to John. Then he started searching through his backpack. He removed a pair of socks and handed them to Alice, who quickly found a log where she could sit and make the change. The dry socks were several sizes too large but felt incredibly good on her cold feet.

A woman's voice called out from the other side of the stream, "Wait up, John. You gave me too much money." Alice turned to see a slightly obese woman, who appeared to be in her early fifties; she had been running to catch up with John and paused at the stream to catch her breath.

"Slow down, Janice. It's no big deal," called John. "Keep the money."

Alice watched as the woman clutched her chest. Grabbing John's hand for support, she quickly crossed back over the stream to reach Janice's side.

The woman's eyes rolled back in her head as she gasped. "I... can't.... get my breath."

"Someone get an ambulance and hurry," Alice called out for anyone to hear. Frank left to summon a park ranger.

Alice began unbuttoning a tight collar around Janice's neck to promote air flow into her lungs. A bystander moved forward out of the crowd and found a place for Janice to lie down. Alice intervened," No! Lying down will make the heart work harder. Right now we want her heart to rest, using as little oxygen as possible. We want to increase the supply of oxygen to the heart muscle and cut back on the amount her heart is using." She turned to Janice saying, "Find your most comfortable resting position." Pausing, Alice looked at the group of onlookers, "Anybody got an aspirin?" Someone supplied an adult, non-coated aspirin. Alice placed it in Janice's mouth with instructions to chew it.

John took a handkerchief from his pocket and wiped the sweat from Janice's face. "How will the ambulance find us out here in the middle of nowhere?" Frank replied that the park rangers were already on the job and would take care of that.

"They'll want her medical history. You got one, Jan?"

Janice dug into her purse and handed a piece of paper to John, who was taking turns with Alice holding Janice's hand and wiping the sweat from her brow. The young woman with Janice watched everything with fear clearly written on her face. Alice guessed she was a relative and tried to reassure her. At one point, Alice caught John looking at her as if he were seeing her for the first time.

The ambulance arrived, lights flashing and sirens screaming. The attendants quickly administered oxygen by prongs through the patient's nose. They placed her on a stretcher with her head elevated and attached her to an EKG monitor. Closing the ambulance door, they would allow no one but the young woman, her daughter, to accompany her on the ride to the hospital.

Alice added, "We'll probably just be in the way until later this afternoon; we'll drop by to check on her then. I was glad to see them do the EKG; otherwise, it might have been erroneously dismissed as a non-cardiac event."

It took quite a while for the group to settle down after all the excitement, and some left, deciding to call it a day. Only the most dedicated birdwatchers, whom some would call diehards, remained with Alice and John.

The group, reduced quite a bit in size by now, continued on the trail, halting whenever they saw a bird or other object of interest. At such times, binoculars went to the eyes, and silence reigned. Alice enjoyed that part of the trip best, feeling that her spirit was united with that of the others. They were giving homage to one of God's humbler creatures. Differences in the group faded as all enjoyed the camaraderie and learned more about their feathered friends. The joy in their hearts mingled with the birdsong in the surrounding woods.

Alice felt at peace with herself and the world around her as she walked with John, at times singly and other times side by side. Words of the old country song described what she was feeling best— *the sweetest thing I've ever known*. She quickly repelled the thought, reminding herself that this was not a date.

The silent times between her and John were never uncomfortable. When they spoke, they talked about Lakewood Rehabilitation Center, the people they both knew there, and its program for addicts. They shared their dreams for the future; Alice still wanted to go to medical school. John wanted to teach and do research.

When they stopped for a late afternoon snack, Alice offered John a chicken sandwich from her backpack. When he took it, their hands met. A frisson of pleasure traveled up Alice's arm, and they stared into each other's eyes. *He feels it too.* She felt her soul joining his through that glance. *Something is there; I can feel it.* But the moment was abruptly ended when John walked away to join friends on the other side of the group.

At the end of the day, Alice realized that they had done nothing to indicate that they were more than friends—no hand holding, not even a peck on the cheek. *It really wasn't a date. Was it? Guess my imagination was working overtime.* So she drew the fetter tighter around her heart.

The conviction that he was not interested in her romantically strengthened as the days passed into weeks. Still she heard nothing. He had returned to the university to finish his doctoral program, *so* she did not even see him at Lakewood.

Chapter 50: After Lakewood

New York, New York, 1973-1974

"Walking the spiritual path...is the unfolding of our attempts to be faithful to our awakened hearts. Although we do not always see down the road, we are granted insight in the next step. Something rings true, something resonates, and our awakened heart confirms and validates what it is we need to do...."

Jonathan Erdman
Forward Day by Day

In November, Alice was discharged as a patient from Lakewood, but Dr. Benson hired her immediately as his assistant. Renting a one-bedroom apartment close to the institution, she walked to work daily and registered for classes at a local university to complete her baccalaureate degree. The holidays came and went. Still no word from John. She thought of calling him but decided it was too unladylike; after all, it was obvious that he just wasn't that interested. She felt good about herself now, telling her mirror that she could deal with rejection. The mirror reflected back a whole person; the wholeness was there on most days. "Just need to put a check on the old imagination," she would say to her image.

Then one evening in January, Alice was heating some chicken noodle soup for dinner when she glanced out the window to see snow falling. Chill bumps were popping out on her arms; so she went to her closet in search of her favorite blue sweater. Shivering as she wrapped it tightly around her, she was starting to button it when the doorbell rang. *Wonder who that could be in this weather,* she thought as she wiped her hands on the apron she had donned for cooking.

Opening the peephole, she tried to see into the hallway. But the light was too dim. "Oh darn, I forgot to report that burned-out bulb to the landlord."

Untying the apron, she opened the door just far enough to peek out. Dropping the apron to the floor, she saw John standing there, holding something behind him.

He grinned. "Sorry, Alice, I'm not skinny enough to get through that crack. If you want me to come in, you have to open the door wider."

She opened the door, and they fell into each other's arms. The roses he had been holding behind him joined the apron on the floor.

They just held each other for what seemed like an eternity. Words, like time, were irrelevant.

He reached down to brush the hair out of her eyes. "I can do what I've been longing to do since I first laid eyes on you: You're no longer my patient."

"You wanted to brush the hair out of my eyes, Dr. Stewart?"

He brushed her trembling lips and then kissed them gently. The world around them swirled and stood still. All of a sudden, he jerked his head back to sniff the air, "I smell something burning, Alice."

"Oops!" She ran into the kitchen and rescued the burning pot with what was left of her chicken noodle soup. "Would you like some soup? I think I have a few cans left in the cupboard," she smiled.

"Toasted chicken noodles. I'm starved." She elbowed him in the ribs.

"No, silly. I'll open fresh cans."

Then, finding her canister of crackers empty, she turned to him again, saying sheepishly, "How about popcorn with your soup?"

"Popcorn and chicken noodle soup. Haven't had that since my grandma died."

"Your grandma fed you popcorn and chicken noodle soup?"

"Only when I was a good boy."

"Bet that wasn't often." He grinned.

They sat at the kitchen table watching the snow fall as they ate what tasted to them like a feast—that is, whenever they noticed what they were eating. Talking about everything that had happened in their lives since the hike, their words tumbled over each other. They never ran out of things to talk about, as one thing led to another.

John grabbed a handful of popcorn as he eyed her. "Oh, do you remember Frank White?"

Alice laughed. "Yeah, I sure do. How could I forget the man who saved my feet from frostbite?"

John frowned. "By the way, did he ever get his socks back?"

"Certainly, what kind of girl do you think I am?"

"I'm hoping, Alice," he winked. Lifting his eyebrows, he quickly added, "Well, old Frank up and got himself engaged."

"Oh-h? Anyone I know?"

He shook his head. "Don't think so. She's another birder, but I don't think you met her on the hike. A Jersey girl, I believe."

Alice began gathering their dishes and taking them to the sink. "Speaking of the hike, how's Janice doing?"

"Okay, as far as I know. She's signed up for the next one."

Alice ran some cold water on the dirty dishes and left them. "Wasn't Jeannie Fordham one of your patients?"

"Yeah! How's she doing?"

"Applying to enter college next fall."

His face registered surprise. "Really?" He looked thoughtful. "How'd she get the money?"

"Dr. Benson is helping her obtain a scholarship."

"Bet he had his arm twisted a bit by you." Alice shrugged her shoulders.

"She's a smart kid. Hopes to get a degree in social work. We've talked about starting a home for abused girls, victims of human trafficking, etc."

"Wow! You're full of surprises. Good luck."

Alice nodded. "It's our passion."

The dishes remained in the sink, soaking—a far departure from Alice's usual habits of housekeeping. At one point, Alice caught sight of the kitchen clock and exclaimed, "Good heavens, it's time for the 11 o'clock news. Where did the time go?" She turned on the small kitchen television. The local weatherman was warning that road conditions were treacherous and that people should stay at home unless it was absolutely necessary to travel.

"Looks like you'll have to sleep on the couch tonight, John." He grinned. "I'll get blankets and a pillow." She stood up and walked toward her bedroom. As she passed him, he stood and pulled her to him. Holding her body tightly against his own, his mouth found hers. She felt his erection as he kissed her passionately. Her body responded with a passion that made her breasts ache for his touch and her nipples stand erect. But she pulled away.

I promised myself that I would wait for a definite commitment, and I intend to keep that promise. I've made bad decisions in the past. I flipped over Jefferson and thought I could hold him with sex. When that didn't work, I thought abstinence until marriage was the answer, but my relationship with Phil was even worse. I've come full circle. Now I'm thinking that once a woman is sure of her own feelings and receives a commitment from a guy she trusts, they should live together for a trial period. If that would minimize the chances of family pain from adultery or divorce, I'm all for it. Returning, she quickly handed him the pillow and blankets before turning around and heading for her bedroom.

Falling into a restless sleep, she awoke about 3 a.m. and peeked through the venetian blind near her bed. Under the distant streetlight, she could see that snow was still falling. A world of white surrounded them.

On the other side of her darkened room, a light was shining under the door, alerting her that her guest was up. Grabbing a robe from her closet, she snuggled into the soft fleece for warmth.

Opening the door, she saw John sitting at the kitchen table sipping from a cup. She cleared her throat to let him know she was there. He looked up. "I took the liberty of making some coffee. Hope that's okay. I'd hate to get kicked out in this weather."

She sat down across from him. "I'll join you, but I think I'll have milk. Coffee gives me the jitters, but milk calms me." Getting up and taking a quart of milk from the refrigerator, she poured a glass, wanting to make sure that her thoughts were well grounded for what she knew was coming.

He reached across the table and took her hand. "Alice, we need to talk."

She looked into his eyes, nodded, and said, "I'm ready."

He raised his eyebrows. "Are you?" Searching her face carefully, he responded, "I believe you are. Good. I'll just cut to the chase and tell you that I can't sleep, knowing you're in the next room. My feelings have been repressed too long. How much of that is lust and how much is true love, I can't say."

She finished her milk and slowly set the glass down on the table. Their eyes met once more and lingered. It was the same look they had exchanged on the day of the hike. In that look, she knew that sex wasn't that big of a deal in what they had found—only whipped cream on the apple pie. They would add the whipped cream when the time was right for both of them.

"I'm sorry, John. I'm not ready for our relationship to move to another level until we know each other better."

They were married in the home of a friend five months later. And the whipped cream made the apple pie even better.

Chapter 51: Alice Finds Her Life

New York and Island of Crete, 1977

John's Uncle Kevin had given Alice and John a wonderful wedding gift: use of his beach house on the Island of Crete, the largest of the Greek islands. All John had to do was get a sabbatical, and they could stay there rent free for a year. John got his sabbatical in 1977 to write a research study he had completed during the academic year. So they were going to Crete.

The beach house was located near the Crete Naval Base, an American facility, so most of their neighbors spoke English. But Alice and John had three exciting years learning as much Cretan Greek as possible.

As they were packing the car for the airport, Alice called out to John, "If you don't hurry, we'll miss our plane." She had worked herself into a nervous frenzy while John, as usual, remained calm and focused.

"Calm yourself, Alice," I have to do a double check to make sure that I have everything I need. Sometimes you get so excited, loved one."

"And isn't that a good thing for you? We'd never get anything done, if you didn't have me as a timekeeper. I do believe that you had never even heard of time awareness until you met me."

"True." He scratched his head, a puzzled look on his face. Turning to her, he said, "I know what I wanted to ask you." He paused. "Did you mail all of the reference books for the statistics?"

"I sent everything to Crete, John, after double checking three times. Don't sweat it. We can always contact the university, if needed."

"Don't think telephone service on the island is very reliable. After all, isn't the remoteness of the place one of the things that appealed to us?"

"Not to mention that it's a freebie for a whole year. And we'll be near your family. Besides, it's a very different culture, so I'll have a chance to strengthen the boundaries of my identity."

He grinned. "Not to mention the fact that you're as weird as I am."

"Don't knock it, John. That's why you fell in love with me." He laughed.

It was an amazing opportunity for both of them. Alice had been John's consultant for statistics as he was conducting the study and would now help him with the writing. Statistics had been her favorite subject at the university, and she had advanced to the highest level.

"I hope they'll let us take all this stuff on the plane, Alice."

An unusual noise attracted their attention to the street out front. The run-on from an old Ford announced the presence of Jeannie Fordham.

"Whoa, Nellie," laughed John.

Jeannie managed to stop the engine of the car and open the door. "You making fun of my car, John Stewart?"

"No way, lady. Wasn't that long ago I was driving one almost as old."

"At least, hers has brakes," laughed Alice.

Jeannie squinted to keep the bright sun out of her eyes as she searched in her purse for her sunglasses. "I was afraid I'd miss seeing you guys before you left." Then turning to John, she gave him a big bear hug. "You got everything you need to write up that study?"

He shrugged. "Naw, we don't worry about minor details like that. Glad you reminded us." She playfully punched him in his middle before turning to Alice and giving her a hug.

"We sent that all over by mail earlier, Jeannie— should get there before we do." She twisted her lips, nodding. "Believe me we've checked everything ten times over."

"Just remember all work and no play…After all, this *is* the honeymoon you never got to take."

Alice took her friend by the shoulders and looked deeply into her eyes "And speaking of work, you have yours cut out for you, girl. You'll need a master's degree, if you want to work at Safe Haven as a social worker."

Jeannie looked thoughtful. "Think I'll worry about getting a baccalaureate degree for now. Maybe take some classes later. Think that'll work?"

"Sounds like a good plan to me. You're needed because no one could provide more empathy to abused girls than you." Alice released her grip. "At any rate, I'm leaving you in charge of our dream until I get back. Don't let me down."

Jeannie grew quiet, a serious look on her face. "Do you think that dream will ever be realized, Alice? I mean Safe Haven."

Alice looked her in the eyes. "Of course, it will. It will happen because we believe in that dream." She narrowed her eyes before adding, "And because we'll make it happen with hard work and the money we're raising."

Jeannie rubbed the palms of her hands together. "Yeah, a few more thousand ought to buy us a place for them to stay. Then what?"

"Whoa, Miss Negative Thinker. We'll concentrate on getting funds for the home first; once we've accomplished that, we'll concentrate on taking the next step. Faith will get us there one step at a time. Believe, Jeannie, believe."

"And how are we going to raise more funds with you on the other side of the world? Will your friend, Martin, the professional fund raiser, take care of that?"

"He will. I trust him, and so should you." Jeannie looked skeptical.

"Believe, my friend. We can do it." Jeannie cocked an eyebrow but nodded. Alice gave her a thumbs up.

Alice and John flew to Rome and took a cruise liner from Citavecchia to Crete. After arriving on the island and consulting with Uncle Kevin, they found their beach house. It was located on a stretch of white sand with date palms lining the blue-burgundy Aegean. The house was a haven where they could work and play—swimming, boating, water skiing, and scuba diving. So they made a schedule for hard work in the mornings, leaving the afternoons free for play.

Alice had learned to be thankful for the blessings in her life, and this attitude alone brought contentment. She looked for the positive aspects of every situation, repelling negative thoughts as indicated, and tried not to distort her viewing lenses. Overcoming her self-centered ways was not easy, but she could see the benefits in the reactions of the people around her. The anger was still there, at times more than others, but the rage was now under her control. Allowing her true self to emerge, instead of focusing on controlling impressions, she found life mysterious and wonderful. And at the most unexpected moments, joy would surface with pride in the person she truly was.

Maintaining a bond with others became one of the highest priorities in her life; the reward was peace of mind and harmony with the world around her. She felt like a fish in water. Freed from ties that had prevented her from being alive in the moment, she could cope with the reality before her.

One Friday morning, Alice finished her work on schedule, packed her typewriter away in its case, kicked off her shoes, and walked into the kitchen to grab a cup of coffee. John was writing on his yellow tablet, surrounded by several open books. She approached, coffee pot in hand, and reached for his cup. "Want a warm up, John?" When he shook his head, she wondered whether he had even heard her.

"I'm going to sprout wings and fly over to Rome," she announced.

"That's nice."

Intense concentration on his work was essential to what he was doing. She respected that.

So, although she wanted his opinion about what she should wear to Uncle Kevin's dinner that evening, she decided to make up her mind without his help. She went into the bedroom and tried on several outfits before settling on a pale blue shift. *Instead of trying to please everyone in order to 'fit in, I will simply be myself and look for common ground with those I choose for my friends, looking for the best in everyone.*

Her thoughts were interrupted by a mail delivery. She couldn't suppress her excitement when she saw a letter from Jeannie Fordham. "Oh look, John, I got a letter from Jeannie," she exclaimed. John put his pencil down, grabbed a cup of coffee, and walked over to her. Alice slit the envelope with a knife she used as a letter opener and began reading. "Guess what her latest project is."

"She donated her old jalopy to Goodwill." He peered over her shoulder until Alice turned and glared at him. He backed off.

"Better than that--she's working in a Family Choice clinic near her campus. She's getting experience as a social worker and earning a little extra cash for school."

His eyes narrowed. "Doesn't Family Choice do abortions?"

"Only when the mother's life is in danger." He said nothing in response.

After dinner that evening, Alice and John sipped coffee with Uncle Kevin, Aunt Sally, and some neighbors on the veranda. Alice made eye contact with the others, frequently smiling and joking. "How many Episcopalians does it take to change a light bulb?" They looked at her. She flicked her eyebrows at them. "Two. One to change the bulb, and another to say that the old one was better." They laughed.

Aunt Sally pointed her thumb and middle finger in the shape of an *o* at Alice. "Good you can joke about your own religion, Alice"

Alice smiled. "Are you telling me I'm okay?"

"I am."

Alice crossed the short distance between them and gave her aunt a hug. "I love to visit you guys— makes me feel like part of a loving family."

Aunt Sally returned the hug, saying, "You're an important part of our family, Alice."

"Couldn't get this research report done without her," added John.

"Where do you plan on submitting your report?" Asked Uncle Kevin.

"I'll send query letters to all of the mags interested in identity. The university has given me a few suggestions."

"How about a little brandy to cap off the evening?" Several of the neighbors accepted the offer.

Alice was gathering up cups and saucers and taking them to the kitchen. Aunt Sally joined her there and picked up a towel to dry the dishes as Alice washed. "I'm happy here, Aunt Sally. Life is so much simpler. Instead of the hustle and bustle of New York, I have an occasional dinner and bridge once a month. Allows me to relax and live in the moment."

Aunt Sally opened the cupboard door and began stacking dishes inside. Laughing she said, "You'll be ready for the exciting big apple again by the time you leave. Gets pretty boring here at times."

As she and John walked home along the beach later, Alice looked up at the stars saying," I realize now that the best way to please people is by accepting them as they are. I don't have to let them control my behavior."

John took her hand, saying, "Good girl!"

"For the first time in my life, I seem to have everything I need—love, family, friends, and satisfying work. That makes me happy, John." He hugged her. "Wish life could stay like this."

"It won't. But you're developing the resources to deal with whatever comes along, and we'll face it together."

The telephone rang just before lunch one day soon afterward. It was the attorney she had hired to handle the legal affairs for Safe Haven. A tingle of fear started at the base of her spine as she asked, "Is something wrong?"

His voice was muffled and barely came through the line. "Mrs. Stewart, we need you back here as soon as you can make it."

The fear traveled up her spine and settled at the base of her skull. "Why?"

"We need someone to take charge of the Safe Haven project."

"Where is Jeannie Fordham? I left her in charge. She is perfectly capable of handling the affairs of the project at this time."

There was a long silence. "I guess you didn't get the news where you are. The story was in all the papers here, so it never occurred to me to send a telegram. I'm really sorry." The fear was spreading like a dark cloud over her brain.

Her voice broke as she said, "What news? What are you talking about?"

He paused. "Again, I apologize for not letting you know; never occurred to me that you wouldn't see a newspaper." A longer pause. "Seems some mental case walked into the Family Choice clinic last Monday and opened fire with an AK-47." His voice wavered, "Unfortunately, Miss Fordham did not survive."

Alice dropped the telephone. Devastated, she went to her bedroom and crawled under the covers, trying to shut out reality.

John tried to comfort her, but he was hurting, too. In his own quiet way, he was as upset as she was. But he had mastered the art of remaining calm in such circumstances. Alice was still working on it.

"How I wish that we had heard sooner," she sighed.

"No need to stew over that, Alice; it only upsets you more."

"I need to talk, John."

"So talk if it makes you feel better."

"My heart is broken, but I've been there many times before. When the emotions have cleared up a bit, I'll decide what to do." She paused in reflection, "I recently recognized something in myself: I have been building a wall around every break in my heart, starting with Belle. Down deep I guess I thought it would protect me from being hurt like that again, but it only ended up hurting me and other people. This time there will be no wall. I'll deal with it the best I can. It may mean that I have to leave you and a life that I love, but Safe Haven is more important."

"Don't worry about the research report. I'm at a point where I can handle it. As for getting along without you, that's a different story."

She hugged him to her. "You're strong, John. You can do it. I'll call frequently, and the separation will only last for a few months. Besides, you'll have your family.... I'll sure miss you and them, but I'll survive." She added listlessly, "I always have."

Two weeks later, Alice was on a plane, returning to the United States. Giving up her newly found happiness, she let go of everything and held onto her Guide. Even with the pain, she had never felt more alive.

Months later, the attorney suggested that the name of their organization be changed to Safe Haven: the Alice Hollister Stewart Foundation.

Alice stared at him for a long time, "A resounding *no"* Let's call it Safe Haven: the Jeannie Fordham Foundation."

Epilogue

Cruise of the Greek Islands, 1999

To celebrate their twenty-fifth wedding anniversary, Alice and John boarded a cruise ship to visit some of the Greek islands they had not seen. After locating their stateroom, John groaned as he lifted Alice in his arms to carry her across the threshold. She had put on a few pounds.

"Put me down, John; you'll injure your back. Look at me; I'm fat and no longer a blushing bride."

"You'll always be my bride, Mrs. Stewart, and you're not fat. Besides, who said I'm not the man I used to be—only better." He dropped her on the bed, a little harder than he had intended.

She laughed and pecked him on the cheek, "Well, I can vouch for the same over-sized ego."

"Did I hurt you?"

"No, are you okay?" He nodded.

"Guess we're getting older."

"Not you, dear, you're younger than the first flowers of spring." Again, she recognized that he was saying what good husbands are supposed to say to their wives, but the words, as usual, lifted her spirits.

Later, they were about to enter the dining room when Alice grabbed John by the arm saying, "Get a load of that sunset." The whole sky was on fire with a bursting rainbow of colors, set against the blue, blue Aegean Sea and the mountains in the distance.

Others had noticed, and people were coming from all over the ship with their cameras in hand. The dining room was quickly emptied as waiters stood with their arms folded while dinners cooled.

"They want to capture the beauty of this moment, John, to share with their loved ones at home." An alarmed expression crossed her face. "But are you sure the ship won't capsize?"

He put his arm around her. "Not likely. But we *are* surrounded by a lot of people, a microcosm of the world, I'd say. I heard several different languages—a phrase of French here, German there and Spanish elsewhere."

"And those are just the languages we recognize. How about those harsh, guttural sounds of the Orientals? Aren't they wonderful? All of these nationalities united by one experience common to us all—enjoyment of a beautiful sunset. Maybe we could all get along in the world better if we looked for common ground with each other. What do you think?"

"Looks like we just found one, Ally. By the way, that woman over by the rail has been staring at you since we arrived. Do you know her?" He paused, waiting for an answer. "Uh oh, she's coming this way. Better put on your thinking cap.

The woman looked Hispanic but spoke with an accent Alice did not recognize. As she studied Alice's face, she asked, "Aren't you Alice Stewart?"

"Guilty as charged. But do I know you? Alice smiled as she searched the woman's face for a landmark to spark her memory.

"I recognize you from your pictures in our Safe Haven, the Jeannie Fordham Foundation."

Alice offered her hand, recognizing the catch in her voice as she spoke, "I'm glad our humble little organization reached you. Where're you from?"

"Brazil, I can't miss the opportunity to thank you for all you have done for the young women in our country. They'd still be on the streets without Safe Haven."

Alice nodded, folding her arms around herself and squeezing. *My life is more than I ever dreamed it could be. Not bad, for a child with such a dire beginning.*

Acknowledgements

I am grateful to Google and Bing for always being there to answer my questions. Wikipedia provided clarity on several issues.

I thank my husband, Steve, for his support, technical assistance, and editing. The book could not have been written without him and the guidance of Danielle A. Dahl and Father J. Phillip Purser. Carol Beery, Betsy Dunkle, Patsy Higbie, Susie Johnson, Dean Kauffman, Linda McKillop, Fran Moore, Vic Rosenthal, Jane Street, and Barbara Williams, were readers who made significant contributions. I also thank three fantastic writing groups: the Oconee Writers' Association, Writer's Ink, and Writer's Muse.

I am especially grateful to Sue Lile Inman and Jamie Langston Turner for their support and suggestions for agents and to Kathryn Hughes, who introduced me to Rumi in her best- selling novel, *The Secret,* published by Headline Review, United Kingdom, 2016. The docents and tour guides for Royal Caribbean Cruise Line provided information about Greece.

I also found the following references especially helpful:

Acadian – Cajun genealogy and history: History of the Acadians. Google.com. Retrieved October 10, 2012 from http://www.acadiancajun.com/hisacad1htm.

Breathnach, S.B. (1998). Something More: Excavating your Authentic Self. New York: Warner Books/A Time Warner Company.

DeCandido, R. *Birds and birding in New York City's Central Park*. Retrieved April 28, 2014 from www.birdingbob.com.

Information on the topic of birding was also retrieved on April 28, 2014 from http://www.centralparknyc.org and http://www.nycaudubon.org.

Erdman, Jonathan (June 26, 2016). *Day by Day*, p. 47. Forward Movement: Cincinnati. Fenwick Lansdowne.Google.com. Retrieved January 23, 2013 from http://www.//en.wikipedia.org/wiki/Fenwick_Lansd owne.
Gouvoussis, G. (No date given*)*. *Greece*. Athens, Greece: 5 Ratzieri STR. 117 42.

Kelly, T.R. (1941). *A Testament of Devotion.* New York: Harper & Brothers Publishers.

Martin, T.R. (1996). *Ancient Greece.* New Haven: Yale University Press.

Special recognition and gratitude is owed to: *Forward Day by Day* 2001-2016. Cincinnati: Forward Movement

The quote by Jonathan Erdman from Forward Day by Day is used with permission from Forward Movement, www.Forward Movement.org.

Made in the USA
Columbia, SC
21 April 2019